PJ AND THE PARANORMAL PURSUERS
&
THE MACKENZIE POLTERGEIST

PJ AND THE PARANORMAL PURSUERS & THE MACKENZIE POLTERGEIST

Jacqui Dempster

The Book Guild Ltd

First published in Great Britain in 2021 by
The Book Guild Ltd
9 Priory Business Park
Wistow Road, Kibworth
Leicestershire, LE8 0RX
Freephone: 0800 999 2982
www.bookguild.co.uk
Email: info@bookguild.co.uk
Twitter: @bookguild

Copyright © 2021 Jacqui Dempster

The right of Jacqui Dempster to be identified as the author of this
work has been asserted by her in accordance with the
Copyright, Design and Patents Act 1988.

All rights reserved. No part of this publication may be
reproduced, transmitted, or stored in a retrieval system, in any form or by any means,
without permission in writing from the publisher, nor be otherwise circulated in
any form of binding or cover other than that in which it is published and without
a similar condition being imposed on the subsequent purchaser.

This work is entirely fictitious and bears no resemblance to any persons living or dead.

Typeset in 12pt Minion Pro

Printed and bound in the UK by TJ Books LTD, Padstow, Cornwall

ISBN 978 1913913 144

British Library Cataloguing in Publication Data.
A catalogue record for this book is available from the British Library.

For Smudge
My own wee Dug and best Buddy of 16 years. I know the rainbow bridge is beckoning. You have my heart forever, in this world and the next, whenever that time comes. May your light continue to burn brightly, here with us, for as long as you choose, my precious little one.

CHAPTER 1

"Look, see, like, I don't wanna be here! I want to go back to Manhattan to the Rosenbaums. If you really want to help me, then p-please book me a flight h-home." I try to sound confident and assertive, working hard to keep my voice steady but unable to keep the tremor under control. It's my first meeting with Aunt Katie as we face off in arrivals at Edinburgh Airport. It's all I've been thinking about. If she cares, surely she won't keep me from my *real* family and my beloved Buddy. I hold my breath, waiting for her to answer. Despite my best efforts to look resolute, I feel my face collapse, my mouth pulling downwards, my eyes brimming with burning tears.

Aunt Katie draws her hands apart, uncertain how to respond. She shakes her head slowly, the pained look deepening as she releases a sob and tears course down her pale cheeks.

"I'm so sorry, PJ," she says weakly. She looks like she's been crying for days. Her eyes have black circles underneath and where they should be white, they're red.

I want her to know that I don't want to stay with her, that I am angry with her for not coming to Mom when she needed her most. But I don't feel any better by making her cry too. I will never be her friend, so what's the point in me staying here and making us both miserable? Surely she'll see that?

Pulling a pack of Kleenex from her pocket, Aunt Katie wipes away her tears and hands the pack to me. I take out a tissue and blow my nose loudly, unwilling to acknowledge the tears in my own eyes while she's still looking at me. She thrusts her hands deep in her pockets and her shoulders stoop. She bends her head, deep in thought before she answers.

"Look, PJ, this is so hard for both of us right now. This isn't the time or the place for us to think things through. You must be exhausted. I know I am. I've been so sad about your mom, and nervous about meeting you and wondering how to help that I've barely slept myself the last couple of weeks. How about we go home, sleep on it and we'll try to figure out what to do between us?" She waits to see how her words have landed with me. Does that mean there's hope? She hasn't outright refused, I guess. I shuffle uncomfortably from foot to foot as I think about it. She's right about one thing. I *am* exhausted. Being this sad, for so long, is like carrying heavy bags and never being able to put them down. If she really means we'll talk about letting me go back to New York, well, it wouldn't be so bad to visit with Aunt Katie for a short while, would it?

"OK, I'll stay for a little while, but you promise we'll talk about this?" Aunt Katie smiles, a full wide grin this time, and OMG, it's as though Mom is standing right here in front of me. I gulp back the torrent of sadness, determined not to show weakness.

"I promise, PJ. One step at a time, OK?"

I nod. "OK."

Aunt Katie grabs the handle of one of my cases and I take the other, and we head off into the wet and windy October night. I shiver miserably as I am soaked in a matter of seconds. I've seen rain in New York, but jeez, this is something else.

We ride in silence all the way back to Aunt Katie's, neither of us even trying to make conversation. I guess we both know that for now at least, there isn't much to say. I am confused. I want to hate her, but something about her (*her likeness to Mom, maybe*), makes it hard to stay totally hostile towards her. And besides, she has the power to give me what I want. A return ticket to Manhattan.

*

It isn't long before we arrive at Aunt Katie's home. We grab my bags from the trunk and she says, "This is it, then! Welcome to Edinburgh New Town, PJ."

We draw up outside an awesome building, a bit like the brownstones (but not as brown) of New York. It has huge windows, divided into squares from which a cosy glow radiates as the lights shine out from high ceilings onto the wet street.

"You own this whole building?" I gasp, wonderstruck.

Aunt Katie laughs. "No, PJ. It's divided into four apartments. One of them is mine. C'mon. Let's get inside."

It's cold out here. We can put the kettle on and I'll make us some tea. Or maybe you prefer coffee?"

I've never tried tea and I sure don't like coffee.

"D'you have any OJ?" Aunt Katie facepalms just like Mom did when she realised she'd done something crazy.

"Doh! Stupid of me! Sorry, PJ, I'm not used to having kids around and I've adopted the British ways in my twenty years here. In the UK, a nice cuppa tea solves everything! I'll go to the filling station and get some if you'd like?"

I shake my head. "Nah, it's cool. I'll try your tea for now. This is some place you have here. You could fit our whole apartment in New York into just this one room." I gaze in awe around the den with the high ceiling into which Aunt Katie guides me. I check myself. I am sounding too friendly. A bit like Mr Rosenbaum exchanging man-type pleasantries with Mom when he came up to fix something in the apartment.

A twinge of anger stirs inside me. Aunt Katie has so much, when Mom had nothing. Why did she not help us? Why did she not ask her, me and Buddy to come to Edinburgh before it was too late? Maybe she could have stopped Mom from dying. She hadn't even bothered to come to Mom's funeral, sending a huge 'Sister' wreath in her place.

I had wanted to stay with the Rosenbaums. They're my *real* family. They've been around Mom and me for as long as I can remember, and they cared for me and Buddy during those dark, lost days after Mom died.

"C'mon." Katie beckons me through the den into the kitchen. "Have a seat." She gestures towards the pine table and chairs in the corner as she turns on the teakettle. She loads a plate with some plain-looking biscuits and some dome-shaped things covered in red and silver striped foil. 'Tunnock's Teacakes', they proclaim on the yellow box she's taken them from. Aunt Katie places a mug of hot, steaming tea with milk (British style, she explains), on the table and tells me to help myself to Scottish shortbread and the teacakes that look altogether more interesting. At first, I don't want to take anything from her; it might give her the impression I'm settling down and being friendly. But then, I gotta eat sometime. I haven't been able to get much past the boa constrictor in my belly in the last few weeks. Whenever I get sad, I feel him twisting, tightening and curling around in my stomach. Curiosity and hunger get the better of me in the end, as I watch Aunt Katie unwrap a chocolatey dome and bite into it with a *craackk*, revealing white, goopy mallow and a cakey, biscuity base. I point at my top lip to tell her she has a sticky white moustache of mallow on hers.

She giggles. "Always happens, PJ. Aren't you going to try one? They're something of a Scottish delicacy, you know."

My willpower gives out and I sink my teeth into the teacake, relishing the crackling chocolate, the sweet, creamy mallow and the texture of the slightly soft, slightly hard base. I'm not so keen on the tea and pull a face as I take a sip of the brown, milky liquid. Aunt Katie suggests some sugar might help, and sure enough, it is a little better.

We sit in awkward silence. I am too darn tired to talk anyway and my eyes droop lazily as the warmth of the room envelops me like a blanket.

"Looks like you could do with some shuteye, PJ. Let me take you to your room. I lit the fire so it should be toasty for you."

The room is awesome. Aunt Katie said she'd re-decorated it for me and that I am to do whatever I want with it. I'm not falling for that trick. I am leaving soon, remember? It's just fine as it is. Nevertheless, I'm grateful for the soft mattress, plump pillows and overawed by the quilt that lays on top, which Aunt Katie tells me she and Mom had worked on for years together.

We say our goodnights and I unpack a few things. Not many. Just what I need to get by for a day or two. Not much point in taking everything out, then having to re-pack.

I run my hand over the quilt and hold it close to my face, happy to feel something that Mom's hands had worked on so lovingly. It would make her happy to know that I will be cocooned inside it, finding safety and comfort in this strange new reality.

I pull out some photos I've brought of Mom, Buddy and me, together in Central Park. The boa constrictor curls in my stomach, waiting for release. I oblige with hot, fat tears and I long for Buddy to lick them away, as he had done every day since Mom had gone. My arms feel empty without his furry body wrapped inside them. I know he is crying too, five thousand miles away. We had shared pain and sorrow, night after night, both of us missing Mom and now, missing each other. The boa constrictor releases his grip and I close my eyes.

CHAPTER 2

I wake up late and stretch luxuriously in the warm soft bed, content; my head is still foggy after a deep, jet-lagged sleep. For a moment, I am PJ Wilson, living in my New York apartment with Mom and Buddy, and the Rosenbaums happily working away in their deli below us. Slowly, I open my eyes and look around me, confused. Then I remember. I am PJ Wilson, orphan, alone and in Edinburgh, Scotland, of all places. The boa constrictor tightens, reminding me with glee that he is still there, and the black cloud of dread and misery hovers ominously above me. I look at the side table where the red digits on the clock tell me it's nearly noon. I stretch out my hand to touch my precious photograph and only the bleak certainty of loss remains.

A quiet, uncertain knock accompanied by Aunt Katie's too-cheerful voice breaks the silence.

"Hey, PJ, are you awake? Can I come in?" I groan. I don't want to see anyone. I just want to be left alone with my thoughts. I want to curl up under the covers and sink into the oblivion of sleep again. Maybe I could just ignore her. But then I remember. She'd promised to talk about getting me back to New York. I have to play nice.

"Uh, yeah, sure," I call unenthusiastically.

Aunt Katie appears in the doorway, stooped over, her elbow on the door handle, a breakfast tray clutched in her hands. "Thought you could use some food, PJ." She smiles, setting the tray on the bed in front of me. "And then, if you're feeling up to it, maybe we could go uptown and get some things to make you feel more at home?" A pathetically hopeful smile spreads across her lips which lasts a nanosecond.

More at home? I don't want to feel more at home here! What does she mean? Something inside me just snaps. *She's trying to trick me. She's got no intention of letting me go back to New York!*

I leap out of out of bed, furiously throwing the covers back, accidentally knocking the tray Aunt Katie has carefully prepared, clean out of her hands. There follows a cacophony of **SMASH! CLANG! SPLAT! SQUELCH!** First the jug of orange juice that she must have fetched especially from the store this morning flies across the bed, spilling all over the quilt and shattering on the laminate below. The plate of bacon, egg, beans and toast hits the newly painted wall and drips greasily and messily to the floor as the knife and fork clang noisily in the same direction.

I stand beside the bed, my fingers clenched, nails digging into my palms as I try to control the waves of anger, sadness and betrayal I feel. Mom betrayed me by leaving me and now Aunt Katie has betrayed me by trying to trick me into thinking she would let me go home.

"PJ?" she says warily. "It's OK. It's OK," she soothes, her hands stroking my hair. I slap her hands away.

"It's not OK!" I yell, my voice raising in volume and pitch to a crescendo of fury. "It's never gonna be OK and nothing you can do, or say, is ever going to make it that way! Go out and buy stuff? I don't want stuff! I'm not staying, remember? Why would we go out and buy stuff? And, and, you come in here, trying to be Mom with breakfast and all. That was our thing! You can't ever take her place, do you understand? You'll never be half of what she was so just keep away from me, OK?"

Aunt Katie nods and stifles a sob as I flop back down on the bed and draw my knees up, wrapping my arms around them, a signal to her to keep away and a signal to the boa constrictor to contain himself. My chest heaves and I sob so hard I think I am having a heart attack. It was the breakfast tray that did it.

When Aunt Katie came through the door looking harassed and smiley, she looked so like my mom. There are differences. She's a little shorter and heavier, her hair brown with highlights instead of plum and it's a little shorter than Mom wore it. But the way she moves, her facial expressions, they were all Mom's.

At weekends, Mom would come to my room in the morning, after we'd slept late and, just like Katie, she'd bring me a tray with orange juice and a plate of fresh-baked pastries she'd bought from the Rosenbaums' deli. The aroma of cinnamon filled the room if she'd brought the pinwheels, drizzled with sweet, warm icing. Other times it would be apple, peach or apricot topping Mrs Rosenbaum's lightest, butteriest, flakiest pastry. The memory is just too raw, I guess, and Aunt Katie hit a nerve this morning.

Aunt Katie clears up as much of the mess as she can and wordlessly leaves the room. It's like a tornado passed through me, creating a torrent of chaos. Eventually, my breathing quietens and becomes more regular, and for a short while the snake is satisfied and relaxes his grip. I groan as I realise what I've done. Mom would be horrified. So much for my 'play nice' strategy! *Oh well, guess she'll be glad to see the back of me now.*

"Sorry, Mom," I whisper.

"*Sorry just won't cut it, PJ. You need to make amends with Aunt Katie. You've really hurt her,*" Mom's voice yells in my head.

I pull on some clothes and find a cloth in the bathroom. I run it under the water and pour some soap on it. I pick up a roll of toilet tissue as well and return to the bedroom. I'm real upset I've spilled OJ on the quilt and I lay out some of the tissue, hoping the juice will be absorbed without leaving a stain. Next, I take the wet cloth to the wall where a greasy stain tinged with orange from the baked beans splatters from halfway up, right down to the floor. Gingerly, I rub it, avoiding a few chips of glass that remain on the laminate. I stand back. If anything, it looks worse. Aunt Katie's efforts to re-decorate are ruined. I'll offer to paint it again if she has any left over. I have a few bucks with me so I'll buy some more if she doesn't.

I lie down on the dry side of the bed and close my eyes. I need some space. I pull on my jacket and creep out of the bedroom, past the kitchen where I can hear Aunt Katie softly crying. I hesitate but decide to face the music.

Hanging my head in shame, I quietly enter the kitchen. She hasn't heard me. She's sitting at the table, her head buried in her arms, her hair flayed out in an unkempt mess. I tiptoe up, shuffling nervously, and clear my throat.

"I'm real sorry, Aunt Katie," I say, keeping my head low. "I know you were only trying to help. I'll fix it up again." She doesn't answer. "If… if you have some of the paint left over, I'll make the wall good again." Still nothing. I've really done some damage here, I think. "Um, if not, we can go to the store and get some more. I have a few dollars with me. I'll pay," I say.

Still she says nothing. Her eyes are blank, faraway. I shift from one foot to the other. I'd rather that she yelled at me than deal with this silence. I turn and walk slowly from the kitchen.

"Where are you going, PJ?"

"Um, I just thought I'd get some air," I say, kinda relieved that she's spoken. "If that's OK with you?" I hear the chair scrape back on the tiles and, clutching her cardigan around her, she reaches up to a rack on the wall and pulls down a key.

"Sure, PJ. There's a park across the way. It's lovely in the fall. Some air will do you good. Do you have your cell with you?"

"Yeah," I say, pulling it from my pocket as proof.

"Don't be too long then or I'll worry. You'll be OK?"

"Sure, I will. When I get back, I'll get started on that wall." She nods weakly and hands me the key. "I'll see you soon then," I say, and head out into the communal lobby.

*

It takes a moment for my eyes to adjust to the gloom, as the door clicks shut behind me. There's a staircase that spirals downwards to the ground floor. An acrid smell of disinfectant burns my nostrils. I lean over the banister and look down through the spiralling, ornately decorated black rails. I lurch backwards, and everything is spinning. I put my hand out and grab the banister to steady myself. *Should've eaten that bacon and egg.* I can't remember when I last had anything other than the Tunnock's Teacake to eat. I realise it was at the Rosenbaums' before we headed to the airport. How could I forget?

No wonder I'm feeling dizzy. The thought of food makes me feel sick, but the lack of it isn't helping much either. My limbs feel weak and I wonder how long it would take to starve to death. I could be with Mom. But I have a vision of Buddy, his trusting eyes imploring me to be strong. For him. *I will, Buddy. I will. I'll be back with you and the Rosenbaums soon, I promise.* I picture my message flying across the Atlantic, hoping that somehow, he'll hear it.

It sure is a long way down to the black and white tiled floor below and I tread carefully, my hands clammily gripping onto the banister, taking each step slowly in case the dizziness comes back. Under any other circumstances, the banister would have been an enticing challenge, and I picture myself whooping with delight and hollering with laughter as my friends and I straddle the shiny handrail and helter skelter down by the seat of our pants. Gee, I miss the guys, Dean and Kyle, and the laughs we had together. If only they could be here now. *Or I could be back home with them.*

When I reach the bottom of the stairs, I see there are

two more apartment doors directly below those on the first floor. Ahead of me is the common door to the outside world. There's a table against the wall to my left and mail sits in a neat pile on the top. There's a layer of dust dulling the shine of the dark wood and I wonder why the cleaners haven't touched this since they've obviously been here today.

I head for the door and stretch up to release the catch. Behind me, I hear a loud *CREEAAK* that makes me jump. Curious, I look around to see that the door next to the table has opened just a little. I wait. There is a soft *swish, swish, BUMP, swish, swish, BUMP* sound, as the door opens wider and an old woman appears, her shoulders rounded, one hand on a cane that she uses to steady herself. She is wearing a robe and slippers. Her hair is silvery grey and sticks up in crazy peaks as though she hasn't brushed it in years.

"Who's there?" Her voice is thin and high and kinda trembles. Something about her makes me want to pretend I haven't heard her and just go on my way, but she turns and stares in my direction. *Darn it.*

"Who are you? You haven't been here before," she barks, gnarled fingers gripping the door frame as she shakes her cane menacingly in my direction.

"Um, my name is PJ, Ma'am. I'm staying for a short while with my Aunt Katie upstairs."

"Have you seen him at all?"

I hesitate, waiting for my chance to escape the crazy lady. "I-I'm sorry, Ma'am, seen who?"

"Azrael, my cat, of course," she harrumphs impatiently. *Of course! Silly me! I knew that.*

"No, Ma'am, no cats around here," I say, looking around the lobby, just to be sure.

"Oh." Her shoulders slump. "He's been gone for days. Can't find him anywhere."

I take a deep breath. I'm a sucker for a lost animal. I approach the old woman, my feet moving forwards, my mind willing me to run in the opposite direction. She looks at me. Only she isn't looking at me, she's kinda looking past me, or through me, I'm not quite sure which. My stomach flips as I see her eyes, which look like nothing human. The surfaces are completely white with only the shadows of her irises visible under the milky fog. She looks like an alien or that scary woman in the wedding dress in a horror movie I'd watched. I know it sounds kinda mean, but I'm freaked out and wanna puke. I swallow hard and breathe deeply.

"I'll sure look out for Azrael," I say, trying to keep my voice steady so as not to betray the queasiness rolling around my insides. I don't look at those scary eyes, preferring to inspect my sneakers instead. "What does he look like?"

"He's black, white and fluffy with emerald green eyes."

Describes just about any cat! That narrows the field a bit.

"He has a tartan collar around his neck with a bell on it," she adds helpfully, still gazing somewhere beyond me.

"Well, I'm just off out for a walk. I'll be sure to keep a lookout for him."

"You'll come back and let me know, won't you? I'll be waiting. Oh, and your mum's here, she has a message for you. Tell you later, when you've found Azrael."

Whaat the…? She 'looks' unseeingly in my direction,

a thin smile drawn across her lips, and I shudder. She's clearly cray cray!

"Um, sure thing, Ma'am." I shuffle uncomfortably, eager to bring the conversation to an end. "I'll be off then, and see if I can find him."

She nods and turns towards her door, the swish, swish of her slippers scuffing the tiled floor, followed by the dull bump of her walking stick, the only sounds filling the lobby.

I breathe a sigh of relief as the door clicks shut behind her and I make a hasty exit from the building.

CHAPTER 3

It's sunny and warm outside, despite it being early fall, and I get my first real glimpse of the 'New Town', as Aunt Katie had called it. The rest of Edinburgh must be prehistoric, I think, as I gaze at the impressive sandstone buildings with columns and carvings, surrounded by wide cobbled roads. The park is just over the road, encircled by railings and trees. The red and golden leaves from trees overhanging the sidewalk crunch under my feet as I trudge aimlessly through the gate, hands thrust in my pockets, my fists clenched and my shoulders tensed. Inside, there's the usual stuff, an expanse of green as far as the eye can see; trees, bushes, benches occupied by tired old folks, chatty mothers with their baby carriages and school kids with their lunch boxes. They all look carefree and happy. *How can the world just go on like this, when my mom is dead? I read somewhere that a butterfly flapping its wings can affect everything that happens in the world, just from the ripples it creates. Surely someone dying must change the whole universe? All the good things Mom would have done, won't happen anymore. That changes everyone's lives, doesn't it? Especially mine. And Buddy's.* I choke back the lump rising in my throat.

I see a girl running around with a dog. She's got one of those ball thrower things and as she fires it off, her black and white collie enthusiastically runs off to find it and bounds back, time and again, never tiring of the game. How Buddy would love to be exploring, running with the wind through his fur, ears flapping and sniffing other dogs' butts right here, right now. I remember how we would run together in Central Park, rolling around on the grass, tussling over a stick or a ball with Buddy trying to outsmart me, dancing around, twisting and turning so that I couldn't get hold of whatever toy he held stubbornly in his mouth.

I gaze at the school kids laughing and joking as they eat their lunch. I was like that once. My homies and I would sit on the grassy area of the school yard on days like this, none of us ever suspecting that life could change in a heartbeat. I didn't like school much. I don't like routine, you know? Sure, I wanna learn, but I don't like routine. I like to find stuff out for myself, not just from books but from exploring and investigating. My idea of hell is sitting in that classroom listening to Mrs Johnson droning on about things that have no relevance to my life as my eyelids droop and my mouth stretches into a deep and satisfying yawn.

"Look out!" A warning voice cuts through my thoughts as the girl with the dog gestures above my head. I see the hard rubber ball arcing through the sky, heading straight down towards me. I run aside, shielding my face just in case I've misjudged its trajectory.

The ball bounces a couple of times and thuds down

next to me, brushing my sleeve as it does so. The collie bounds up and skids to a halt to retrieve his toy. He stands looking expectantly up at me to join in the game. I tease the ball from his mouth and throw it in the direction of the girl who is running awkwardly towards me, her long skirt flapping around her ankles. Again, the dog picks it up and this time heads back towards me.

Breathlessly, the girl reaches me and bends over, hands on knees as she recovers from the run. She's about my age, I guess. Maybe a little older, but it's hard to tell for sure as her face is made up in goth style. Her hair is black; dyed from the look of it, as her eyebrows are a lighter brown shade. She looks really pale. Her nails are painted black and she wears a long black skirt with a black T-shirt and leather jacket. Her sartorial elegance is completed by Doc Martens on her feet. Her eyes are lined with thick black pencil and her lips painted with deep red lipstick. She's quite scary to look at. *Vampire much…?* She wouldn't be out of place in *Twilight*, I think.

"So sorry," she gasps in a surprisingly gentle Scottish lilt that contradicts her 'out there' appearance. "I didn't see you as I threw the ball. I don't usually fire missiles at other people in the park." She grins.

"Hey, it's cool. No worries. It didn't touch me. And I get to play with your dog. What's his name?"

"Archie," she says. "He's a big daftie. Loves to play and loves it when he gets everyone involved. You like dogs?"

"Sure, I do. I have my own dog, Buddy, back in New York."

"New York? Gosh, I'd love to visit that city. Must be exciting. You must be missing Buddy, though?"

"I am," I say. "But it's only for a few weeks. Just visiting my aunt here. I'll be going home soon."

"That's nice," she says. "You'll have fun here. Lots to see and do. Make the most of your visit."

"Oh, yeah, I shall," I say as there is a sudden commotion between Archie and something that's caught his eye in the bushes. He starts to growl and bark. The girl and I run over to the bushes to see what's going on.

As we approach, I hear hissing and spitting, followed by a yowl from the bush. Archie's head is tilted as he pushes his nose inquisitively into the undergrowth. He leaps back in shock as a black furry claw jerks out from the leaves and scratches his snout. Archie cowers back then barks angrily. 'Twilight Girl' grasps him by the collar before he sustains any more injuries.

"It's a cat," the girl says, unnecessarily, as she grabs Archie's collar to clip on the leash.

I kneel on the ground while the girl and Archie stand back, their heads tilted, watching intently as I lift the bottom leaves of the bush to reveal a fluffy black and white cat. More piebald than black, I notice. Its ears are pulled backwards and its tail swishes wildly from side to side. It arches its back, hissing and spitting at me. This is not a friendly feline, I think. It has been scared, though. I speak softly.

"Hey, it's OK, fella. Don't be afraid. The dog won't hurt ya. He just wants to play, that's all." I try to soothe the cat with my quietest whisper. "You're safe now." The cat relaxes a little, its eyes flashing in the shadow of the bush "Sshhh, it's OK." The cat moves suspiciously towards me and I see it has a tartan collar around its neck.

"Azrael?" I try the name to see if it fits. The cat meows as though answering my question. "Would you like to come home with me now?" I ask gently, and carefully stretch my hand reassuringly towards the cat. I am wary of those claws poised like razors that could come at me any moment. The tail stops swishing and the cat's body fully relaxes, no longer arched for attack. Slowly, warily, Azrael creeps out from the bush, looking in all directions, and eyes Archie suspiciously. He approaches me and rubs his head then the length of his body along my knee as though we were old friends. I tickle him under his chin and run my hand along his wild, soft fur.

"Did I hear you right?" The girl frowns. "Did you just call the cat Azrael?"

"Yup. At least, I think it's him. He belongs to my aunt's neighbour. Said I'd look out for him as he's been missing a while."

"Cool name," she says. "Angel of Death."

"*Say what*?" I glance up at the girl questioningly.

"Azrael. The name means 'Angel of Death.'" She must have realised she's spooked me because she quickly adds, "AKA Angel of God, or Help from God. He's a good angel, not a bad one."

Archie's attention is caught by something good to sniff in the grass and the girl extends the leash so that he can wander more freely behind her. She bends down to stroke Azrael.

"I think Azrael is here to help and comfort us," the girl says mysteriously, a wistful smile on her lips. She seems far away in her thoughts.

"Um, yeah, maybe," I say, not really knowing how I should respond to this.

She lingers for a few moments more, stroking Azrael's head and chin, which he relishes, his eyes closing as he rubs his head, this way and that, against her palm.

"Well, I'd best be off before Archie causes any more havoc." The girl gives Azrael a final tickle under the chin and he purrs contentedly. "What's your name, by the way?"

"PJ. PJ Wilson."

"I'm Freya. Pleased to meet you, PJ." She grins, her black kohl-lined eyes creasing warmly. Maybe we'll bump into one another again if you're ever in the park?"

"Yeah! Sure. That'd be cool, Freya." I return the smile, but as I look closely at her eyes, I see she has a kinda sad, haunted, faraway look. Like she's trying to hide something else, just below the surface. I recognise that look. I've seen it in the mirror gazing back at me so many times lately. I think she recognises it in me too, because she reaches out and squeezes my hand and says, "Maybe Azrael introduced us for a reason, PJ," before turning away to catch up with Archie, who is still nuzzling the grass.

"Bye, PJ. See you!"

"Catch ya later!" I wave as Freya and Archie meander off into the distance.

"Poor li'l guy," I say to Azrael. "You were just frightened, weren't you?" Azrael nuzzles and shoves his head further into my hand. "C'mon then, let's get you home and see if you really are Azrael." Not trusting to chance that the cat will follow me, I carefully pick him up. He sits willingly, cradled in my arms, and seems happy to be transported back to the town house, purring contentedly as we go.

With Azrael tucked under one arm, I put the key in the door and enter the gloomy lobby once more. I wish I didn't have to knock on the old woman's door again. Why couldn't she just have a cat flap like everyone else? Well, there's nothing else for it. I lift the brass door knocker and rap it loudly.

Swish, swish, bump! Swish, swish, bump! The familiar signal that the old woman is approaching echoes behind the heavy door.

"Is that you, PJ? Is Azrael with you?" Her reedy voice calls from inside the apartment.

"Yeah, it's me. I think I have Azrael. I have a cat, anyway," I reply uncertainly.

The door creaks as it slowly opens and the woman's face appears. She opens the door wider and reaches out her gnarled hands. I place the cat into her arms and her hand brushes mine. It feels papery and cold. I flinch. I don't like the touch of her skin, which reminds me of dead leaves.

"Azrael!" She smiles happily, revealing a gummy smile, which, together with the milky, almost sightless eyes, reminds me of every creepy film I've ever seen. "You've done well, PJ. Now I must reward you. Come inside for a moment."

"No! Really. It's fine. You're welcome. Just happy to have helped, Ma'am," I say. "My aunt will be wondering where I am, so I'd better get back," I add, hoping that she'll just leave me alone. Strangely, though, I am reluctant to turn and head up the stairs. It was what she said earlier. About Mom and a message? I wait a moment, hoping that she'll say something without me having to go inside the apartment.

She just stands there, stroking the cat, burying her face into his fur.

"I knew you would find Azrael. Only you could do it."

"Huh? I'm sorry, say *WHAT*?" I blurt out somewhat rudely.

"He is a good angel. You found each other because you need an angel to look after you, PJ."

I am rooted to the spot, my jaw clenched, a cold tingling making its way down my body.

"I-I don't know what you mean," I reply, although I do have an inkling of where this is going.

"We know that you've lost a loved one, PJ. Azrael wants you to know that your mother's soul is at peace but that she is still with you and taking care of you. She has sent you signs. White feathers, I think." My eyes widen and I forget to blink. *How does she know that? About the feathers?* Ever since Mom died, white feathers have been appearing from nowhere. Mom always told me that when a loved one dies, they go to the angels and leave white feathers so that you know they're still with you. I have five perfect white feathers that I've found in the weeks since Mom died, in a box by my bed. The woman appears to be in a kind of trance as she speaks, her glazed eyes looking beyond into the distance.

I want to run now and my breath comes in sharp gasps, but my feet feel like lead, as though something is holding them down.

"Yes, yes, I see it now. She was sick, wasn't she, PJ? But not for long. It was a quick departure. One day here, the next, gone. But they are never gone, PJ. Your mother says, oh…!" She hesitates and tilts her head as though listening intently. "No. Wait. She wants to speak to you herself." I shriek in terror, as the woman throws her head back sharply and breathes noisily and deeply. I think she might be having a heart attack, and I'm about to run upstairs to get help when her head snaps back up and her gaze, if you can call it that, meets my eyes and she speaks.

"Hey, kiddo, how are you doing?" My mouth drops open and I feel the blood rush to my head. The woman's twee Edinburgh accent has given way to Mom's New York twang. My eyes grow wider and my jaw gapes open. There's a sort of faraway echo and the voice comes and goes. "I can't stay long, PJ. I want you to know that I'm OK and I'm always by your side. And by the way, give Aunt Katie a break, will ya? Things will come right, PJ, I promise. We'll sort it, like we always did. Just know that I'll be there to fight your battles with you. I have to go now. She can't keep this up for long. Keep looking for the signs, PJ. Luurrve ya, honey!"

My hands are shaking out of control. *Mom? Was that really you? Don't go!* I want to laugh, cry, stay, run, all at the same time. I unclench my fists and see the nail marks left on my palms. The way she said *luurve ya, honey*, all stretched out and sickly sweet, that was her joke to embarrass me, usually when I was with the guys back home.

I swallow hard as the old woman's head slumps forward. Jeez, her neck must be like elastic! Her eyelids droop. She still grasps Azrael, who's been licking his paws uninterestedly throughout the last few moments.

"I'm sorry, PJ. I must go inside. I must have taken a funny turn there for a moment. It happens sometimes. Need to sit down for a minute. Thank you for returning Azrael." The old woman turns inside the apartment and lets the cat down. He runs inside and disappears into the room beyond. There is a musty old odour that comes from inside.

The door clicks shut behind her and I stand there a few moments in disbelief. Have I really just heard Mom? It sure seems like it. My fear and confusion give way to curiosity. I want to know more. Clenching my fists, I steel myself. I can't just walk away after that, can I? I want to, but something is pushing me to stay. Finally, I pluck up enough courage to confront the old woman for answers. I don't much like the thought of seeing her again and a chill runs through me as I lift the brass knocker. Before I have a chance to let it fall, the door opens so suddenly that I lurch inside, still gripping the brass circle in my hand. Expecting to see the old woman behind the door, I am shocked to find that no-one is there! I figure she can't have closed it properly moments earlier.

I call out and peer into the gloomy room that Azrael had run into. "Hello? Erm, hi? Anyone there? It's me, PJ." At first there is no reply, but then I hear the old woman's signature *swish, bump*, and I feel a tap from behind. I swear I jump clean outta my skin! I turn, and there she is, standing in the doorway of another room off the corridor of her apartment.

"Gee! You gave me a scare!"

"I could say likewise, young man. Do you often enter people's houses without invitation?" Her lips stretch into an amused smile. "Not to worry. I was expecting you'd want to speak further."

Well, it's more than I was expecting, but hey! This day has been full of surprises.

"Yeah, sorry. I mean, no! The door just opened as I held the knocker and I kinda fell in."

"Well, you're here now. Won't you come through and

take tea with me? I think you have some questions."

She's right. I do have questions. *But how does she know that?* I am more than a little afraid.

Go on, you wuss. What harm can a little old blind lady do? Are you a man or a mouse? Squeeeakkk…! That was one of our favourite catcalls when my homies and I were daring each other to do something and any of us showed any fear. I could just hear Dan and Kyle hooting with laughter at me being scared of an old dame. I take a deep breath and go in. The musty smell hits me again. It's combined with an odour of vegetables. Cabbage soup, maybe? I try not to gag. It's not pleasant in here. There's a kinda sweet aroma as well. I shudder. It's a bit like rotting meat. *Maybe she hasn't put the trash out? Perhaps I should ask if she needs any help.* After a few moments, I adjust to the atmosphere and the smell becomes less noticeable. The old lady ushers me into her den, which I had briefly seen from the doorway. It is full of brown leather furniture, cracked, with foam peeking through, lace doily things – *antimacassars*, I think the Rosenbaums called them – over the backs of the chair. A clutter of glass ornaments, carved wooden things, ancient photographs in curly metal frames, china animals adorn every surface. A lamp, in the middle of a round table in the centre of the room, catches my eye. The base is shaped like an elongated black and white cat that looks a lot like Azrael. It has big black wings opened out at either side and I guess this was a representation of the cat as the Angel of God or Death, or whatever it was. It sure does look like the real Azrael, though.

"Please sit, PJ." The woman gestures to a seat at the table. I oblige. I can't take my eyes of that elongated cat.

Something about it spooks me. "Now, can I fetch you some tea?"

"Oh no, please don't worry," I say, wondering how she manages to use a kettle with her poor eyesight. I'm really not keen to eat or drink in here anyway. The old woman slumps awkwardly into the chair next to me.

"Now, give me your hand, PJ," she says. I groan inwardly, dreading that dry, papery touch again. Reluctantly, I stretch out my hand which she grasps with unexpected firmness. The air becomes heavy in the room and I find it difficult to draw breath. I am cold and it's getting colder until it feels like an ice box. OMG, my breath is now a fog, just like it had been in the early-morning air. How can that be?

"Would you mind lighting the candle, please, PJ?" She points to a red candle, half burned, and a lighter that lies next to it on the table. I flick the lighter and hold it next to the wick until it starts to burn. She closes her eyes. The flame sways this way and that, creating shadows in the dimness of the room. Azrael stretches lazily from the sideboard, his eyes orange with the reflection of the burning flame, which dances wildly now. I feel a whoosh of a breeze that comes from nowhere I can identify and I am getting nervous. The old lady has closed her eyes and her bony fingers dig deep into my flesh. As I watch, her face seems to change and I gasp. Different features swim into focus then blur into an indistinct mess. Every few moments she looks like a different person as though they're all fighting to be seen only to be quickly dismissed. I see young people, old people, kind faces, evil faces, their mouths twisting and black, their eyes sad, desperate, murderous even. My heart is racing and I snatch my hand away, desperate to run but equally desperate to understand. I squeeze my eyes nearly shut so that I am just squinting at the woman's changing features, fearing something even more loathsome might appear on her face. Suddenly, the old woman's head jerks back, and when she straightens up, I swear I see Mom's face covering hers. I let out a cry of shock. "Mom?" I exclaim. Mom's face blurs and it is the old lady again.

"Oh, PJ. So much heartache." She shakes her head sadly. "So young to feel so alone. But – now you know you're not alone." The old woman smiles, then hesitates, and closes her cloudy eyes like she's thinking hard. "She has unusual-coloured hair. Very modern. Like a deep purple shade. She has it pulled back. She likes to laugh a lot and she describes herself as *'feisty'*. Wait a minute. She's coming through to speak with you herself.

"Hey, honey! It's me again, Mom." The voice changes to New York twang and I see Mom's face more clearly in the old woman's features.

I feel my eyes widen and my heart beats faster. *Oh my. Surely it can't be. Can it? Yes! It's true, it really is Mom! But how?* My entire body trembles, yet weirdly the fear is less than the warmth of comfort I feel seeing my dead mom here, wanting to talk to me.

"Now listen up, PJ. I don't have much time. She can't keep this up for long. Honey, you're about to start a whole new adventure and things will get better. I'll never be far away from you, PJ, and I'll try to let you know whenever I can that I'm there, looking out for you and Buddy. Don't even think about running away, PJ, *please!* You'll understand soon enough, but Katie is the best person for you right now. Everything will turn out just fine. Have faith, PJ. I gotta go now, hon! She's running outta steam. Just look and you'll find me whenever you need me." Mom's voice becomes distant before I hear her call, "And remember to wash behind your ears!"

My world rocks. What have I just witnessed?

"Mom? Is it really you? Mom! No, don't go! I need to understand, please! Just stay a while longer." But Mom has faded, and it is the old woman's voice I hear.

"Ooch, sonny." The old woman stares ahead, her head tilted as though listening intently to someone whispering in her ear, her glacial, vacant eyes freezing my bones. Those eyes fix themselves on me now. Her features seem to melt and mix until fleetingly, she is Mom again, before teasing themselves back into the ancient, loose-skinned cragginess of the old lady.

How can this be happening? I saw Mom! Maybe it's just the lights and the shadows playing tricks? This is just so freakin' weird. Half of me wants to run to the door and get outta here, but half of me is transfixed and rooted to the spot. If it really is Mom, I wanna know more.

The old woman pats my hand, breathes deeply, and her head falls to her chest. I don't panic this time; I'm used to the routine. Her hand, dry and cold, falls on top of mine and I shiver with disgust, as though creepy-crawly bugs have just walked all over my flesh. I want to pull my hand away but decide to wait until the woman comes round.

I glance at Azrael. As usual, he is busy cleaning himself. It's just another day to him, it seems. The old lady coughs and her head kinda nods a little. Her shoulders heave and she draws in a noisy, lung-filler of a breath. She lifts her chin and blinks. A smile spreads across her face as she leans back in the chair.

"Sorry, son. I can't always control the spirits so well these days. So many of them trying to speak and get their messages across. It's like Waverley Station here sometimes." She cackles. "I have to work hard to connect with the right one." Finally, she releases my hand and I rub it down the leg of my pants, desperate to wipe away the sensation of creepy bugs and dead leaves.

"How did you do that? How did you change your face to my mom's? And you spoke with her voice! How do you know so much about me?"

The old woman cackles again.

"I am a medium, PJ. I'm clairvoyant and clairaudient. Sometimes when I am in contact with the other side, my face will transfigure into the person speaking with me, if they want to show themselves to their loved one. It's a gift I've had all my life, son. Nothing unusual."

Nothing unusual? Well, in a usual day, I've never seen anyone talking with dead people before.

"Er, what *is* a medium exactly? And what's clair… clair…?"

"Clairvoyant and clairaudient?"

"Yeah. Those…"

"Well" – the old woman clasps her hands together, quite relaxed, as though we're chatting about the weather – "a medium is just something used as a way of communicating. A radio is a medium. A television is a medium." She laughs. "I'm a kind of radio and I connect with the dead, just as we use radio waves to connect to the stations. I'm also like a TV set and I channel the pictures."

She chuckles, amused by her explanation. "Clairvoyance and clairaudience just literally mean I can see and hear things clearly, except that they're things that most other people can't see or hear."

"Wow. It sure is scary. Aren't you afraid when it happens?"

The old woman shakes her head. "I've become used to it, PJ. I was afraid when it first happened, way back when I was just a young girl. But not anymore. I've learned to control my gift and those who wish to use it. I think it was very important to your mum that you should come to me, PJ, and I hope that you can take comfort in the fact that she's here, watching over you. The dead are never gone, you see. They just live on a different plane to the living."

Mom's watching me? What – all the time? That could be awkward. I'm not so sure I'm entirely comfortable with this idea, but it is kinda cool to think Mom's OK and even existing somewhere where maybe I'll see her again one day. It does make me feel a little happier, I guess.

I have loads of questions, but the old lady yawns widely. "Ooch, forgive me, PJ. It fair takes it out of me these days, talking to the spirits. Now, if you'll excuse me, I need to rest."

I thank her and take my cue to leave. "I'm sorry," I say, "I never asked your name."

"It's Mrs Anderson," she says.

"Well, I'll be seeing you Mrs Anderson. And, er, thanks again."

She follows me to the door, shuffling in her usual rhythmic style and as it clicks shut, I hear the rattle of chains and bolts as she secures it behind me. I wrap my arms around myself as a cold shiver runs down the length of my spine and head upstairs to Aunt Katie's apartment, glancing uneasily behind me.

What just happened? I rub my forehead. *That was Mom speaking. No doubt about it. But – how…? What does it mean?* I am too shocked to think straight. My head hurts. I shake my head as though to clear the jumble that's inside. Maybe I'm dreaming? Yes, that must be it. I'll wake up any minute now and find I've been in a nightmare. But no. I don't truly believe that. Was the woman playing a prank on me? But then how did she know about Mom? Maybe she spoke to Aunt Katie. *Yes, that's it! Has to be the answer, doesn't it?* This was just too freakin' strange.

I trudge slowly and heavily up the spiralling staircase, thoughts whirling around my head so fast I think it will burst. I just heard my mom speak. It's funny, but for all the weirdness, I feel better. It was her. In my heart, I am certain of it, even if my head is telling me there has to be another explanation. I am suddenly grateful to the crazy lady and Azrael. I reach Aunt Katie's door and a big fat fluffy white feather sits on the mat. I frown and with still-trembling hands, I reach down for it. I swallow hard. "*Thanks, Mom, I hear ya.*"

❋

"PJ? Is that you?" Aunt Katie's voice comes from the kitchen. *Shoot! I was hoping to sneak in without her noticing.*

"Yeah," I call back, shrugging off my windcheater. I bite my lip, considering whether to go straight to my room or face the awkwardness of seeing Aunt Katie. In the end, I decide I have to see her sometime and the longer I leave it, the worse it'll get.

"Um, hi," I say, uncertainly.

"How was your walk? Did you find the park OK?" Aunt Katie smiles as though nothing had happened earlier.

"Yeah. Good." There is silence for a moment. I thrust my hands deep into my pockets, trying to appear casual, unconcerned.

"What have you been up to? You've been a while." Aunt Katie is sitting at the table, a laptop open in front of her. A pair of glasses are perched at the end of her nose and she clutches a mug of coffee in her hands. Her hair is piled high and messily, just like Mom used to wear it when she was working at her desk.

"Oh, I just went to see the old lady from downstairs. I met her earlier when I found her cat in the park."

Aunt Katie pulls the glasses from her nose and gives me a questioning look. "Old lady? What old lady?"

"You know, the one who lives in the apartment below this one?" *Surely, she must have met her at some time?*

"But that apartment's empty, PJ," Aunt Katie says gently. "There hasn't been anyone in there for the last six months, since Mrs Anderson died."

CHAPTER 4

My stomach leaps right up into my chest. *What does she mean? Mrs Anderson died? Haven't I just been talking to her? She's as alive and breathing as me and Aunt Katie!*

"Look." Aunt Katie rises and takes a set of keys from the hook by the kitchen door. "I have the keys to keep an eye on the place and let the cleaners and workmen in. The family are remodelling it a little before selling. I've been down several times in the last couple of weeks. There's nothing and no-one in there, PJ."

I'm stunned into silence. I don't know what to say. I know what I saw and I know that Mrs Anderson is there!

"Um, maybe it was one of her family, then," I say.

"No, that can't be it. They live in England and they always contact me for the keys if they're visiting." Aunt Katie is frowning, puzzled. "Hey, c'mon," she says, "let's go down and take a look. If there's someone in there, I need to know about it."

She sounds braver than she looks as we creep down the stairs, fearing that the slightest noise is going to alert the 'intruder'. We hesitate outside the door and Aunt Katie looks nervous as she shuffles through the keys on the ring to find the one for the front door. Eventually, she clasps a mortice key and puts it in the keyhole and turns the doorknob. The door creaks open and Aunt Katie feels for the light switch. The room is suddenly illuminated and I inhale sharply at what I'm seeing.

The apartment is totally empty. I can see through the door to the den where I'd been sitting only minutes earlier. The dowdy furniture is gone; the table with the Azrael looky-likey has disappeared, and even the carpets and rugs have been taken up. It smells of fresh paint. We stand on the bare floorboards for a moment, before warily checking out the rooms. In each, it's the same story. Empty, except for decorators' ladders and a few paint pots awaiting their return to finish the job that is already well in progress. I shake my head in disbelief. *This can't be happening! It's me who's gone cray cray!*

"Are you OK, PJ?"

I can't speak. I just stand, my mouth opening and closing like a goldfish, my palms upturned, my head shaking in denial of the obvious.

"C'mon, outta here," Aunt Katie says decisively. "You don't look well right now, PJ." She ushers me through the lobby and out into the communal hallway, locking the door firmly behind her. She shudders. I think she senses that something is way off-key here, as she eyes me with a quizzical look, brows knitted together.

I don't remember climbing the stairs back to Aunt Katie's apartment, or the moment when she wraps a blanket around my shivering body. She turns on the gas fire and I gaze into the flames, trying to find a rational explanation for the events of the day.

Aunt Katie brings a hot chocolate and I manage to grasp the mug in my freezing cold hands and gratefully sip on the sweet, creamy liquid. It does the trick and I feel a little better…

"Do you want to talk about it, PJ?"

I nod. "When did Mrs Anderson die?"

"It was around six months ago. It was all a bit of a shock, really. She kept herself to herself mostly. She didn't get out and about much because—"

"She was blind, wasn't she? Her eyes were all kinda misted over and milky white."

Aunt Katie's mouth drops open and she looks at me dumbstruck. "But, how could you know that? I mean, yes, that's right. She had cataracts and she had difficulty walking."

"Uh huh. She used a walking stick, didn't she?"

"Yes, that's right, PJ. It was terrible when they found her. You see, she'd been dead for over a week and no-one noticed. It was the postman who alerted us, seeing the mail piling up on the table outside her apartment."

"Was there, like, a sickly sweet sorta smell, mixed with vegetable soup in the apartment?"

"Why, yes, that's exactly what it was like. She had a pan of soup on the hob, come to think about it." Aunt Katie pulls a face and shakes herself, trying, I guess, to rid herself of the memory.

"Did she have a cat called Azrael?"

"Yeah, only it wasn't in the apartment when we found her. I guess she must have let it out before she died and it's gone elsewhere by now."

"I found him earlier. He was in the park. She said she'd lost him. I brought him back with me. That's when she invited me in and told me, she told me…"

"Told you what, PJ?" Aunt Katie says gently.

I am feeling real weird about this. Aunt Katie knows Mrs Anderson is dead, *I* know she's dead, and yet I'm describing a meeting with, well, what? A ghost? *Really?* Aunt Katie must be thinking I'm completely crazy!

"Well, she kinda turned into Mom and she knew stuff. Like, she knew about the feathers, and Mom said I had to give you a chance and that everything would be OK and…" It just all comes out. I can't stop the tears any longer, remembering Mom's face and her voice in Mrs Anderson's apartment. My body is trembling and I feel scared. *Real scared*. What's wrong with me, I wonder? Aunt Katie warily reaches out, puts her arm around my shoulder and draws me to her. I don't resist. She gives me a full hug and for the first time in ages, I feel safe. We sit like that for a while, as I soak Aunt Katie's cardigan with my tears.

Finally, when I'm all cried out, Aunt Katie releases me and strokes my hair.

"I'm sorry, Aunt Katie, I've been a monster, haven't I?"

She smiles softly and shakes her head. "Not at all, PJ. I expected a bumpy ride. After all you've been through lately, it's natural and just part of the grieving process. It's OK, hon."

"Aunt Katie?"

"Uh huh?"

"Do you think I'm going nuts? I mean, I've just told you I've been talking to a dead old lady and my mom. It's kinda out there, and I-I'm scared."

Aunt Katie takes a deep breath. "PJ, I don't for one moment think you're nuts. Something clearly happened down there in the apartment. How else could you have known about Mrs Anderson? I think, sometimes when people have heightened emotions, they can kinda 'tune in' to things. Have you ever seen the movie *The Sixth Sense*?"

I nod. I saw it a coupla years back when I watched it with my mom. Jeez, is she saying it really *was* a ghostly encounter I'd just had? That makes me feel really uneasy, but something Aunt Katie just said reminds me of how the old woman had described what happens to her.

"Mrs Anderson said something about 'tuning in,'" I tell Aunt Katie. "Like on a radio or a TV. She called it clairvoyance and when she just heard stuff, clairaudience." Aunt Katie nods, as though I've just said the most normal thing in the world. "How come you don't think I've lost my mind, when I'm telling you this stuff?"

"Well, believe it or not, PJ, my job is to study just this subject at the university. I'm a parapsychologist. We have a whole unit there, set up to look at these sorts of experiences. Mostly, they have a perfectly rational explanation. Our minds are really sophisticated things, PJ, and we don't really know much about how the brain works. But I would hazard a guess that your senses are sharp just now and it's just possible that you picked up on something because of that."

"*Wow!* Are you telling me you're a professional *ghost hunter*?"

Aunt Katie laughs. "No, PJ, that's not it at all. I'm a scientist primarily. I don't go ghost hunting or ghost busting or whatever you want to call it. I study the mind and the experiences of people who claim to see ghosts, talk to the dead, have telepathic and telekinetic abilities—"

"Whoa! Slow down, Aunt Katie! You 'study their minds'? How d'you do that?"

"As I said, it's all very scientific, PJ. We carry out controlled experiments in laboratory conditions to see if people who tell us they can communicate with the dead, or read minds or move objects just by thinking about it, can replicate their claims under closely regulated and closed circumstances."

"Wow! Just wow!" I exhale deeply. This was taking things to a whole new level of coincidence. "So, do you believe in ghosts or life after death now that you've carried out experiments?"

"Hmm…" Aunt Katie hesitates, as though trying to find the right words. "To answer your question, I'm prepared to be convinced, but if I'm honest, whilst I've seen some extraordinary things, there's nothing yet that I could say gives me one hundred per cent proof positive that there is life after death or that people have superpowers. It's sure interesting, though."

Well, how d'you like that? Who knew my Aunt Katie was so darned cool?

"Anyway, enough of this for now. How about I go get us some tea, or OJ and a Tunnock's Teacake? We can talk more, if you're interested, once you've gotten over the shock of all this."

I grin, and realise I am warming to her more by the day.

"Just one more question, Aunt Katie?"

"Shoot!"

"I'm kinda weirded out. Scared. What if the ghosts all come back and haunt me?"

"Well, think about it for a moment. Did Mrs Anderson try to hurt you, honey? Or Mom, when you saw her?"

I think for a moment and shake my head. "Nope. Mrs Anderson just seemed like a regular old lady, who just looked a bit scary, I guess. And Mom. Well, she was just Mom."

"So, it was a *good* experience, PJ. Nothing to be afraid of, huh? If Mrs Anderson and Mom *did* visit you, it was to help you, not hurt you."

I see the sense in what Aunt Katie is saying. And yeah, now I think of it, it's nice that Mrs Anderson showed me that Mom is OK. But I remember something else.

"The bit with Mom and Mrs Anderson, that's kinda cool, I guess. But, when Mrs A's face changed, I saw some really scary faces. Some looked bad."

"It's just like life, PJ. There are good people and bad people. But I don't believe that ghosts can harm you, unless you let them get to you. The only thing to fear is fear itself, as good ol' President Roosevelt said in his inaugural speech. I think you should think of what happened as a gift, PJ. Your mom needed to speak with you and, somehow, she found a way."

"I guess. Jeez, she always did have to have the last word."

Aunt Katie and I laugh at that. She promises to talk more about parapsychology another time, but for now, well, I'm bushed and I head for bed, keeping one eye over my shoulder at all times.

CHAPTER 5

I wake up from a thankfully uneventful sleep, undisturbed by any spooks visiting with me. I never believed in ghosts before. I thought it was all Caspar the Friendly Ghost, or Scooby Doo fake spooks. But now, I think, I've seen the real deal. Dead people who still walk among us and even come visit to say 'hi' every so often. I can tell you, it's a real mind freak.

My head is mush. Is Mom watching me now, I wonder? And Aunt Katie – a… what did she call it? *Parapsychologist, that's it!* Someone who studies ghosty stuff for a living! Who even knew that was a thing? She didn't seem to think taking tea with a dead woman who changes into your mom (and various others) was anything to get het up about! Gee, my family sure is one in a million!

As I drag myself up from under the covers (I kept my head buried under the quilt last night), and stretch out with a satisfying yawn, my hand touches something. I peer over to my side and see a parcel, wrapped up in ribbon and with a card tucked inside.

It's rectangular and kinda heavy. I shake it a little, but it doesn't give me a clue as to what's inside. I tear off the paper and there is a white box inside with a silver apple on the lid. *Wow. Just wow! This has gotta be…* I lift off the lid. *It is! It's an iPad. Mom always wanted to buy me one of those. Said she would when she was qualified and got herself a good job.* I hold the screen and press the button. It's charged up and ready to go. I can't help but feel a flutter of excitement. I can do my journal on here. Take photographs, make videos, all kinds of cool stuff.

I pick up the envelope and pull out the card inside. It says:

> PJ   a little gift from me to welcome you to Edinburgh. I sent the Rosenbaums one of these too. Thought you could keep in touch with them and Buddy over FaceTime as I know how much you're missing them. Hope it makes you feel a little less homesick. Love, Aunt Katie xxx

Wow! I haven't thought of that! FaceTime! I can see Buddy and the Rosenbaums and they can see me! I can't wait to get it set up. I think back to yesterday when I flipped out at Aunt Katie. She's been thoughtful and I've just been a jerk. She was so cool last night. Didn't laugh at me when I told her about the ghost. And now this. *Got some making up to do. Not just playing nice, but BEING nice!* After all, it's what Mom wants. Isn't it?

I throw on some clothes and bound through to the kitchen where I find Aunt Katie working at her laptop, a mug of steaming coffee next to her. She looks up at me and, boy, does she look like my mom! The way she's pinned up her hair with a pencil, the way her eyes sparkle when she smiles, even the way she holds her chin on the back of her hands remind me of Mom. My heart lurches but I dig deep and manage a grin.

"Thanks so much for the iPad, Aunt Katie." She smiles, and completely without warning, I find myself giving her a hug and planting a kiss on her cheek. She reddens but smiles with pleasure, as she touches her face in surprise.

"You're welcome, PJ. I thought it might cheer you up. Just a little," she adds quickly. "I mean, I know it's not going to help bring Mom back, but, well, you know…"

I beam my brightest smile at her to let her know I understand. "It's a great idea," I say. "I'm gonna call the Rosenbaums and Buddy tonight. You bought them an iPad too?"

"Yeah." Katie laughs. "You should've heard the controversy it caused about how to set it up and get it going. I had to go through a whole tutorial with them, while they argued and bickered about whether Mr Rosenbaum was doing it right and Mrs Rosenbaum worried about how she'd look on the screen. It was hilarious. They're wonderful people, though, PJ. And they're missing you and Mom dreadfully."

I laugh, picturing them with the iPad, trying to work it out as though it was some magic object. They had enough trouble working the TV remote; they have no chance with technology! I wonder how they'll cope with a live FaceTime. I'll find out later, I guess.

With our new-found friendship, I feel comfortable enough to ask Aunt Katie about her relationship with my mom.

"Aunt Katie, what exactly happened between you and Mom? Why didn't you help her when she was sick? You didn't even come to the funeral."

Aunt Katie's eyes glisten as she sweeps her hand through her hair. She shrugs helplessly.

"Life happened, PJ. When I came over here to study, I wanted you both to come with me. I'd looked after your mom when our parents died, and then, as she got older, she wanted to lead her own life with you. I think she wanted to prove she could do it. She refused to come here and I guess we just drifted apart. Nothing dramatic, just five thousand miles and different lives separating us. When Mom's attorney called me to say she was real sick, I wired over some money to make sure she got the best medical treatment, but it was too late. We did speak every day, though, after that and I promised I would be here for you when I was needed. When the end came, it was so fast."

I nod, remembering how Mom had been kinda tired but OK for a few weeks, then suddenly, she collapsed, right there in front of my eyes. I remember flying out of our apartment and down the stairs yelling for the Rosenbaums to come help. The paramedics came and Mom was taken to the state hospital. She never came back out. I push back a sob, thinking of her, all wired up to machines, barely able to speak, and her weak little hand holding mine as she gently slipped away.

As though reading my thoughts, Aunt Katie grasps my hand now. "I'd been planning to fly out to New York that week, after I'd sorted things out over here. Then I got the call. I was devastated that I hadn't made it in time. I booked a flight right away to get over for the funeral but my flight was cancelled – a storm in the Atlantic, they said. When it all subsided, late the following day, the funeral was over. I called the Rosenbaums and we agreed that it was best that you fly over here. And that's it, really. I can't turn the clock back, PJ, but I'm here for you, and her. I can't tell you how much I regret what's happened. I sure wish things were different. All I can do is my best in the here and now to help you through this and take care of you. You're the only family I have now."

We sit there, in silence, our hands still clasped together. I don't want to pull away. I smile and I feel, for the first time, like it really will be OK.

CHAPTER 6

"Say, I have to go to my office at the university for a while this morning. Will you be OK if I leave you alone here for a couple of hours?"

"Sure. No worries." I shrug. I'm actually quite relieved to be alone with my thoughts for a while. "Do you have any spare paint for the bedroom? I could try to fix up the wall I messed up while you're out."

"That'd be great, PJ. Yeah, have a look in the cupboard behind you. It should be near the front of the first shelf."

I find the paint, a tray and a foam roller from the cupboard and head off to the bedroom as Katie throws on her coat.

"Won't be long," she calls. "I've left my cell number on the table in case you need me for anything. Save it to yours."

"Cool. Thanks. See you later."

I'm glad to have something to occupy my mind as I roll the paint over the yukky mess on the wall. This has been one freaky old week and I can't stop thinking about how the old woman mimicked Mom's voice so darn accurately.

I step back and check out my work. Not bad, I think. I had to do the whole wall to blend in the paint, but it's looking almost good as new now. After cleaning off the roller and the tray, I pour a glass of OJ, just as Aunt Katie breezes through the door. I tell her I've finished the painting and she's real pleased with my work.

"Great job, PJ. Looks as good as new. Now, I'm sorry to be a pain, but I have to finish this paper I'm working on. Do you have any plans for the rest of the day?"

"I think I'll take another walk in the park for a while. I met this girl, Freya, walking her dog, Archie, yesterday. Maybe she'll be there again today."

"Great idea. How about I treat you to fish and chips for dinner tonight? Another great British delicacy!"

"Sounds cool. But the British eat chips with their fish?"

"Yeah, but not the ones you're thinking of, PJ. What we call 'chips' here are what you call fries. They're much better than the ones you get in NYC! You'll see!" Aunt Katie grins.

I grab my windcheater and head off out. The communal lobby is silent as I go down the stairs and my heart is thumping with fear as I near the bottom. I don't stop and I don't look at Mrs Anderson's apartment as I literally sprint to the door. I'm breathing heavily as I step out into the crisp fall sunshine again.

The door clicks shut behind me and I hear a shuffling sound, followed by insistent meowing. It's Azrael! He's perched on the base of the column and when he sees me, he stretches lazily and jumps down, rubbing himself against my legs and winding his body in and out between them. I bend to stroke his head and chin. He sure feels real.

Poor little guy. He must be wondering what happened to his mom and his home.

"Hey, Azrael. How you doin' today? Got the same idea as me, have you?"

The cat stretches his chin upwards and his mouth pulls into a grin as I scratch the underside. He purrs contentedly.

"Well, that's enough for now. See you later, huh?"

I head off down the stairs and stride towards the park. I look back and see Azrael following behind me. I stop. He stops. I walk on; he starts jauntily padding behind me. I turn and smile at him, bending once more to stroke his head.

"Are you 'fur' real?" I ask, admiring my own joke as Azrael nuzzles his head further into my hand. "OK then, you can come too," I tell him. As though he knows permission has been granted, he takes his place by my side, rather than his furtive five steps behind.

We reach the park and Azrael disappears into the bushes. I sure hope he'll get home OK. I decide I'm gonna ask Aunt Katie if he can come stay with us.

It's a crisp fall day and there is a chill in the air this morning. It isn't dissimilar to fall in New York, although it is usually a little warmer than this. My breath is visible, as my warm air hits the chill and creates a foggy cloud from my mouth. I have a lot to think about, but I guess with one thing settled – I'm not heading back to New York anytime soon, no matter how much I want it – my options are now clearer. If I'm honest, I'm down to one – stay here in Edinburgh with Aunt Katie. *Would it really be so bad?* I decide here and now, I'm gonna make the best of things, and in a funny sort of way, with that resolved, I feel a lot better.

Freya and Archie aren't anywhere to be seen in the park today. I wait a while in case they show up, but nada! Disappointed, I head back to Aunt Katie's, and just as I'm crossing over the cobbles back to the apartment, Azrael appears and jumps up onto his perch on the column.

"Azrael! I think you're spying on me!" *Or watching over me, maybe?* I stretch over to scratch his head again, then warily turn the key in the door. Azrael follows me in and stops for a moment outside Mrs Anderson's apartment. I'm already taking the stairs two at a time, when I hear the tapping of little paws behind me. He really *is* following me.

"I guess you read my mind, little guy. C'mon then, let's see what Aunt Katie says!"

I wander casually into the kitchen, where Aunt Katie is still working. Azrael stays firmly behind me.

"Hey, Aunt Katie, I'm back," I say unnecessarily. She's already looking past me and staring at Azrael, who eyes her warily.

"Uh huh, and who's your friend?" She raises an eyebrow.

"Um, it's Azrael. I think he's been homeless since Mrs Anderson passed away. He's been following me everywhere I go." I squirm a little, as Aunt Katie's eyebrow disappears into her fringe. "I was wondering if maybe he could stay here? Even until we find him a new home? Er, maybe…?"

Aunt Katie smiles. "Well, since you ask so nicely, PJ. I guess we can't leave him out in the winter cold, can we?" She stoops down and stretches out her hand. Azrael, as usual, can't resist the prospect of attention and he approaches her quite happily and rubs himself against her knees as she scratches his head.

I'm relieved and happy that Azrael is staying. He is,

after all, my guardian angel. I'm sure that Mom and Mrs Anderson cooked this one up for me.

I head off to my room, with Azrael following close behind me. He stops every so often to inspect his new home. I sure hope it meets his standards! I lie on my bed and Azrael leaps up and promptly curls up on the quilt, where he soon drifts off into a contented sleep. I reach for the iPad and spend the rest of the afternoon playing around with it.

Eventually, I look at the bedside clock. Wow! It's 5.30pm. That means it's around twelve noon back in New York. I picture the Rosenbaums in the deli, making pastrami or salt beef on rye sandwiches with pickles and slaw and packing them up in wax paper for the lunchtime rush of customers. Not a good time to call now then, I think. I make sure the iPad is set up to use FaceTime later. The shop closes around six NY time, so I'll call then. I smile as I think of speaking to my fur baby Buddy later. If only I could FaceTime Mom, but this time, without Mrs Anderson's help!

I hear Aunt Katie calling me for dinner and Azrael jumps up, sniffing the air as a delicious fishy smell wafts through the apartment. She was right about one thing, British fish and chips are a thing of wonder. Squishy fat chips, covered in vinegar, with golden battered cod appears from white paper-wrapped packages. I could live on this forever, I think, as Katie and I tuck in amiably. I watch movies for a while on Netflix (some habits are hard to break). Neither Katie nor I have mentioned Mrs Anderson or ghosts today. I think we just want to find some normality for a while. All the same, my mind wanders off, thinking about Mom and how she came to see me. I hope I'll see her again, but the thought of going near Mrs Anderson's apartment scares me rigid.

Finally, it's time to FaceTime. Aunt Katie called the Rosenbaums by phone earlier, to give them advance warning that I'd be on the iPad tonight. I set up the call and wait for them to answer. Moments later, our chaotic first attempt begins.

"No, Ezra, that's not it! Look you have to push this button, here…"

"Push this button, swipe this bit. I swear I'll never be used to this new-fangled stuff…" Mr Rosenbaum shakes his head in bafflement.

"Mr Rosenbaum, Mrs Rosenbaum – can you hear me?" I say as loudly as I can over their argument.

"Say! Yeah, I hear ya, PJ!"

"You can hear him, Ezra? You can hear PJ? Can you see him too?"

"Yeah – it's easier than I thought, Rachael. Look, can you see PJ?"

Mrs Rosenbaum comes over to the screen and peers down so close I can see right up her nose.

"Mrs Rosenbaum – hold the iPad away from you. I can only see your nose from here." I giggle.

"Oh, PJ, PJ! I've missed you so. How are you? Have you been eating enough?"

I assure Mrs Rosenbaum that yes, I'm fine and I'm eating enough. I make light of things as I don't want them to worry about me, especially as I know about Mr Rosenbaum's heart condition now.

"You look sad, PJ. Tell me now, are you real sad? You need to tell people if you are, you know. You mustn't suffer in silence."

"Rachael – of course the boy's sad! He's just lost his

mom; how do you think he's feeling?" Mr Rosenbaum scolds his wife.

"Well, yeah, it's hard, I guess," I say, downplaying how I really feel. "I miss you both and Buddy, so much."

"We'd love you to have stayed with us, PJ. Ezra, wouldn't we have loved for him to stay here?"

"Sure would," says Mr Rosenbaum. "But PJ, we couldn't have done what Aunt Katie can do for you now. Besides, you needed someone younger around you. You wouldn't want to be with a pair of old fogies like us."

"I-I'd really like to come back and be with you both," I can't stop myself from saying.

"You're not getting on with your aunt?" asks Mrs Rosenbaum. Both of their faces are too close to the screen and they look a little like comic book characters.

"I didn't at first," I say. "I felt real angry at her because she didn't come and help Mom," I tell them.

Mr Rosenbaum shakes his head and looks at Mrs Rosenbaum.

"Don't be harsh on your aunt, now PJ," he says. "She's desperate to do right by you. Sure, everyone makes mistakes in their lives, but it wasn't just her. Your mom confided in us that she was just as much to blame for losing contact. In fact, she said it was mostly down to her. She was real happy when, close to the end, she and Katie were reconciled and speaking. It was a huge relief to her that Katie was going to look after you. For your mom, PJ, give things a chance."

Mrs Rosenbaum is nodding vigorously.

"For once, he's right, PJ. And you know that's not something I say often, huh? I don't often say that about you, do I, Ezra? Besides, when you get more settled and organised, you can come stay with us in the school vacation. Wouldn't that be nice? Wouldn't that be wonderful, Ezra?" Mrs Rosenbaum clasps her hands eagerly.

I laugh, feeling so much lighter than I have in days.

"That'd be just great." I grin widely. "I can't wait to see you guys. Now, how's my boy Buddy? Is he OK?"

"He's fine and dandy." Mr Rosenbaum moves from the screen and I hear him calling, "Hey boy! Buddy! C'mere! PJ's here to see you." I hear the thud of paws and as Mr Rosenbaum moves the iPad towards Buddy, he bounds up and licks the screen. He sniffs it and tilts his head when hears my voice. He can't quite work out where I am, but his tail is wagging and he gives a happy bark. After a little doggy chat, Buddy gets distracted by something behind him and, relieved that he seems contented enough and that he isn't pining away, I wind up my FaceTime with virtual hugs and kisses and settle down to sleep with Azrael softly purring next to me.

CHAPTER 7

I wander sleepily into the kitchen, rubbing my eyes. "Hey, Aunt Katie, have you seen Azrael? He went to sleep on my bed last night but he's not there now." Aunt Katie looks up from her laptop.

"Nope, he hasn't been in here. Did you sleep well?"

"Yeah, I guess, thanks. Wonder where he's gone?"

"Probably hiding in a closet somewhere. Here, come sit with me, I want to talk with you for a minute."

Uh oh, sounds ominous. I slump down in the chair opposite and pour some OJ from the jug on the table.

"Wassup?" I grin, waiting for her to spill whatever she wants to say.

"Well, I got to thinking last night. I think it would be good for you to meet some other kids."

"Uh huh." *There's a catch coming…*

"Yeah, so, I thought it might help if you met kids who are in a similar situation." She looks at me, waiting to see how this piece of news is going down. I don't say anything. I'm not sure that's such a great idea. I mean, how miserable would that be? Not the kids, that is, just the '*situation*'.

"So, I called up this support group where you can share your experiences and talk about how you feel. It's all set for you to go this evening." Aunt Katie bites her lip, warily, waiting for my reaction.

I know she's trying to help and although I'm not enthusiastic about the idea of wallowing in a mutual pity party, I guess it might be good to meet some other kids.

"OK, I guess we can try it at least."

Aunt Katie grins with pleasure and heaves a sigh of what I think is relief. She's probably worried about my old friend the boa constrictor rearing his ugly head again. But no, I'm oddly relaxed and decide to go with the flow.

"Great! Well, it's all arranged for six o'clock tonight. Why don't you go look for Azrael? He might be hungry. I'll fix him something just now and then pick up some cat food while you're at the group."

Well, I look high and low for that darned cat, but he's done another of his disappearing acts. Where could he have gone? I scratch my head. Maybe Aunt Katie opened the door and he's gone out. That must be it.

"Aunt Katie?" I poke my head around the door. "I can't find Azrael anywhere. Did you open the door this morning?"

"Nope, I haven't been out at all today. It's *raining cats and dogs* out there!" Aunt Katie giggles at her little joke. "I'm sure he's just found a cosy nook to hang out in. Cats are pretty clever when it comes to finding the warmest spot to curl up in. Don't worry, he'll show up when he's hungry enough."

I'm not convinced but say, "I guess," before heading off to my room to play on the iPad. The rain is bouncing down on the pavement below. No point in going to the park today. Freya and Archie probably won't venture out in this downpour, I think.

By 5.45, we're ready to set off for the support group. *Gee, it sounds so lame. Not something I'll be mentioning to the guys back home on FaceTime, that's for sure!* Azrael still hasn't appeared and I'm getting real worried about him. Maybe he'll show up by the time we get back.

It's only a couple of miles drive, and already I'm regretting this. I'm still not sure how Aunt Katie got me to agree so easily. If Mom had suggested such a thing I'd have argued endlessly and, if that didn't work, I'd have resorted to whining and wheedling my way out of it. Or at least tried! Tbh, if Mom decided something, it took a lot to change her mind. Oh well, nothing for it, I guess. I'll go this once and work out the best path of resistance later.

We arrive at some kind of community hall and I drag myself out of the car.

"See you in an hour," Aunt Katie calls after me. "I'll be waiting right here for you."

"Uh huh," I manage disdainfully as I slam the door shut a little too forcefully. A woman is at the reception desk and she greets me like a long-lost friend.

"Hi, come on in," she says, altogether too brightly, rising from her chair to come around to my side of the desk. "Now, then, you must be PJ."

"Uh yeah, that's me," I respond bleakly.

"Nothing to be worried about, PJ. We're all friends here,"

she says, leading me through a set of double doors into a room that smells like school after the cleaners have been in. A piano stands in the corner of the room and about eight kids of different ages between eleven and sixteen sit on chairs set out in a semi-circle. They aren't chatting amongst themselves but sit quietly on their chairs, scuffing the floor with their feet, studying their nails or playing on their cell phones. They look as though they want to be here as much as I do. Only one of them pays any attention to me. He's a ginger-haired boy, around my age, his hair unkempt and more fidgety than the rest. As our eyes meet, he gives me a cheeky grin and raises his eyes as if to say, '*I don't know what I'm doing here either*'. I manage a mealy grin in return and sit down next to a girl who is playing with her cell phone and doesn't stop to acknowledge me. I give a sideways look and darn nearly fall off my chair! OMG, it's Freya! I was so wrapped up in myself I hadn't noticed her. How I could miss her, I don't know. She's still engrossed on WhatsApp.

"Er, Freya?" She looks my way and her face lights up in recognition.

"PJ! Hi! What are you doing here? How's Azrael?"

"My aunt made me come. And, well, he was OK, but I can't find him today."

"Oh, he'll turn up. Guardian angels are always close by." She grins. "No, when I said, 'what are you doing here', I meant, *why* are you here? I mean, it's a bereavement group. You know, to talk about people that you've lost, and you're sad about."

"Yeah, I know. My mom. She died a few weeks back. It's why I'm here in Edinburgh. Aunt Katie had this brainwave that spreading my misery with others would help. Can't see that it'll do much good, though. But what about you? Why are you here?"

Freya hesitates. The smile has faded from her face and she bites her lip. Her hands grip her cell phone and her voice is quiet as she eventually finds the words that are so hard to say.

"My twin sister died recently. We were really close. Like your aunt, my mother in her infinite wisdom thought this would make me feel better. It's the most conventional thought she's ever had!" Freya rolls her eyes disdainfully, but I can see the hurt in them as I recall the haunted look I'd noticed back in the park.

I give up the bravado I've been trying to show the world and I manage a whispered, "Gee, sorry, Freya."

Freya nods and sighs deeply. "Thanks, PJ. Likewise. It's tough, isn't it?"

"Sure is. But, I'm glad to see you. A familiar face and all that."

Just then, the overly chirpy woman from the desk comes in and sits in the chair facing us.

"Great to see you all tonight. So, welcome! Some old faces and a couple of new ones too. Now, I want everyone to feel comfortable. This is your safe space where we can exchange thoughts and ideas about what's brought us here and just let rip with whatever emotions you're feeling about it. There's no shame in crying or being angry and confused. All of that is absolutely normal when you've lost a loved one so don't be afraid to show it. So, let's get started, then. First, I think we should introduce ourselves and just say who it is we're remembering here tonight."

I groan, inwardly. I had hoped to slither out of here without having to say a word. She goes around the circle and I discover the ginger-haired boy is called 'Shuggie'. Weird name, I think, as he blurts it out confidently in an almost unintelligible Scottish accent.

"My name's Shuggie and I've lost ma maw," he says.

Freya is next as she quietly explains that her twin sister died of a childhood heart condition.

It's my turn and I feel my face redden as Morag, who had introduced herself first as leader of the group, nods encouragingly.

"Uh, I'm PJ," I say. I hope comes across as nonchalant and confident. "And, um, well, my mom died of cancer a few weeks ago." My voice cracks just a little and ends in a whisper. I don't get to wallow for long, though.

"PJ?!" Shuggie exclaims. "Whit kind o' name is that when it's at hame? PJ? Like ye call yer jammies when ye cannae be bothered tae say pyjamas?"

There's a murmur of laughter and Morag intervenes with, "Shuggie, I don't think this is the time for jokes. Please, everyone, PJ is trying speak."

I'm not sure whether to be angry or laugh. I choose humour.

"Uh huh, just like PJ in pyjamas," I agree. Only they're my initials (as I'm sure he well knows). "Short for Phillip Joel," I add.

"Aye, well, I can see why ye call yersel' PJ, eh?"

I am about to answer in what might be less than complimentary terms considering his name was '*Shuggie*' but bite my tongue instead and ask if it's his real name.

"Naw – it's longer than ma real name. Hugh is ma real

name, so ye can tell why ah prefer the nickname. Frae America, are ye?"

Well, duh-uh, I think, but don't say. "Yeah, from New York."

"So how come ye ended up here?" he asks.

I shrug. "Misread the departures board at JFK Airport," I say, casually folding my arms. "Meant to go to Edinburgh" – which I pronounce the American way, *Ee-din-berg* – "Indiana, but ended up here by mistake."

"*Really?*" he asks in all seriousness. *Gullible much?* Can't spot sarcasm when it hits him. I grin, pleased to have scored a point. One all!

"No, I was just kidding. My aunt is my only relative so after my mom died, I came to live with her."

"Ah right. Yeah. Ye just get shoved from pillar tae post when yer ma dies, eh?" He shakes his head philosophically. "It's just a pile o' poo, eh?"

Morag decides at this point to interrupt the *PJ & Shuggie Show*. She wants to get down to business, saying, "Right, well, PJ, I'm sure you want to tell us about your mum and what it's meant to you."

Personally, I'm happier with the distraction and I'm enjoying Shuggie's cheeky humour. Better than dragging us all down to the misery we're supposed to be trying to escape. However, Morag is determined.

"So, PJ, how do you feel about losing your mum?" Morag speaks softly and sincerely. *Jeez, really? How does she think I feel? Overjoyed! Couldn't be better!* Shuggie rolls his eyes and shakes his head. He knows what I'm thinking. I feel I have to say something.

"I, er, I feel unhappy, I guess. I feel like I have a horrible snake in my stomach that tightens up whenever I think of Mom and my dog Buddy. I'm angry and I want to hurt people sometimes. I feel lonely and empty and I don't know how to be me anymore." I shrug. What else is there to say?

"Thank you for sharing that with us, PJ. How about you, Freya?" She looks up from her cell again. She'd lost interest after Morag shut me and Shuggie down.

"Me? Well, same as PJ. Although, I don't feel my sister, Alana, is really gone. We were so close. I feel she's still with me."

I look sharply at Freya. *What does she mean?* She looks at me and smiles and I think she knows. She knows I feel the same, but I don't know how.

"So, open to the whole group," Morag continues. "Someone explain how all these feelings affect us." There is a communal shuffling of feet, heads down, everyone trying to avoid Morag's gaze in case she picks on one of us. It starts to feel awkward. I think she is gonna let us squirm until someone answers, so just to get it over with, I chip in again.

"Um, I feel angry that Mom was taken away from me and sometimes even angry at her for getting sick and dying. I know it sounds bad, but that's how it is. I feel angry when people are nice to me, because no-one can be as nice as my mom was. I feel guilty for being angry at Mom especially, and guilty for being nasty to nice people. I feel guilty that I was sometimes horrible to Mom and I wish I could take those times back. I try to stay numb, because it's easier not to feel anything."

"Aye, that's the same wi' me," Shuggie chimes in. "I should've helped ma' maw instead of giving her grief all the time. I stressed her oot. Always in trouble at school an' that. She was stressed cos of me when she left the hoose that morning. Didnae look where she was going and stepped oot in front of a motorbike. We'd been arguing. It's my fault. I feel like I killed her."

The room is silent. I glance at Shuggie, seated beside me, and I see the tears rolling down his cheeks, which are hot and flushed. I grip his shoulder as I feel his pain. Freya offers him a tissue.

"Hey, man, it wasn't your fault. Everyone knows that. It's just how it gets us sometimes," I whisper in his ear.

"Thanks, pal. I know. Ye just get tae thinking sometimes, eh? That's no' something I do on a regular basis." He grins. "Thinking, that is. I knew it was a bad idea coming here."

"Maybe not," I say. It kinda does help to know that others are going through the same thing.

We spend a few minutes hearing from Morag how it's OK and normal for us to feel numb, angry and guilty when we lose someone. Morag tells us that none of the things we did, or didn't do, ever killed anyone and behaving differently wouldn't have made any difference. She says all kids do and say stuff that they maybe regret but when all was said and done, we were loved by our moms, sisters or whoever, and we shouldn't blame ourselves for what happened.

It's a relief when Morag calls time for a break. There's some orange and shortbread biscuits laid out for everyone.

"Ah'd have preferred some Irn Bru tae this diluted orange muck," Shuggie comments, unimpressed by the offering.

"Excuse me?" I say.

"Irn Bru, man! Ye ken? Yer other national drink? Made frae girders?"

"Sorry." I laugh. "It's like you're speaking another language, Shuggie." Shuggie raises his eyebrows in mock disdain for the stupid Yank. Freya comes to my rescue.

"What he's trying to say is that he would prefer Irn Bru. It's a fizzy fruit-flavoured drink originating in Scotland. You'll like it. Better than Coke. *I* said that last bit, not Shuggie." She laughs.

"Uh right, OK. So, what is all this other national drink and girders, then?"

"Och, it's all advertising speak. Shuggie's just quoting what they used to say in the adverts. The first national drink is whiskey, as you probably know. I'm not quite sure about the girders, though – just that they're usually iron or steel and sit on top of cranes." Freya shrugs.

"I can tell you about the girders," pipes up a boy who is standing next to us and introduces himself as Sundeep. He wears glasses with thick black frames that make him look really intelligent. "Yes, well, you see, the story goes that the maker of Irn Bru, AG Barr, saw some steel workers reconstructing Glasgow Central Station and that they were struggling. He 'brewed' the drink especially for them with caffeine in it to give them strength. The sugar also boosted their energy. A rumour grew that iron was also one of the ingredients and that it came from an iron girder which they kept at their factory. That's how it became Irn Bru."

"Wow, that's a real cool story," I say. Even Shuggie looks impressed.

"Aye, ye'll need to take a swatch at their adverts on YouTube. They're really funny, man! Ye'll like the drink. Ask yer auntie tae buy ye a bottle next time she's oot doing her messages."

Freya adds helpfully, a mischievous glint in her eye, "He says to have a look at the Irn Bru adverts on YouTube and you're to ask your aunt to buy it when she goes shopping next time."

I laugh gratefully. "Yeah, I'm kind of getting the gist of what he says now, but thanks, the translation is really helpful."

Shuggie shakes his head in mock disgust. "I dinnae ken whit ye're on aboot! I'm speakin' the Queen's English, am ah naw?"

"Say – what?" I smile, shaking my head.

Freya giggles. "He's doing this on purpose, I think, PJ. But anyhoo, '*Dinnae ken*' means I don't know, '*whit ye're on aboot*' is 'what you're talking about'. I'm speaking the Queen's English, am I not—"

"Uh, yeah, Shuggie. Definitely the Queen's English." I laugh. "With Freya around we'll manage a full conversation sometime!"

Soon, the break is over. I'd enjoyed the chat and there is, I guess, an air of camaraderie amongst us. Survivors of tragedy.

There are a few more stories. Sundeep (or Sunny, as he prefers to be known) explains that his father had passed away very suddenly and unexpectedly after getting sick with a terrible headache one night after returning home from work.

"The headache got worse and worse and by the next day it was so bad my dad could barely see and he was crying with pain and being sick. He was taken to hospital immediately and a scan showed he had bleeding on the brain. He was dead within the week." He also tells his story in a very solemn but matter-of-fact kind of way. I think we all have a kind of shell around us when we speak, careful not to let others get too close to the rawness we really feel, fearing the pain if anyone breaks through.

It's close to finishing time and it feels like Harry Potter's Dementors have sucked all the life out of us. We all just sit there, limp, like raggy dolls propped up lifelessly in a bedroom corner. It's a relief when Morag makes her closing remarks and asks if anyone wants to say anything else. I hope that no-one does, but my hopes are dashed when Shuggie pipes up again.

"Ah just wanted tae share with you a wee story aboot when ah last went to visit ma maw at her grave."

"Of course, Shuggie," Morag says solemnly and all supportively.

"So, I was just layin' oot some flowers for her, eh, and havin' a wee chat with her, when I saw the gravedigger tidying up the cemetery. He must have felt sorry for me, cos he gave me a wee grin. I recognised him from maw's funeral when he was filling in the grave. I asked him if he'd been busy lately. He looked awfy sad as he shook his head and said, 'Naw son, *I havenae buried a livin' soul* for six weeks.'"

There is a stunned silence for a moment and Morag's mouth opens and closes like a goldfish. Then a stifled snort comes from Freya's direction. I look first at Shuggie, who grins and shrugs with an air of innocence, and then, at Freya, whose barely concealed laughter makes her shoulders go up and down. She can't hold it any longer, and when she looks from me to Shuggie, the three of us snort out a bellow of laughter at Shuggie's ridiculous joke, its so *wrongness* making it all the funnier. Sunny's expression goes from open-mouthed shock to one of total joy as the whole atmosphere changes and the group giggles mercilessly. Morag fails to crack a smile, clearly unamused by Shuggie's cheek. None of us care, though. We all feel better and no-one is offended by his 'Scottish graveyard humour', as Sunny describes it.

Morag stiffly says her farewells and ends the evening saying that she hopes we've all gained something from sharing our insights and experiences, and that we should come along for as long as we like until we feel we can cope alone. I feel a little bit guilty having joined in the fun, so before joining Freya, Sunny and Shuggie, who are gathered in the reception area chatting, I do what Mom would have wanted and thank Morag for her help. To make her feel better, I tell her that I feel a little better. I think she's grateful for the comments but bemused that her bereavement group walks out laughing and giggling together.

"Shuggie wasn't being rude," I say. "It's just his way of coping with stuff, is all."

Morag smiles. "It's good that you've all bonded, PJ. Actually, it's a bit of a tonic hearing the laughter. We have to remember that it's OK to laugh," she says solemnly.

When I get to my group of newly formed amigos, I say, "Good one, Shuggie. You sure warmed up the proceedings there."

"Aye, well, ye cannae go around with a face like a slapped backside all the time, eh?"

We all nod in agreement.

"So, will you guys be here again next week?" I ask.

"Maybe," Sunny says uncertainly and without enthusiasm.

"Depends," says Freya but doesn't expand upon what it depends.

"Naw, naw, naw," says Shuggie emphatically.

Disappointed, I say, "Shame. I used to have pizza parties and Netflix. Now those days are gone I hoped maybe I'd have you guys in my newly founded pity parties."

Shuggie laughs. "Aw, man! We can still get th'gether but can we no' have a support group that's a bit cheerier? Why no' meet up on the ootside and see if we can do a better job of it? Ah just dinnae feel comfy speakin' oot like that."

Freya perks up, a smile lighting her face. "Oh, Shuggie, what a great idea. I'd really like that. It does all feel a bit forced here, doesn't it? I mean, sometimes you want to talk about it but not necessarily at the times Morag wants to dredge it all up. Like tonight. I just wasn't feeling it at all."

Sunny agrees enthusiastically. "Oh yes, guys, that would be great! Then if one or two of us are down, the others might be able to cheer us up. We can just be us and talk about things when we want to."

I'm up for it and feel grateful that the session has brought us together. "Great, what are we thinking then? Meet up this weekend, maybe?"

We agree that Sunday afternoon is good for all of us and we arrange to meet up in Starbucks on Princes Street at 1pm. I realise that I feel good – well, not *good* exactly but you know what I mean? There is some light on the horizon and something to look forward to.

Aunt Katie is waiting for me in the carpark and waves as I leave the community centre. Just as I wave back, I catch something out the corner of my eye. Movement on the fence. *No! It can't be! Azrael?* I run over to the fence and the cat jumps down on the other side. I peer through a gap and the cat looks up at me with his feline grin. *It is Azrael, I'm certain of it! But how?* I call his name, but the cat runs off into the bushes. *More like Macavity the cat from that poem we learned in school. The one that's always up to no good but has an alibi every time to prove he wasn't there.*

Puzzled, I walk over to the car and get in.

"What was that all about?" Aunt Katie wants to know.

"Nothing. I just saw a cat. Looked like Azrael."

"Can't be." Aunt Katie frowns. "He's not left the house today. No way he could have done, without one of us seeing him. Anyway, how would he have gotten here? I've bought some cat food. Let's go home and see if we can find him."

"Yeah, sure. OK, let's go."

"How was it? The group, I mean?"

"Well, it was an experience, I'll say that! You sure do have some funny people here in Scotland." I tell her all about Shuggie, Freya and Sunny.

"So, will you go back next week?"

"Don't think so. The four of us really clicked and kinda figured that we'd maybe just meet up outside the bereavement group. We've arranged to meet up Sunday. Would that be OK with you, Aunt Katie?"

She beams. "Of course it's OK with me. And for what it's worth, I think that's a really great and mature way of doing things."

I'm happy that she's pleased. I thought she might get hissy when I told her I didn't want to go back to the official group. Going there tonight had been difficult but it had been a good idea of Katie's, because now I have a bunch of new friends to hang out with.

We arrive home and Katie makes us some hot chocolate while I go look for Azrael. I switch on the light in my room and guess what! There he is, curled up on the quilt. He looks up at me sleepily and yawns widely before jumping off the bed. A couple of wet leaves remain in the spot he's vacated.

"Azrael! You're some guy! You *were* there tonight, weren't you? You're no ordinary kitty cat." I stroke his head, marvelling at the teleporting cat. He follows me to the kitchen where Aunt Katie has put out a plate of food for him. I decide to keep quiet about the leaves on my bed. Maybe he'd managed to get out and perched on the car. Both ways. *Yeah, sure he did, PJ. He probably went ice skating and had a coffee while he waited. Maybe took in a movie too…*

"You found him, then? Told you he'd be skulking around in a warm spot somewhere."

"Um, yeah. He was on my bed. Aunt Kaaatie?"

"Yee-sss, PJ?"

"Can we get some Irn Bru when we go to the store next time?"

"Oh sure!" She laughs as I tell her all about the Glasgow workers and the iron girder.

I finish my hot chocolate and go to my room to FaceTime Buddy. I can see every bit of fur and every contour of his body as his head comes too close to the screen. He looks like he has a humungous-sized nose as he licks the screen. I burst out laughing. It's a perfect end to a great day. If only Buddy was here now, I think, I would be almost sorta happy.

As I draw the covers over me and lean over to switch off the light, another perfect white feather drifts down onto the quilt.

"G'night, Mom. I miss you." I know that she hears me.

CHAPTER 8

"Hey PJ, over here!" Freya is perched in a corner booth at Starbucks, next to the window, with Sunny and Shuggie, who wave at me. I grin, pleased to see them and looking forward to the day ahead.

"So, we were just having a wee chinwag about what to do today," Shuggie says. "Freya was sayin' it might be good to give you a wee tour of the town hotspots as you havenae been here long."

"Ayuh, I'd really like that. You're right. I've only been in Princes Street with my Aunt Katie so far and that's just a bunch of stores like you get back home. It'd be cool to see some other places in Edinburgh."

We set off in the fall sunshine in the direction of Waverley Station and onto Market Street.

Shuggie is slightly ahead of us, leading the tour. He stops at an archway between buildings and as we catch up with him, I see an old-fashioned street sign that says 'Fleshmarket Close'. I shudder, picturing great globs of bloody flesh sitting on stalls and hanging from the walls, unsure if it's human or animal. Shuggie halts and we stand looking upwards at a dark, dank alleyway, with ancient grey stone buildings flanking what must be centuries old, uneven steps.

"What the heck…? Fleshmarket Close? What's that all about?" Tbh, I'm not sure I really want to know as I think it can't be anything good.

"This is what the Scots call a close," Sunny tells me. "It's just an alleyway surrounded by houses, or rather tenement flats. This is a really old close, as you can probably tell."

"Aye, see, people lived in the closes and in the olden days, they also carried out their trades here. PJ, can ye guess what trade this close is famous for?" Shuggie's eyes are gleaming, clearly enjoying our first port of call.

"Um… cannibalism?" I say the first thing that comes into my head, thinking about the name of the close.

"Naw, ya bampot. We might be a bit rough round the edges in Scotland, but we didnae eat people."

"What about Sawney Bean?" asks Freya.

"Och aye. Right enough. I forgot aboot him, Freya." Shuggie shrugs. "I stand corrected. Sawney Bean *was* a Scottish cannibal, but he's another story and nothing tae dae with Fleshmarket Close, which, for your information, was where the butcher's trade was carried out, back in the day."

I picture the carcasses of dead animals hanging in this gloomy alleyway and think, not for the first time, vegetarianism might be for me. One day.

"It looks real creepy," I say, peering in at the shadowy, winding stairway that stretches ahead of us. "I sure wouldn't want to walk up there on my own on a dark night."

"Aye, there's many a mystery hidden in the streets and

closes of Edinburgh," Shuggie says solemnly and with just a hint of menace. He lowers his voice to a whispered growl and puts his arms out to draw the three of us together. "Burke and Hare, for instance." He nods, one eyebrow raised, and pauses dramatically for a moment. "Aye, ye can just imagine those two creepin' aroond these stairs, lugging their deid bodies aboot the toon!"

"Er, dead bodies? Why? Who are they? When was this?"

"Burke and Hare were notorious Scottish body snatchers," Sunny explains. "They famously supplied Dr Knox, a well-to-do surgeon, with dead bodies for medical research. It was only legal in those days, you see, to use the bodies of anyone who committed suicide, died in prison or who were orphans for medical research."

"Yes, but there was a shortage of bodies from the legal categories, so Burke and Hare improvised and started to rob graves in the churchyard and sold the bodies of any freshly dead people to the doctor," Freya continues, her eyes widening. "But then, the authorities got wise to it and clamped down, securing the graveyards, so it became really difficult to get bodies to dissect."

"Aye, that's right," Shuggie agrees. "So, Burke and Hare saw a wee money-making opperchancity, as ye might call it, and decided to create their own supply of bodies for the doctor."

"Um, right. You don't mean…?"

"Aye, PJ. That's just whit I mean, MURRRDERRRR!" Shuggie speaks in a menacing whisper. "Hare and his wife took in lodgers and it started when one of them died of an illness. Hare didnae report the death and instead, just took her body straight to Dr Knox, who paid £7 and 10 shillings for her. That was a shed-load of money in they days. Burke and Hare put their heads together an' decided if they couldnae get deid bodies from the graveyard, they'd improvise. They murdered sixteen people during the early nineteenth century."

I listen with growing horror at the stories that just this one shadowy alley in downtown Edinburgh was throwing up. I peer into the close and shiver, imagining the dark shadows of Burke and Hare heaving bodies up and down these stairs. "So, what happened to Burke and Hare then?"

"Ach, they got caught. The police suspected what they were up to and arrested Hare first of all. They told him if he confessed and dobbed in Burke by giving evidence against him, he wouldnae be prosecuted. So that's what he did. Burke was hanged and guess what! His body was given to the medical school for dissection. Believe it or not, ye can still visit the Edinburgh Medical School an' see his skeleton to this day."

"Um, I think I might have puked a little in my mouth…" I say.

"C'mon, then. Let's go up to the Royal Mile," says Shuggie brightly.

I let the others lead the way as we begin the steep climb up through the close. I can almost feel the sights and sounds of past centuries as I brush against the uneven, blackened stone of the buildings around me. I am transported for a moment into the nineteenth century, when illness and death must have oozed from these walls.

Strangely, we reach halfway up and there is a tiny bar (or pub, as they call it here), appropriately named The Halfway House. It's a cheery relief from the gloomy black and grey walls. It's brightly painted, with hanging baskets and a welcoming light from inside. I glance at the menu posted outside the pub. "What's Cullen Skink?" I ask, wrinkling my nose, as it sounds like something nasty.

"It's a sort of creamy fish soup. And look – there's haggis too. I don't like that. It's made up of the innards of some poor animal and wrapped up in stomach lining." Freya pulls a face.

"Urgghhh! Gross! You Scots are monsters from what I've heard today!"

Freya giggles. "Yeah, we are a bit ghoulish, I suppose. There are lots of nice things here too," she assures me. "Princes Gardens are beautiful, especially at Christmas, when the market comes to town and the Ferris wheel goes up. My sister Alana and I used to go there every year to buy our Christmas presents and goodies to eat. Maybe we can go there when it comes?"

I smile. "Yeah, that'd be good." I know how it feels when you did something regularly with that special person who's no longer there. Freya probably feels the same. Lost and a little bit lonely.

"Hey," she says, "they're nearly at the top now." She points to Shuggie and Sunny, who are waving down at us. "Shall we go and get on with the tour, then?"

"Sure, let's go."

Eventually, we arrive at the Royal Mile, a cobbled road that leads up to Edinburgh Castle. I am totally entranced by the feeling of being surrounded by ancient history. In stark contrast with the ancient street and buildings, there are loads of modern shops lining the road on either side. Shuggie beckons us over to one of the touristy shops which is full of tartan kilts, scotty dogs, highland cows and all the usual tat found in big city tourist shops. New York is full of them.

"PJ! Try this on!" Shuggie is holding a tartan hat with a ginger wig attached to it. I take it from him and pull it onto my head. The others crease with laughter, and when I look in the mirror, I can see why. I am a true comedy Scot with tendrils of orange hair falling to my shoulders.

"Well, I look just like you now, Shuggie." I grin.

"Aye, just naw as handsome, though, eh?"

"That's what we call a 'Tam O'Shanter', PJ," says Freya. "There's a poem by Rabbie Burns, one of our most famous poets, that tells the story. It's another spooky one! This guy Tam O'Shanter gets leaves his local bar one evening, and sets off on his mare, Maggie, to go home. Witches and warlocks chase him from the haunted churchyard and one of the witches grabs poor Maggie's tail and yanks it right off! Witches and warlocks can't cross running water, though, so he manages to escape over the river. The hat is named after him."

"Wow, is the whole of Edinburgh just made up of spooky stories? Now it feels like Mrs Anderson is…" I clamp my mouth shut before saying more. I don't want my new friends to think I'm crazy. Not quite so soon, anyway. Freya is the only one who hears me.

"Who's Mrs Anderson?" Freya asks.

"Oh, no-one. Just someone my aunt knows."

"What about her? You were going to say something."

I shrug and shake my head. "Nothing. I forget. Can't have been important." Freya seems to accept my explanation and drops it.

"There's certainly a really dark history here," Sunny agrees. "Just look around you. You have the castle up there at the top of the Royal Mile and just up here" – Sunny walks along the cobbles a little – "we have Mary King's Close. Edinburgh is built on top of the old city. There's a whole town below our street level, some of which has been excavated. The story goes that bubonic plague broke out in the seventeenth century and the whole close got bricked up to stop it spreading. All the residents died there. You can walk up and down the close now, where they say all the earth-bound spirits still roam."

"Och, I'd like to have a wee swatch at that sometime," Shuggie says, his eyes shining with anticipation. We all agree it would be good to go inside one day, but we've had our fill of Edinburgh ghosts and ghouls for now, and Freya suggests we head down to the gardens for a stroll.

We give Fleshmarket Close a miss on the return journey, and instead, take the longer route down Cockburn Street. Freya and I walk together, lagging behind, with Sunny and Shuggie, as usual, leading the way. Freya stops every so often to look in the stores, which are kinda boho and gothy. They definitely suit her style.

"My sister, Alana, would have loved that dress," she tells me, pointing to a pretty '50s-style dress.

"Guess she had a different taste to yours, then?"

Freya smiles. "Yeah. We were identical twins. We got tired of being dressed the same and people never being able to tell us apart, so we expressed our individuality by wearing different style clothes. She liked the frothy girly stuff and I like the goth style. We never got mistaken for each other again after we changed our dress types." Freya lingers a little, staring in the shop window. A tear mingles with her black eye make-up, creating a dark rivulet that runs to her chin. I put my hand on her shoulder and she turns towards me, her eyes sad and her face downcast.

"I know, Freya. I know," is all I can say. She pulls a Kleenex from her pocket and we meander slowly down to catch up with Shuggie and Sunny, our shoulders touching companionably every so often. We don't need words to say how we're both feeling.

*

We're sprawling on the grass in Princes Street Gardens and I am already feeling a bond among us that I am sure will grow real strong. We sit quietly for a few moments, without awkwardness, each absorbed in our own thoughts. Shuggie, who can't sit still for long, leaps up. "Right then," he says, "who's for a can of Irn Bru?"

"Yes please." Freya's eyes light up.

"Sure thing!" I say.

"I'm in." Sunny stretches lazily.

Shuggie heads off to the nearby ice-cream van, leaping up to catch tree branches and jumping over stones and obstacles in his way. I'd laid into a whole bottle of Irn Bru when Aunt Katie got back from the store yesterday and I wonder how it isn't a thing back home. It's awesome!

"It's kinda weird, isn't it, how we all got caught up in 'City of the Dead' stuff" (I've seen a poster for 'City of the Dead' tours) "instead of enjoying the lively stuff that's going on around us," I say to no-one in particular.

"Maybe it's because of what's happened to us all," Freya

reasons. I hadn't thought of that. Are we really so obsessed by all things dead because of our loss, or are we just being normal kids enjoying all things scary, I wonder?

Sunny's brows crease in deep thought. "Hmm, perhaps when we think about ghosts and death and stuff, it's just a way of expressing our deepest hopes that life goes on in some way and that those we've lost are still around us."

Deep, Sunny. But maybe he's right.

"So, what would you think if I told you—"

There's a *whoomph* beside me as Shuggie plonks himself down, grasping four cans of Irn Bru. Shoot! I nearly told them about Mom and Mrs Anderson. The moment's gone, as I don't want Shuggie to spend the rest of the day goofing on about it. I'm sure he'd never take me seriously.

But, opening his can with a crack and a fizz, he says, "It's Hallowe'en in a couple o' weeks' time." *Wow! So it is.* I haven't even thought of that. Back home in NYC you couldn't forget it throughout the whole month, with every shop and house decorated from just about the beginning of October with pumpkin heads, broomsticks, fall leaves, broomsticks, orange, black and white lights.

"How come you don't have any decorations up around here? Hallowe'en is a big thing where I come from."

"Ach, Christmas is bigger here. It starts early when you catch the first Christmas tree of summer round aboot the end o' September! Easter starts around January…" Shuggie shakes his head in bewilderment. "Ah mean, whit's that all aboot? There's something no' right aboot decorating yer Christmas tree in yer swimmies, eh? Anyway, I wis just thinkin' aboot what we could dae? How aboot going on one o' they ghost tours to see what happens? We could book it up for Hallowe'en night. It'd be a good night oot, eh?"

Freya's eyes light up and Sunny nods enthusiastically. "Oh yes, I've lived here all my life and never done that. It'd be fun."

My stomach leaps, just a little bit. I'm not so sure I want to see any more ghosts, but more than that, I sure don't want to be left out.

"Uh sure," I say. "Sounds cool."

Shuggie is animated now. "I didnae want tae say too much before, because people might think I'm a wee bit weird, but I *love* all that stuff. It's always fascinated me. Dae ye ever watch the ghost huntin' stuff on the telly?"

We all shake our heads and Shuggie looks kinda sheepish, maybe thinking, as I was earlier, that we might all rip his chain about it.

"Och, ye's dinnae ken what yer missing! Tell ye what. Why do ye's no' come over to mine now and we'll watch some on catchup TV? It'll get us all in the mood for Hallowe'en! It's October break, after all, and we don't have school tomorrow. We can get the bus tae my bit. Stay for a sleepover if ye's like."

"Won't your dad mind three of us turning up and lounging around your house watching TV all night?" Freya looks uncertain, biting her bottom lip.

"Nawww. He's cool. He works until late an' when he comes in, he goes tae his bed most nights. He'll be glad not tae feel he has tae entertain me. We can get popcorn and Irn Bru an' crisps and that. It'll be braw fun!"

That settled it, although I was a bit wary after all that had happened. Still, it would maybe be a good time to see what the others thought of what happened to me. Any other time I'd have been right up for it. A night of scary stuff, probably spooking each other out and playing tricks on each other. But for me, it had taken on a whole new level. But hey! I'm not gonna be the party pooper. I'm the party guy, remember?

I call Aunt Katie and clear it with her. I give her Shuggie's address and she agrees to drive over in the morning and take the rest of us home. We head out of the gardens and back onto Princes Street.

"What's that great big tall thing?"

We passed the bottom of the huge monolith earlier, when we were in the gardens, but I hadn't actually taken note of how high it stretched. Looking at it now, it's kinda like a huge stone spaceship.

"That's the Walter Scott Monument. He was a famous poet," Freya explains.

"Wow, bet you get a great view of the city from up there."

"Aye, but ye have tae climb nearly three hundred steps tae get there," Shuggie replies dismissively.

"Actually it's two hundred feet high and gets narrower and narrower as you get to the top," Sunny adds, looking up and shielding his eyes from the sun.

"Aye, and whit aboot the story of the guy who dropped a ten-pence piece from the top?"

We look at Shuggie, waiting to hear just what did happen.

"Well, what happened to him?" Freya asks the question on all our lips.

"It's no' so much as whit happened tae him, but the coin

came doon with such velocity, it hit a tourist on the head and killed him."

"Such a waste." Freya shakes her head sadly.

"Aye, it wisnae so good for the tourist either." Shuggie explodes into laughter as his punchline hits home. "Ye fell right intae that one, eh, Freya?" We groan at yet another of Shuggie's spectacularly awful jokes. "The auld yins are the best, eh?"

I laugh, shaking my head, as we clamber on the bus and head to Shuggie's.

CHAPTER 9

We arrive at Shuggie's house in Portobello a while later, and as he turns the key in the door, there's a frantic scuffling from the other side, followed by an assured warning bark.

"Get doon, ye daft mutt," Shuggie affectionately scolds the surprisingly little dog, who is now springing up with excitement, circling the floor and enthusiastically wagging his tail that makes his butt waggle comically. I kneel down on the floor to receive the kind of fur baby welcome I have missed for so long. I reach down and scratch his ears as he rolls over on his back, paws waving in the air. I smile, remembering how Buddy would leap to the door with excitement whenever we arrived home and would roll over for tummy tickles, just like this little fella. A completely useless but cute guard dog, as he did the same thing, whoever came to the door. The little dog licks my face and gambols around me now, holding a rubber ball in his mouth which he drops next to me. He pretends to let me try to grab it before he lunges for it himself, victoriously running away and back to me for round two.

"Aww, he's a great little guy," I say to Shuggie, who is leaning against the door frame, watching the fun.

"Aye, he's a daftie alright," he replies affectionately.

"What breed is he?"

"Jack Russell. Goes by the name of Dug."

"Doug? That a strange name for a dog."

"Not at all," replies Shuggie. "It's what he is. A dug!"

I must look a little vacant for minute, until it dawns on me. Of course! In Shuggie's language, a 'dug' is a dog. I roll my eyes in mock disdain and laugh. "Not the most creative name for the li'l guy, is it?"

"Och, c'mon, it's functional. He does what it says on the tin! He's a dug, so Dug fits him well."

I can't argue with the logic and to be fair, it is quite funny.

"I had to leave my dog back in the States," I tell Shuggie glumly as I nuzzle my face into Dug's warm fur.

"Aww, man. Nae luck. That's bad. I couldnae have survived withoot Dug these last few months. He gives me a reason tae get up in the mornin', after ma maw died." He kneels down and hugs Dug, scratching his cheeks. "Yer ma bestie, eh, Dug?" The little terrier responds by licking Shuggie's face. The love and affection they have for each other is clear as he gazes at the lively little terrier whizzing around us.

"Whit's your dug called, then?"

"Buddy." Seizing his moment of revenge, Shuggie says, "That's a strange name for a dug. Why d'ye call him that, then?"

I smile, catching his knowing grin. "Cos he's my buddy, dill brain." I laugh.

"Ah rest ma case on functional names, then."

Of course, I have to agree.

Shuggie ushers the three of us into a small den as Freya and Sunny continue with the oohing and ahhing over Dug. There's a big couch, an armchair, a sideboard and a massive TV hanging on the wall. Big speakers are attached to it which makes it sound like we're at the movies when Shuggie switches it on. It's kinda cool. He beckons us into the kitchen where – guess what? – a bulk tray of Irn Bru cans is sitting on the table.

"Help yersels." Shuggie gestures at the Irn Bru while he grabs popcorn, potato chips of various flavours and a bag of Haribo candies that he pours out into various dishes. He delves into the freezer and brings out several pizzas and places them on trays after turning on the oven.

"Right then, grab yerselves a plate each and dig in. This'll keep us going 'til the pizza is ready." We dive into the dishes and follow Shuggie back into the den, where we settle down. Freya, Sunny and I perch on the couch while Shuggie takes command from the armchair. We all chat in eager anticipation and I wonder what to expect, as Shuggie sets the TV to the channel with the remote control, which he calls 'the doofer'. He dims the lights.

"OK, guys," he begins, whispering solemnly, "I thought we'd start off with *Most Haunted*, the UK's most famous ghost investigation programme, and then we'll do a selection of some of the American ones, too."

I must confess, my heart is thumping a little in my chest, as I wonder just how scary tonight's viewing will be. Will this tell me more about what happened to me in Mrs Anderson's apartment, I wonder?

The eerie and dramatic music comes on after the presenter of *Most Haunted*, a woman called Yvette, does a piece to camera about the house they are going to investigate, which she calls *East Drive*. It's in a place in England, called Pontefract, and the team speak to a woman who lives next door to the house that is no longer lived in. She explains how the house has a violent poltergeist, a noisy ghost that throws things around, and had scared the owners so much they left, fearing for their lives. It looks just like an ordinary little house, similar to Shuggie's.

Freya shudders and says to no-one in particular, "It's weird to think that ghosts can be in ordinary modern houses, isn't it?" She sits between me and Sunny and hugs her legs, which she's drawn up protectively in front of her.

Sunny, in his thoughtful but practical way, says, "It is possible that the land on which the houses are built is very old and has a lot of history beneath it."

Shuggie interrupts with exasperation: "Ghosts dinnae just come frae the long distant past, ye ken! Ghosts of the recently deid can come back an' haunt ye as well! It's no' like they have tae be Roman soldiers all the time."

I say nothing, but watch, entranced, as Yvette squeals quite a lot and two dudes called Karl and Stuart, the cameramen, who we discover both like to carry out daring 'vigils' on their own, move into different rooms and call out for any spirits within them. I keep an open mind, as we watch the two-hour special, mouths gaping, during which the investigators discover a massive kitchen knife that apparently appeared from nowhere, sticking up through the couch. Things move around in one of the bedrooms, strange shadows are caught on camera and weird knocking sounds can be heard. At one point, Karl is sitting near the top of the stairs and gets dragged by the hair around the landing.

"They've actually made a movie aboot this place and the same thing happened to one of the young girls who lived in the hoose before. It's why they had to leave." Shuggie is riveted, transfixed by events unfolding on the screen.

Freya keeps her legs firmly in front of her so that she can peer through them or hide behind them, with eyes half open when something scary happens. Sunny seems quite relaxed, with his legs crossed, and appears to be approaching the whole thing with his usual quiet intensity. He is probably the least affected by the events on the TV, although the slapstick comedy of some of the team doesn't suggest the investigators are totally serious. I think if you're going to do something like this, you ought to give the dead people some respect, rather than taunting them and screaming all the time. As the closing credits run, I'm really not sure what I've just watched. It was a bit scary, sure, but I did see a note on the screen at the beginning to say the show was for entertainment purposes only. It makes me wonder just how much of the activity was staged. I say this to the group.

Shuggie shakes his head. "Naw, naw, naw, PJ. These guys are for real, I'm sure of it."

Freya's eyes dart around the room, maybe looking for any flying daggers that might be heading our way. "Have you ever seen a ghost in this house, Shuggie?"

He hesitates and reddens and looks away kinda shiftily, I think.

"Naw. Nothing," he assures her, "never seen a ghost in ma puff."

I blurt out uncertainly, "I have." Everyone's eyes are on me now.

"Eh? You've seen a ghost?" Shuggie mutes the TV. "Well, come on, spill." He sits forward, eagerly waiting to hear what I have to say. I'm not at all sure this was such a good idea.

"A coupla days ago. In the apartment below my aunt's. I met this woman, Mrs Anderson, who'd lost her cat—"

"Azrael!" Freya interrupts.

"Um, yeah. Well, she invited me into her apartment because she said my mom had a message for me. I went in and her voice and face changed to Mom's. Mom spoke to me through Mrs Anderson and she told me everything would be fine. I've been feeling real homesick, you see. I wanted to go back to New York. Mom said I had to give it time and it would get better. Mrs Anderson kinda went into a trance and then came out of it. She explained she was clairvoyant and clairaudient."

"Aye, like the psychic mediums they have on the ghost-hunting programmes." Shuggie is hanging on my every word.

"So, I went back up to Aunt Katie's apartment and just mentioned that I'd been with Mrs Anderson in the apartment downstairs. Anyway, she looks at me like I'm cray cray and then tells me that apartment has been empty for ages, since Mrs Anderson died."

The others let out a collective gasp. "Anyway, Aunt Katie is looking after the place and has the keys, so she and I went down to take a look. When we went in, the whole place was empty. None of the furniture that had been there only minutes earlier was in there. It was completely unlived in."

"OMG." Freya looks at me in horror and, I think, disbelief. "What did your aunt say?"

"Well, that was kinda the oddest bit. She seemed to believe me. She told me she's a parapsychologist and studies this stuff at the university where she works. She says mostly this kind of thing comes from people themselves. Like it's not really ghosts, but sometimes, when you're in a real emotional place, as we are, we can get sensitive and pick up stuff."

Shuggie exhales loudly and throws himself back in his chair. "That's amazin', PJ." Sunny meanwhile, looks deep in thought, rubbing his chin with his fingers, his brows knitted together.

Shuggie suddenly jumps up outta his chair. "Well, I say, we should check this out and find out for ourselves whit's goin' on. What about you guys? Are ye in?"

"Now, hang on, just a minute, Shuggie. We can't just let ourselves into private property and go hunting around," I say uncertainly. I'm not so keen to revisit Mrs Anderson's apartment if I'm honest.

Surprisingly, Sunny agrees with Shuggie. "Well, you do have access to the keys, so it wouldn't be like we're breaking in," he says reasonably. "And it would be an interesting scientific exercise, don't you think? Maybe we can debunk what happened. Or maybe we will find proof of the afterlife. I mean, your aunt sounds really cool and she's a scientist. Maybe we could just have a look around and see what evidence we can find, then maybe talk to her about it."

"Seriously, Sunny? You're up for this?" He shrugs and nods at the same time. I look at Freya. "What about you, Freya? What do you think?"

"Here's what I think," she begins, trying to find the right words. "We've all lost loved ones recently. I am convinced that my sister, Alana, is still here. I hear her sometimes, when she has something important to say. Occasionally, I feel her brush next to me. Let me tell you all, I come from a family who not only believe in the supernatural but live and breathe it. I'm not sure what any of it means, but I'd like to find out. Can you imagine – if we could all hear from our loved ones, just like PJ has, well, how awesome that would be?"

"Aye, right enough, Freya. What I'd give to tell ma maw how sorry I am and that I love her and miss her."

"It seems like an opportunity to study a real-life haunting that's too good to miss," adds Sunny. "And just for the record, if I could say goodbye to my dad, it would make me really happy. I didn't get to the hospital in time, you see."

I look at all their faces, these new friends of mine, and I see the longing and the hope in their eyes. I can understand where they're coming from, but what if nothing happens and they're disappointed? What if this was all just my imagination because I was wishfully thinking I could see Mom again? Also, what would Aunt Katie say? They're all looking at me, waiting for an answer.

"Well, I guess we could go take a look. I don't think I'm gonna tell Aunt Katie about it, though. She's going to a meeting tomorrow night and won't be back until late. How about we all get together at our apartment then?"

"Fandabbydozy, that's braw for me," Shuggie says enthusiastically.

"I can be there," says Freya.

"Me too." Sunny looks pleased.

"Right then, that's settled. So how about we get some Irn Bru and pizza, then get back into the ghost-hunting programmes? If we're gonna be ghost hunters, we need tae pick up some tips."

After a quick trip to the kitchen, where we load up on pizza, potato chips and other goodies, we settle back down to watch *Ghost Hunters*.

"Aye, these are ma heroes, Jason and Grant. Ghost-huntin' royalty, they are. True professionals," Shuggie tells us admiringly.

They sure do seem slicker in their investigations than the *Most Haunted* team, using 'night vision' cameras and darting around like characters from *Mission Impossible*. They use all sorts of equipment and seem to take a very scientific approach to their investigations. It sure is creepy when they pick up EVPs (digital electronic voices that are recorded, even when they can't be heard with the human ear), K2 meters that light up seemingly when ghosts are near or in response to questions. They take base readings with thermometers so they can tell when the temperature changes and pick up electrical fluctuations with EMF machines.

"Wow," says Sunny. "They have some really cool equipment. I like the way they investigate so thoroughly and debunk some of the stuff they find."

Shuggie, who has been quiet for a while says, "Aye they're amazin'. Hey, I've been thinking, we could maybe just start with PJ's apartment block, and then maybe do other ghost hunts." Everyone laughs and agree it might fun to do something as a new hobby.

"We could get some equipment as we go along, from eBay, maybe?" Sunny seems particularly excited by the thought of scientific investigation.

"Well, I think it sounds a really cool idea. We can maybe find some answers for ourselves and possibly even help other people if we get really good at it." Freya catches my eye and gives me an encouraging nod.

"Uh, yeah, sure. Sounds fun," I say, not altogether convinced. "I was the editor of our school magazine back home. I like to investigate stuff."

"Och, PJ, that sounds fab." Freya claps her hands. "Maybe you could start a blog or a website and document stuff that we find?"

That appeals to me. I'm beginning to get the vibe now.

"YouTube!" Shuggie yells excitedly. We all look at him, waiting for him to elaborate. "We can do a YouTube channel. Ah could be the frontman on that, giving it my slightly comic, you know, slightly serious, wee bit entertaining narration. We can do pieces to camera and show any footage and EVPs and that? It would be so cool. Meanwhile, PJ, ye can be lead investigator and writer in residence, so to speak. Sunny, ye're the perfect scientific dude. Ye can work all the fancy equipment and Freya. Er, Freya, you could, er…"

Freya is frowning, looking slightly irritated that Shuggie hasn't thought of a role for her.

"I can be the spiritual adviser and use lots of techniques deriving from the elements," she says decisively.

"Er, aye. Right. That would be great. Only, whit dae ye mean exactly? Just so we understand."

"I told you, we eat, sleep and breathe the occult or supernatural in my family. My mother's a white witch, my uncle is a druid and warlock and various other members read tarot cards, practise candle magic and communicate with the dead. I am still developing my own medium skills. It's why Alana is trying to contact me. She's helping."

My head is quite honestly reeling with all this, now. It sure is a strange coincidence that we've all gotten together like this. All kids with experience of or interest in the paranormal. Maybe Mom has a hand in this, I wonder.

"Holy moly," I say, as I digest everything Freya has said. "Is that how you knew about Azrael and his angelic name?"

"Huh? Who's Azrael when he's at hame?" Shuggie looks confused.

"Ah, we never mentioned it, did we? Freya and I met before the group. In the park, near Aunt Katie's. I was looking for Mrs Anderson's cat, Azrael. Freya told me his name meant he was a messenger from God or an angel of death."

"Och yes. One of my mum's pet projects just now – angel cards. She practises readings on me and Azrael is one of the names on the cards. That's how I knew. But – not only that, I had a *feeling*, you know? That something was odd with the cat. And you, PJ."

"With me?"

"Yes, nothing bad, you understand. Just a feeling – Alana was whispering to me that day – that there was something deep about you. I felt we were on the same page, somehow. The cat too. Something a wee bit strange about him. He's sort of there, but not there. I don't know how to explain it. Archie picked up on it too. He doesn't usually bother about cats, but Azrael spooked him."

I exhale loudly. "Wow, Freya. You're right about Azrael.

I found him again the day after Katie and I went into Mrs Anderson's. She agreed to let me give him a home but he kinda disappears every so often and even though he can't have gotten out of the apartment, he's nowhere to be seen. The other night, I swear he managed to be at the community centre where our group met and then got home before we did. There were even wet leaves on my quilt. Aunt Katie was certain he couldn't have got out, though."

Freya nods knowingly. "I think he is a spirit, PJ. A real angel who is there when he needs to be."

Shuggie and Sunny are staring at us in open-mouthed wonder.

"Naw. Too much. Cannae be. Cat angels that teleport tae follow ye aroond? Ghosts, aye, but *angels*?"

"You'd be surprised at what's around us, Shuggie. You've heard the ghost hunters talking about demons, haven't you?"

"Well, aye…"

"And you believe they might exist."

"Mebbes."

"So, angels are just the good version of them. It's not so far-fetched, is it?" Freya sits smugly, arms folded, chin raised haughtily, having made her point.

"Well, when you put it that way… Aye, I can see where ye're coming from. Anyway, are we settled, then? Off tae PJ's tomorrow evening?"

Everyone agrees, the conversation so far having given us a great deal to think about. We carry on with ghost-hunting TV for a while.

Ghost Adventures is up next. They're a bit of a mix between the antics of the *Most Haunted* crew and the serious investigations of *Ghost Hunters*. They add a bit of unique drama to their investigations. We sit in awe when they bring out an 'SLS' camera that shows computerised mapping of ghosts not seen by the human eye. That gives me the chills, not helped by Dug, who has been barking at the screen every so often. Can he see what we can't, I wonder? They say dogs have a sixth sense, don't they?

Dug jumps up excitedly and sits between me and Freya on the couch. I put my arm around him, stroking his smooth white coat, which is dotted with perfect black and tan patches. He's a great little guy, with deep brown soulful eyes and the suggestion of a smile beneath his black button nose. I feel sad that Buddy is so far away and I know exactly what Shuggie meant when he said that Dug gave him a reason to get up in the morning. I remember, just like Shuggie, that I have to keep going, for Buddy's sake, after Mom went. I feel grateful to our unsung doggie heroes and hope that someday, Buddy and Dug (and Archie too), might all get to play together. I mean in this world, not the next. I let out a one of those involuntary, long, sad, deep sighs that really expresses the way I feel. Shuggie catches my eye, winks and gives me a kinda *keep your chin up* look that tells me he knows how I'm feeling. I give him a grin. We're all kindred spirits here. We don't talk in depth about our experiences, but we're all fighting the same war and trying our best to make sense of it.

Shuggie's dad arrives home and peers round the door to greet us. He tells us he's tired and excuses himself, deciding to go to bed rather than join us. We've all had a long day, so we lay out blankets on the couch and sleeping bags that Shuggie produces from a hall cupboard.

I'm lost in my thoughts as we hunker down for the night, hopeful that no ghosties or ghoulies are going to show up tonight. The lights are off and only the streetlight shines a little through the curtain.

"Do any of you really think it's possible that there's some sort of parallel life going on? Like where our moms, dads, sisters and other family still live on but can somehow interact with us?" I throw the question out to everyone from my cocoon.

"I'm certain of it," says Freya. "But I'm not sure that all dead people want to interact with us. It seems to me that it's mostly when they're unhappy, or maybe have an urgent message, that they come through. I'd rather think that wherever our people are, they're happy and at peace. I wouldn't want to do anything that might disturb that."

Sunny agrees. "That's a very valid point, Freya. However, from a scientific view, it would be very interesting to investigate and try to discover why those who still appear to be around aren't at peace. Can you imagine what the implications are if we did discover there's another plane of life that we go to after death? Science would go into meltdown."

I think about Mom and hope she is in a good place where she can still see me and knows that we'll see each other again someday. It's a nice feeling.

Without planning to voice my thoughts, I say, "Once upon a time, to me, death was something that happened to other people; something that was talked about but couldn't actually happen to us. I mean, how could you just suddenly not be here? But then, Mom suddenly wasn't there and I had to get my head around the reality."

"Aye," Shuggie says quietly, thoughtfully, almost. "An' then you have all these questions in yer head, eh? Like, will we see each other again? Does it hurt tae die? Do ye ken that yer dying? Is it scary?"

Freya nods. "And then do we go to heaven if we've been good but go to a bad place if we're bad? And then you wonder which place will we end up in?"

"And then the paranormal hunters, who seem to believe there is somewhere that we go to, but that we might come back to this world sometimes," Sunny adds.

My mind is in overdrive. "Jeez, it's mind-blowing, this death business, isn't it?"

Everyone agrees it certainly does mess with your mind. We all want to believe in the good bits of what we've heard and it's clear that we're all harbouring the hope of maybe reaching our loved ones again. I've given them that hope, by telling them what happened at Mrs Anderson's. I fear the unknown, though, and I wonder what we might unleash by dabbling in the other world.

I listen to the sounds of the house settling and realise that we are, quite possibly, embarking on something really momentous.

CHAPTER 10

Next morning, I call Aunt Katie.

"Hey, Aunt Katie," I say as she answers her cell after a couple of rings, "I was just wondering—"

"Hey, PJ, sure. Shoot!"

"Well, you know how you said you were going to be out until late tonight?"

"Uh huh. Should be back by eleven latest, I should think. Why?"

"I was wondering if I could bring the crew back with us this morning? Thought we could go to the park, maybe the coffee shop in the street near us and they could keep me company tonight. Er, if you were OK with it, perhaps they could sleepover? They'll leave early next morning."

"Sure, PJ. Why not? Sounds a great idea and it will be company for you when I'm out this evening. You can watch some Netflix and you could order some takeout if you'd like. Just make sure they all clear it with their families, OK?"

I tell the others that it's all cool for their visit with me and they hurriedly make their arrangements before Aunt Katie arrives to pick us up.

I'm sure looking forward to having my friends stay over, but I'm worried about sneaking off to Mrs Anderson's behind Aunt Katie's back. I guess she'll never know, but if she does find out, she'll probably get hissy about it. We tidy up Shuggie's den, watch some TV for a while, and soon Aunt Katie arrives for our ride home.

We all clamber into the car, me upfront and the others huddled in the back. Aunt Katie turns and introduces herself to her three new passengers.

"Aye, it's braw tae meet ye, Auntie Katie, ma name's Shuggie." He grins his cheekiest toothy smile. I laugh at how comfortable he seems, calling her 'Auntie Katie', as though she's his aunt.

"Lovely to meet you and thank you for having us over." Freya smiles sweetly, her black eyelashes framing her big brown eyes.

"And I am Sunny." Serious as ever, Sunny stretches out his hand, which Aunt Katie shakes. "I would also like to thank you for your kind hospitality and for giving us a ride back."

Aunt Katie beams at them. "Well, aren't you a cute and polite bunch of kids. It's so great to meet you all. PJ's told me a little about you all and I'm so happy he's found such lovely friends."

Freya blushes. Sunny breaks a smile. Shuggie, turning on the charm, replies, "PJ's lucky tae have such a pure barry aunt."

I look quizzically at Freya. "Edinburgh phrase. Means utterly wonderful and fantastic," she says.

Aunt Katie laughs. "Well, I've heard it said around here, but I never actually knew exactly what it meant. But thank you, Shuggie. I think, anyway…"

"Aye, ye're welcome." says Shuggie dismissively. "PJ was tellin' us that ye're one o' they parapsychologists, Auntie Katie?"

"Was he now?" She looks in my direction and winks. "That's right, Shuggie. I work at the Koestler Unit at Edinburgh University."

"Turns out we're all interested in all things spooky," I explain. "Freya's mom is a white witch, you know."

I glance at Freya, who rolls her eyes upwards, then gives me a look that says I shoulda kept quiet.

"Really? How cool," says Aunt Katie.

"Is that something you study at the uni?" Sunny's ears have pricked up at the mere mention of universities and 'ologies'.

Aunt Katie shakes her head. "No, that's outside our field of study, Sunny. We don't look at UFOs, witches, fairies or anything like that. They're generally just folklore, stories that people create to explain what they don't understand. We study people who appear to have powers beyond the normal. That's not to say that people who claim to be witches don't have paranormal powers, by the way, Freya. But we would study the human abilities they have, which might have led to people thinking they are witches."

"Hmm." Freya hesitates. "I guess it's true to say my mum is kinda, well, *unconventional*. I don't tell most people what she does, but I have seen her do things that are hard to explain."

"Well," says Shuggie, "I'd be tellin' everyone ma maw

was a witch. I think she'd be a legend, eh? No-one would cross ye if they ken yer maw is a witch!"

Freya shrugs. "It's not something I put out there, Shuggie. People can be really funny about things like that. They have a picture of a woman in a black pointy hat, a broomstick and warts, who casts bad spells on people to do them harm. My mum is a white witch and she does healing and spells to help people."

Aunt Katie nods, adding, "Yes, that's how the wise women of old were so badly persecuted, Freya. People are afraid of what they don't understand. The reality is that they were often herbalists or very empathetic people who made natural potions that could heal sickness, or make people feel better. Sometimes just believing that they're getting something special can make people better. Even doctors do that sometimes. It's called the placebo effect."

Puzzled, I ask, "You mean that just *thinking* something is good for you can help, Aunt Katie?"

"Yes, PJ. Again, it's just a thing of the mind. The brain is almost a magical thing in itself. We know so little about what it can do."

"My mum has a witches' shop in the Grassmarket." My eyes nearly pop out of my head, I'm so surprised by Freya's matter-of-fact declaration. "She has lots of spells and potions there."

Sunny, who is listening intently to the conversation, chimes in, "My uncle dabbles in Hindu mysticism. He's been trying to help me come to terms with losing my dad." *Another* strange revelation, I think – who'd have thought Sunny, of all people, would admit to that?

Shuggie asks doubtfully, "How's that working for ye?"

"Well, he says that our religion, Hinduism, teaches that whatever we believe determines how we act, and that how we act, creates our destiny."

"Eh? Whit does that mean?"

Patiently, Sunny tries to explain. "So, Hindus believe that everyone has a soul and that even animals have souls that are equal to humans. My uncle says that all souls should strive to be with the leader of souls, *Parmatma*, a Hindu god. Do you know what *karma* means?"

I think I know the answer to this and jump in quickly. "Isn't it a word that means what goes around comes around? Or, whatever you do has an effect? Like if you do something good, you'll get something good back, or if you do something bad, a bad thing will happen to you?"

Sunny nods at my explanation as my mind works up an example.

"So, you could leave here as a human and come back as a dung beetle, kinda thing?" I'm warming to the theme.

"Yes," says Sunny. "Exactly, PJ. And a dog that saves his master and showers him with love might come back human next time."

I could believe that. Sometimes when I look into Buddy's eyes, I swear he knows much more than he lets on. He understands like a human and does things like a human, you know?

Sunny continues: "You see, Hindus believe that our souls are reborn, or *reincarnated*. The karma means that when we die, our souls are judged on what we did in our lives. If we are bad in this life, then we will suffer for it in the next life. This cycle goes on as we are continually reborn until we have learned our lessons and have been fully punished. We can never be fully happy in our lives until then."

"Jeezy peeps!" exclaims Shuggie. "Ah'm gonnae have tae start doin' some good deeds, then." His brows knit together in thought, before he asks, "So if that's true, and we're all reborn after we die, how dae ghosts fit into this?"

Sunny picks up his explanation. "Ghosts in the Hindu religion are generally believed to be the souls of people who died a violent death and didn't get the proper death rituals. Their souls cannot be reincarnated because of this and they're doomed to roam the earth forever."

"Aye. Right, right. I can see the sense in that. It's like we see on the ghost-huntin' programmes. It's the same with most religions, eh? Like, people who die unexpectedly or violently often have unfinished business and they stay around as ghosts until they get it sorted."

"Yes, I think so." Sunny nods. "Anyway, it helps me to think that my dad will either be happy and content where he is, or that someday, he will come back, reborn and have another chance at life. He was a kind person, so I feel sure he will be rewarded."

I wonder why Mom might still be around, if Sunny's beliefs are true. She was a great mom! *Unfinished business*, I think. She left me unexpectedly and probably knows I need to hear from her.

Freya adds, "It's funny, isn't it, how we all have this interest? And how we all got together like this?"

"I was thinking exactly the same thing, Freya," I nod in agreement. "It's like we were all meant to meet each other."

"Aye, it's almost more than normal coincidence, eh? It's like one o' they *synchronicities*, I've been reading about in my *Unexplained* book." Shuggie's eyes are bright, excited by the chat.

"What's that mean?" I have to ask. Sometimes Shuggie comes up with some really strange stuff.

"It's, like, coincidence, plus, plus. *Meaningful* coincidence." Shuggie smiles, pleased to show off his superior knowledge. "Like, ye cannae see a cause for things that happen, but when ye put them all together, there's a reason that connects them. Like with us."

Aunt Katie, who's been quietly listening in as she drives, joins the debate. "Yes, but when you think about it, you've all had a shared experience in losing someone close to you. It wasn't such a coincidence that you all met up at the group, or that you might all be asking questions about what happens to us after we've gone, is it?"

Undefeated by Aunt Katie's unintentional bubble bursting, Shuggie says emphatically, "Naw, naw, Auntie Katie. Ye're no' seeing it right." I can see her point, though.

Freya says, "Well, it's not *so* much of a coincidence, is it? Like Aunt Katie says, we met at a perfectly usual bereavement group and it's not like we've *all* had experience of ghosts or paranormal stuff, is it? I mean, what about you, Shuggie? I know you like watching *Ghost Hunters* and you've introduced us to it, but have you ever had a ghostly experience?"

Shuggie reddens. "Well, aye. Actually, I have – but I didnae want tae say before. I thought ye'd all laugh at me. Not recently, though. When I was a wee laddie. I used tae have imaginary friends. That's whit ma maw and dad called them. But they werenae ma imagination. They were there. I could see and hear them as clearly as I can see and hear you lot. They were wee bairns. Two of them, Heather and Jamie. When I was a wee bit older, I used tae see other ghosts. Adult ones. They were all lookin' for help an' askin' me tae pass on messages. They terrified me when they'd turn up in the middle o' the night, next tae ma bed."

"I thought you said your house wasn't haunted." Freya's eyes widen and she looks a bit scared.

"It's not. It was *me* that was haunted. No-one believed me until I told ma maw the names of the bairns that used to come and play with me. I could tell she was rattled and it was only a couple of years ago when she told me. She had two babies that died shortly after birth. They were called Heather and Jamie."

"Wow! Just wow!" I am amazed by Shuggie's story. Really? What are the chances of nearly all of us having ghostly encounters and Sunny, with his scientific interest in the paranormal, all getting together?

Freya asks, "When did you stop seeing the ghosts, Shuggie?"

"Once I hit aboot eleven years old, they all stopped coming. They were doin' ma heid in, so I was kinda glad."

Aunt Katie looks in her rear-view mirror, a slightly concerned expression on her face, I think. "Now don't get too carried away, you guys. There is often a very rational explanation for this type of thing."

I ask, "Well, how do you explain Shuggie's story about his brother and sister, then?"

"Easy," Aunt Katie begins. "Even though he was young, he might have heard his mom and dad talking about it. There might have been photographs that he doesn't remember seeing. If they were upset, Shuggie might have picked up on what happened and then his imagination convinced him that his brother and sister were there. Happens a lot."

Aunt Katie seems annoyingly determined to debunk everything. I guess that's what scientists do. Never accept anything until proof hits them in the face. It makes me more determined to find out as much as I can, though. Not saying she's wrong, but…

Shuggie is shaking his head emphatically. "Nope. They never spoke aboot it tae me or ma sister. It was like they felt it might bring bad luck tae us, so they kept it quiet so as we didnae get freaked oot."

Katie raises her eyebrows but keeps quiet as we draw up at the apartment.

Shuggie looks out of the window. "Why are we stoppin' here?"

"This is it. We're at Aunt Katie's."

Aunt Katie touches my shoulder and says quietly, "And at *your* home, PJ. Don't think of it as just mine." She smiles and I nod, finally accepting that yes, this is my new home.

"Get tae France!" Shuggie blurts out.

"Huh?"

Freya explains, "No exact translation, PJ. He just means he doesn't believe you live here."

"It's a mansion! PJ, ye never telt us ye were fae the aristocracy!"

Everyone laughs as we bundle ourselves out of the car and head into the apartment, chattering excitedly. No-one gives Aunt Katie any clue what our plans are for the evening.

CHAPTER 11

"OK, guys, she's gone!" I'm peering through the curtains of our apartment, watching as Aunt Katie drives off to her meeting.

"Great! Where are the keys to Mrs Anderson's flat?" Shuggie whispers.

"They're hanging on the rack in the kitchen," I whisper back. "But, Shuggie, why are we whispering?" Everyone laughs.

"Ah dunno." Shuggie grins. "Maybe cos we're doin' something clandestine and it just seems the right thing tae do! Away and get the key, then, PJ, before yer auntie gets back."

I retrieve the keys and the four of us head for the front door, armed with cell phones and a flashlight I found in the drawer. We tiptoe down the staircase, when Freya lets out a yell, cutting through the silence. I'm already like a coiled spring and I just about jump outta my pants.

"Freya! Haud yer weesht, will ye?" Shuggie tuts in annoyance.

"Well, *thanks*, Shuggie, don't worry about asking if I'm OK or anything."

I look back at Freya, who is smoothing down her long skirt. "What happened?"

"Och, my boot got caught in the hem of my skirt. I thought I was going to trip down the stairs. I'm OK now, though. I'll lift it up a bit." I sure hope Freya can stifle the screams if Mrs Anderson decides to show herself tonight, otherwise I'm toast when Aunt Katie gets to hear of it.

We reach the bottom and my heart is beating hard. I can hear it *thud, thudding* in my ears. I check the other apartment doors, uneasily, fearing we'll get caught. My eye stops at Mrs Anderson's door and I imagine it creaking open to reveal something horrible. I shake myself. This is no time to get weedy.

My hand is shaking so hard, it's difficult for me to get the key in the lock, but eventually, it's in and it turns, pulling back the mortice. I twist the brass knob and the door creaks open. It smells of paint, just as it did when Aunt Katie and I came in the other day. I take a quick glance back where the others are all behind me and I'm satisfied no-one else has seen or heard us.

"OK, quick, come in," I say, and everyone shuffles through the door, which I shut quietly behind me.

"We could maybe put the light on for a minute," Freya suggests, as the darkness enfolds us. The curtains are all closed inside and there is barely a chink of light.

"But someone might see the lights outside. A neighbour, or someone who knows there is no-one here," Sunny says urgently.

I pause to think about this and say, "I guess they might

think it's just Katie checking up on things? Still, better not to take the chance. I'd have a lot of explaining to do if they came to the door or mentioned it to her."

"Here, I'll put my mobile phone torch on," Shuggie says, as the screen eerily lights up his face while he sets it to the flashlight app. Sunny switches on the flashlight in the meantime and sweeps the room.

"It's really cold in here." Freya whines a little and rubs her arms uneasily.

"Well, there's no heating on and it is winter," I say, persuading myself that the cold is quite natural. "So, what are you thinking, Shuggie? I mean, you're the ghost-hunting expert around here."

"I think we should split up into different rooms and start with a call out." He is back to whispering again. Probably a good idea at this point, I think. "How about I take the kitchen? PJ, you take the living room. Freya, you go into the main bedroom and Sunny, you go into the small bedroom. Put yer mobiles on tae record and just ask questions, like, 'Is there anyone here that wants tae speak? What's yer name? Can ye give me a message?' You know, stuff like that. We can check the recorders later. If you see anything strange, get yer video on."

"Um, PJ, did you say Mrs Anderson actually died in the flat?" Freya's voice is kinda trembly.

"Yeah. She was found about a week after she died, Aunt Katie told me."

"D-do you know what room she was found in?"

"In the den, I think," I say, remembering that's where I'm going to investigate. It sure is weird being in here without all the furniture I saw and knowing I've already had a long conversation with a dead woman. I feel she's watching me. She knows I'm here. I don't know how I know that, but I do.

"Uh, OK." Freya sounds a little calmer. "I just didn't want to be in the place her body was found."

"What's that smell?" Sunny is holding his hand against his nose and he's pulling a face.

"I cannae smell anything," Shuggie says, sniffing the air.

We all lift our noses in the air and sniff.

"Urgghh. Yes, I can smell it." Freya holds her nose. She's right, an aroma kinda whisps into the air around us. It's that sickly sweet aroma, mixed with the cabbage soup smell I'd noticed before.

"Ach, poo!" Shuggie exclaims. "Aye, I can smell it too. It's like the smell o' death and auld vegetables," he adds helpfully.

I shudder and Sunny says, "Guys, do you really think we should do this? I mean, it seems, well, *disrespectful*. If Mrs Anderson really is here as a ghost, she might not be very pleased at us disturbing her."

"Stop bein' a wuss, Sunny. Anyway, she's PJ's pal. She'll be chuffed tae see ye, eh, PJ?"

I'm not so sure. Sunny may have a point, but at the same time, I'm eager to see what happens. Still, I apologise to Mrs Anderson, silently in my head.

"Right, c'mon," says Shuggie impatiently. "We've no' got much time, let's get on with this."

I agree. "Yes, we haven't much time. Let's get into the rooms and see if anything happens. We'll regroup in, say, fifteen minutes. Call out if you need help."

Everyone sets their cells to flashlight. Sunny keeps the

other one in case anyone loses battery power, and we turn on our audio recorders. We all head to the rooms we're going to investigate. *What am I doing? What am I doing? Sorry, sorry, sorry, Mrs A.* I'm chanting in my head as I push down the handle to the familiar den, now empty of the contents that I know had once been there. My feet clunk on the floorboards, which creak a little under my weight. Fear is making my hand shake as I pass the cell flashlight around the room, my eyes half closed, terrified of what I might see. Shadows are cast around the room, but there doesn't seem to be anything out of the ordinary. I decide to call out, with some trepidation, "I-is there anyone here with me?" My voice sounds squeaky and timid. I hunch up, defensively, hoping not to hear any answer. I wait. *Phew!* Nada. I try again, a little more confident this time. "Is there anyone here? Mrs Anderson? Can you hear me?" I hold my breath. As I exhale, it forms a fog in front of me. *Huh? Can't be that cold inside, surely?* I hear a shuffle and something brushes lightly past me! I can't help it. I yell out. "Aarghhh! *OhmyGod, ohmyGod, something's in here with me!*"

Freya is the first to reach me. "What's happened?" I see her in the light of my cell flashlight, a look of terror in her eyes.

"Something just brushed past me, I'm certain of it." We cast our flashlights around the room but see nothing.

"PJ! Look! It's Azrael!" And sure enough, there's that darn cat, who I haven't been able to find all day, cleaning his paws, unconcernedly, in the corner of the room.

"Whaaa? But how did he get in here?"

"Well, it was dark as we came in. Cats are pretty nimble. I'm guessing we were all so preoccupied, he must've slipped in between us." Freya's explanation sounds possible, but I'm not so sure. Azrael finishes his grooming and wanders over to us, tail swinging high, and rubs himself against my leg, purring loudly. Freya and I both reach down and tickle his head.

"You sure scared the heck out of me, boy," I say, feeling his warm fur between my fingers.

Sunny and Shuggie have arrived from their rooms.

"Well, thanks for rushing in to help me," I say, unimpressed at the time it's taken them.

"Aye, nae bother," Shuggie replies nonchalantly, not catching my sarcasm or choosing just to ignore it.

"Sorry, PJ. I was concentrating on calling out and I heard Freya going past so thought you'd be OK," Sunny adds apologetically.

"So, whit's up?" Shuggie passes his cell torch around the room.

"Just Azrael, Mrs Anderson's cat. He must have snuck in behind us without us noticing."

"Where is he?" Shuggie is frowning as his flashlight roams the corners of the room.

"Right here, at my feet."

"Naw. He isnae." I look down where Azrael had been rubbing against the leg of my pants and see that he's gone.

Freya also looks around, puzzled. "Well, he was here a moment ago. That's odd."

We all search for Azrael, going from room to room, but he's nowhere to be seen.

"Ah think yer lettin' yer imaginations run wild. There's no cat in here," Shuggie says decisively.

"Well, he does have a habit of finding places to hide," I

say. I'm really beginning to wonder about that cat. I glance at Freya, who shrugs as though to say she's stumped too.

"Ach well. Never mind. He'll probably turn up later," Shuggie says, his attention switching to other things. "Any luck? Did ye see or hear anything strange?"

The others agree it's all very uneventful so far. Shuggie, who is carrying his backpack, unzips it and produces some cans of Irn Bru, which we accept gratefully and sit on the floor to drink.

"Aye, it's a wee bit disappointing, eh? After your experiences here, PJ, ah really thought we'd find something."

There is a **BANG, CLATTER, CHING** from the kitchen and I swear we jump five feet in the air.

"Ooft! Nearly lost ma Irn Bru there. What in the name o' God was that?!"

I scramble to my feet, followed by Shuggie, Freya, and Sunny, all of us edging closer to each other. "It came from the kitchen, I think. C'mon!" I beckon the others to follow me.

We tiptoe closer to the kitchen door, as though hoping whatever might be in there won't know we're here. Unlikely to fool a ghost, I'm thinking, but anyway, I keep as quiet as possible. We point the flashlights inside and together we gasp in terror and amazement. The kitchen cupboards have all flown open and the cutlery drawer is being pulled by an unseen hand, so far that it clatters onto the floor. We stand like statues, unable or unwilling to move in case whatever has created this mayhem in the kitchen comes after us. My feet feel like lead, rooted to the spot. Freya's hand grabs my wrist. Sunny, recovering himself, is frowning, as though considering the possibilities.

"*Get tae France!* Did that really just happen? Am I believin' what I'm seein'? Ah think we should skedaddle aff oota here!" Shuggie, the intrepid ghost hunter, seems unusually anxious to leave.

"Well, we can't just leave it like this. Aunt Katie will be wondering what the heck's been going on when she comes to let in the decorators again."

I hesitate, fearful of entering the kitchen that seems to have a life of its own. Freya and Sunny hang back behind me. Shuggie is wandering away, flashing his cell around the darkened corners behind us. It's all gone quiet now, but we're not rushing to set things straight again. Finally, I take command and usher everyone into the den again. Sunny excuses himself, with a sudden need to use the washroom.

Freya, Shuggie and I stand together in the den, our breathing hard and fast, Shuggie bending, hands on his knees.

"Well, I guess it's what we came for," Freya says. "All the same, I wasn't expecting that to happen."

"Maybe it was Azrael?" As I say the words, I realise how darn stupid it sounds. How could a cat, even one as wily as Azrael, throw open overhead cupboards and pull out a drawer?

Shuggie gives me a look that confirms how cray cray I sound.

"Right," I say, taking command. "Let's just catch our breath and I'll go in and sort things out."

"That's really brave of you, PJ," Freya says admiringly. "Are you sure you want to go in alone? We should all go together."

"Look, Shuggie obvs doesn't want to go in there. I'll go," I say, with a bravery I don't feel.

"Naw, naw. Ah'm no fearty. Don't forget I've watched all they ghost-huntin' programmes. They always come out unhurt. It'll be fine." I would be admiring his courage, but something is off. I hope Mrs Anderson hasn't gotten really hissy about us being here.

"Maybe Mrs Anderson just wants us to leave her alone," I suggest to the others.

"Aye, we might have disturbed her, I suppose," Shuggie says. "Look, I'll go and get the kitchen tidy and then we'll go and review the audio evidence back in your bit, eh?" Freya and I nod as Sunny appears in the den doorway.

"Shuggie, how could you? This was supposed to be a serious investigation." Sunny sounds angry as he stands with his hands on his hips, giving Shuggie a death stare.

"What? What do you mean, Sunny? How am I gettin' the blame? And for what?"

"You know very well, Shuggie. This!" Sunny triumphantly holds his hand up high and appears to be holding something that none of us can actually see.

"What is it, Sunny? What are you holding?"

"Follow me," he says, clearly irritated about something. Sunny heads back in the kitchen and strides towards the open cupboard doors and the drawer, still lying on its side on the floor. We follow him and huddle together as he shines his flashlight on his palm. It's difficult to see, but there is a thin, see-through thread across his hand. He traces this one to the drawer handle where the other end is knotted through it. He shines the light on the cupboard handles and again, shows us long strands of near-invisible thread dangling from them. He shuts the cupboards and puts the drawer back in place. Gathering the threads from each in his hand, he leads us back out of the kitchen into the den. He tugs hard on the threads and we hear the clattering noise back in the kitchen. He gives the other one a good yank and we hear the sound of a drawer sliding from its frame. He doesn't pull hard enough to drag it out onto the floor. He looks at Shuggie.

"I didn't go to the bathroom. I decided to go back to the kitchen myself and take a look. Well? You were investigating in there. How do you explain this?"

"Ach, it was just a wee joke." Shuggie turns his palms up and shrugs, his face reddening. "I snuck down earlier when yer Aunt Katie was getting ready and you were all on Netflix. The label was on the key, so it was easy to partly set up. I finished it when we came in earlier."

"A joke?!" It's me who exclaims angrily, now. "I'm not seeing the funny side, Shuggie."

Freya has her say too. "You flippin' well scared the heck out of us all, Shuggie! Why did you do that?"

"Ach, it wasnae so much a joke as something tae keep ye's all interested," he says weakly. "I thought if I convinced ye that something would happen, ye'd all be keen to dae more investigating. If nothing had happened, ye's might have decided no' tae carry on. That's all." Shuggie looks dejected and shamefaced.

Sunny shakes his head in disgust. "Right, let's get cleared up here and go back to PJ's. It's getting late and we don't want to be caught doing criminal damage to Mrs Anderson's house."

We all head back to the kitchen to clear up.

"Right, here's the key to our apartment. Sunny and Shuggie, you get back upstairs and wait for us. Freya and I will give the place a once-over and follow you up. I want to see if Azrael is still hiding somewhere in here. I don't want him getting stuck here for days."

I stand at the door of Mrs Anderson's apartment to see Sunny and Shuggie off the premises, while Freya and I watch as they trudge up the stairs, a frosty silence between them.

"Whatever did he think he was doing?" Freya shakes her head in bemusement.

"Shuggie likes to be the centre of attention and I think he just gets over-excited. He probably does think we needed immediate evidence to keep us onside. I *know* what happened to me here, though, Freya. I don't need any more evidence to keep my interest." A sudden breeze comes from nowhere, catches the front door from my hand and it slams shut.

"What the…?" Freya jumps in shock. I try to open the door to see if someone had come through the external door, bringing the breeze in with them.

"It's stuck! I can't get it open!" I tug and heave with all my strength, but the door won't open.

Freya sharply inhales and lets out a squeal. "Look! Over there!"

I turn quickly and there is a shadow in the den doorway. It sort of becomes a mist and there are twinkling lights flying around it. We stand stock still, too scared to move. We watch in terror and amazement, as the mist twists and turns, until it finally forms a human shape. I hear the familiar *swish, swish, bump* noise as the mist becomes Mrs Anderson. Briefly, I see her face, Mom's face and, finally, the face of a young girl, who looks around Freya's age. I look sharply at Freya, wondering if she is seeing what I'm seeing. Her mouth is wide open and she is staring, unblinking, at the shape in front of us. The shadow mist swirls around and three round twinkling lights dart around it, and finally disappear through the walls. The mist slowly dissolves, leaving nothing but the open doorway in the den.

"Freya?" I say quietly.

"I saw it, PJ. I heard the swishing and thudding. I saw Alana! She was here."

"I saw Mom, too." I touch Freya's wrist reassuringly. "And Mrs Anderson."

Freya nods, still too shocked to speak, I think.

"C'mon. Let's go. We can talk about this later." I pull as hard as I can on the doorknob and fall backwards on my butt as the door flies open easily and unexpectedly.

"Guess Mrs Anderson has decided it's time to let us outta here," I say, rubbing my backside, which hit the floor hard. I usher Freya into the lobby, letting the light flood in. "Wait here. I'm just going to check the rooms for Azrael."

Warily, I look into each room, casting my flashlight into every nook and cranny in case Azrael is hiding somewhere. Something tells me he isn't here. Probably never was. My search done, I close all the doors and give the corridor one last sweep. My flashlight catches something bright falling downwards from the ceiling. I put my hand out and – guess what? A perfect white feather lands in my upturned palm. I smile. Mom.

"I'm gonna find you again, Mom," I whisper. "Even just to talk to you one last time." I grip the feather and meet Freya in the lobby.

"Find him?"

"Nope. He sure is the cat that wasn't there."

"You know, right, there's something weird about Azrael?"

"Yup. But then, there's something weird about everything right now, huh?" Freya smiles thoughtfully and we head back to Aunt Katie's for a debriefing session and a showdown with Shuggie.

CHAPTER 12

There's still an icy silence between Sunny and Shuggie, who are sitting in the den at opposite sides of the room when Freya and I return. It's uncomfortable, and despite feeling a little sore at Shuggie, I like him. I decide to try and be a peacemaker.

"Say, guys, how 'bout I get us some eats and Irn Bru and we can have a debriefing session on our first investigation?"

Shuggie looks at me gratefully. I think he was expecting a hog roasting from me. "Aye, sounds braw, PJ." He grins sheepishly. "Nothin' like a wee can o' fizzy juice and some scran tae make everything feel better."

"Fizzy juice? Scran?" Sunny uncharacteristically explodes at Shuggie, who slumps back into his chair. "You really think that will make everything OK? Do you realise how badly you compromised our investigation tonight? And *you* are the one who started all this, remember? The least we could expect is that you took it seriously and not try to scare the life out of us just for giggles."

Shuggie looks at each one of us in turn, his eyes warily

scanning us for our reactions. "Sorry…"

"Well, sorry just doesn't cut it, Shuggie," Sunny snaps. "How can we trust you in future investigations?" Shuggie fails to meet anyone's gaze. He cuts a lonely figure, biting his lip and sinking further into the cushions of his chair.

I hold up my hand, signalling a stop to this, and then make a 'T' shape with my index fingers. "OK, guys, time out. Enough already. Let's just cool it. Sunny, you're quite right to be sore at Shuggie, and Shuggie, what you did was real stupid. Now, we can't fix stupid, but we just have to try and live with it in Shuggie's case."

Shuggie snorts a laugh, Sunny tries to resist a grin and Freya giggles.

"You can't fix stupid? That's so funny, PJ," she says, laughing and gazing affectionately at Shuggie, like he's a naughty pup.

I shrug. "He can't help being a dufus."

"Och, ye'r too cruel." Shuggie grins. "Ah wuz wrong. Sunny, hand on heart, I promise, on the Irn Bru factory's life, ah will never, ever, dae anythin' like that again. I will be a pillar o' the ghost-huntin' community fae this moment on."

"Well," Sunny's arms are folded in front of him, "one more strike and, as far as I'm concerned, I will not be ghost hunting with you again. We can't be scientific and objective if some… some *clown* contaminates the evidence."

"So, guys," Freya joins in, "shall we all kiss and make up now? Shuggie's learned his lesson, I'm sure. Anyway, we've got some exciting stuff to talk about." Sunny rises from his chair. Tight-lipped, he nods reluctantly. "OK, let's forget it. This time…" He throws a warning glance at Shuggie, who is looking suitably apologetic. "Great," I say. "Shuggie, let's work on fixing stupid, huh? Maybe you'll be the exception to the rule."

"So, what's the exciting stuff you want to talk about, Freya?" Sunny asks. Freya glances at me and signals that I should answer.

"When you two had left Mrs Anderson's, Freya and I saw her."

"You saw her?!" Sunny exclaims. "But why didn't you come and tell us? It's what we were there for!" He rises to his feet and looks from me to Freya, shaking his head incredulously.

"We couldn't, Sunny. The door slammed shut and we couldn't get it open. It was like we were being kept there," Freya explains.

"So, whit happened?" Shuggie wants to know.

"Well, it started with the *swish, swish, bump* sound, so I knew it was Mrs Anderson coming," I say.

Freya's eyes widen as she explains the events we'd witnessed. "Yes, I heard that too, then this mist sort of appeared and there were some twinkly lights flashing around it. Then the mist formed into an old lady and her face kept changing."

"I saw my mom's face again, then she changed into a young girl that Freya says was Alana, her sister."

"What happened after that?" Sunny asks.

"Well, nothing much," Freya shrugs. "The mist just broke up and disappeared. The twinkly lights moved to the wall and seemed to go through it. Then we tried the door and it opened so fast, PJ landed on his butt."

"Did ye's record it on yer mobiles?" Shuggie asks.

"Ah. No." I realise this was a glaring omission and facepalm. Why didn't I think to do that? Stupid!

Shuggie rolls his eyes and mutters, "Pair o' bampots."

Freya looks equally shamefaced. "I guess it just didn't occur to us, Shuggie. We were caught up in the moment, just watching what was happening. I kinda forgot we were there to investigate tbh, especially when I saw Alana. I had so many feelings running through me, it just never occurred to me."

"Ditto," I say. Even though I'd seen Mrs Anderson's talents before, she still held me in her thrall and all thoughts of investigating melted away when she and Mom appeared.

"Aye, well, a fine pair o' investigators you two turned out tae be."

"And whose fault was it that we'd wrapped up for the night, Shuggie?" Sunny stares accusingly at Shuggie, who shuffles uncomfortably from foot to foot.

I decide that food might be the antidote to the slightly frosty atmosphere and head into the kitchen to fix us those eats I'd promised. Aunt Katie's been shopping and left hotdogs, nacho chips, southern fried chicken and slaw in the fridge. I pop the hotdogs in the microwave and pour some cheese on the nacho chips, ready for warming. I nearly drop the whole lot as Freya shrieks in the other room.

"PJ! PJ! Come here. You need to come here now!"

"What is it? What's going on?" Freya is ashen-faced. Sunny looks stunned and Shuggie is jumping around, yelling, "Yaas! Ya dancer!"

"Sshh, Shuggie." Freya puts her finger to her lips. "Let PJ hear this." Her hand trembles as she swipes the screen of her cell onto the audio recorder.

I listen closely. At first, there's just a sort of normal background hissing, then Freya's voice says, "*Hello. I'm Freya. Mrs Anderson? Are you here with us tonight? I'm sorry if we're disturbing you, but we were hoping you might put us in touch with our loved ones, just like you did with PJ? Just talk into this mobile phone if you can't show yourself.*" As Freya goes silent, the hissing noise returns for a few moments.

I look at Freya quizzically and shrug, my palms up. I can't hear anything.

"Wait. Any second now."

Then suddenly, I hear, "MACK-ENNN-ZIEEEE!", followed by a real scary growl.

"Wow! *Shut. Up. No!* What the heck was *that?* What did it say? Play it back, Freya." She rewinds to the start and we all listen intently to the disembodied voice.

"Well, I think we can safely say it wasn't one of us." Sunny shoots a disdainful glance of disgust in Shuggie's direction.

"You're darn tootin' it wasn't one of us," I say, a whistle escaping my lips. "It wasn't Mrs Anderson, either."

"I think it quite clearly says *Mackenzie.*" Freya looks at me, puzzled.

"Well, what's that supposed to mean? Is there anything else recorded?"

"Dunno." Freya shrugs and looks at the others to see if they have any ideas. Sunny and Shuggie look as bemused as us.

"Well, it's just a common Scottish name," Shuggie ventures. "Mebbe someone else lived in that apartment who was called Mackenzie?"

"Could be, I guess. Weird. I wonder where Mrs

Anderson was when you were in her room. I really thought she'd be reaching out to us," I say.

"Well, she did. Later." Freya says thoughtfully.

"Aye, aye, I ken," says Shuggie. "But still! Were ye's no' terrified oot yer wits when she appeared?"

"Strangely, no," Freya admits, "she wasn't scary or anything. She felt kind of comforting. It was just a bit… well… odd, I guess."

"Ah think we should go back doon there an' see if we can get some photos. Maybe she'll turn up on oor cameras." Shuggie pockets his cell and starts moving to the door.

"No. Wait," I say. "Too late now. Aunt Katie will be back soon. We can't take the risk. Have you all checked your cells for any messages?"

"Yes," says Sunny, "nothing on them."

"Hmm – OK, so we need to find out anything we can about Mackenzie then. I'll see if I can find out anything from Aunt Katie. Maybe the name's familiar to her. Look, dig in, guys, the hotdogs are ready. I'll go fetch them and then we can check out my cell too."

I lay out the food on the coffee table and everyone leaps towards it. I pull my cell out of my pocket and set off the audio player. The enthusiastic chomping around me stops as I press play. The first few moments are the same as Freya's. A bit of hissing.

"Did ye's hear that?" Shuggie jumps closer to me to hear better.

We all heard it. I replay and there it is again. The soft crying of a woman or maybe a young child. I let it run on. Another voice. A familiar one this time. It's Mrs Anderson!

"Help needed. Danger… Mackenzie. Beware!"

We have to play the recording back several times to fully decipher it. The voice certainly has Mrs Anderson's lilt, but the words are kinda indistinct. We all agree that it does sound like she's asking for help. The Mackenzie word is clear. And that's it. Nothing else on the tape. I wonder why Mrs Anderson didn't just come and give me and Freya the message like when she spoke to me the other day. I say so out loud.

It's Freya who now offers her opinion. "Well, maybe it was just that you were particularly receptive to her last time, PJ. Perhaps tonight you weren't on the same, well, you know… och – I can't think of how to say it…" She looks helplessly at the others.

"Wavelength?" Sunny offers.

Shuggie suggests, "Plane? No' the flyin' kind, ye understand?"

"Yes," Freya agrees, "something along those lines. I'm just thinking maybe the conditions weren't right for her to appear to us fully tonight. Maybe one of us was blocking her or something, you know?"

"Well, we're not going to get any answers tonight. I need to find a way of broaching this with Aunt Katie, without letting her know we were in Mrs Anderson's apartment. What say we just park this for a while and think it through over the next day or two? I'm kinda ghosted out for tonight."

"Aye. Fairy nuff, PJ," Shuggie agrees resignedly. "What I'd give to back down there and take another wee swatch around, though."

"Well, we can't," I say decisively, but all the same, I kinda agree with Shuggie.

"Yes – we need to do some research," says Sunny. "I

can maybe check on local records to see if there's been a Mackenzie registered at this address in the past."

We agree that we'll take a methodical approach to this, and next time Aunt Katie is due to be out, we can try to get back in for another investigation.

The door to the den creaks and, wide-eyed, I see it opening slowly. There's no-one there!

"Man alive! What the…?" Shuggie jumps.

Freya laughs as we both look round and, on the floor, Azrael is peeking in.

"It's OK. It's just Azrael," I say as I stand up to let him in. Shuggie and Sunny breathe a sigh of relief.

Shuggie yawns deeply and widely, stretching his arms. "It's been one beezer of a night, eh?"

"Sure has, Shuggie. How about we watch some TV before bed?"

Everyone agrees and when Aunt Katie arrives home, it just looks like we've been here eating and Netflixing all night.

"Hey guys. You had a good night? Looks like it's been a lazy one!"

We all reply together, our voices mingling in our haste to keep it normal and not arouse suspicion.

"Yeah!"

"Cool, thanks."

"Pure barry, Auntie Katie."

"Yes, indeed, thank you."

"Great. Imma get me a coffee and head for bed, then. Don't stay up too late, will ya?" We all assure Aunt Katie we'll be heading for my room soon, where Shuggie has laid out the sleeping bags he brought from his house. Soon after, we all head in. I'm sure tired, but I don't know if I'll sleep with all the drama that's happened spinning round in my head. I take my bed and the others huddle in their sleeping bags.

"Night, guys. Sleep well."

"Night. You too, PJ." Freya yawns.

"Aye, I'm fair jiggered. Think I'll be oot like a light the night."

"Night all. And thanks for having us, PJ." Sunny never forgets his manners.

CHAPTER 13

It's still dark when I awaken. Something's disturbed me, but for a few groggy moments, I can't work out what. I glance at the clock. It says 3.33. I hear the high-pitched insistent beeping of a fire alarm. At first it sounds distant, as though coming from elsewhere in the building, outside our apartment, but it gets real loud and I realise we need to move.

"Guys! Wake up! FIRE!" I have to shout now to get Shuggie to wake up.

I pull on my pants and hoodie as the others are now scrambling around to find shoes and warm clothes. I run down to Aunt Katie's room. We meet at her door and nearly crash into each other as she's rushing out of her room just as I am about to run in.

"Quickly, PJ, where are the others?"

"They're coming," I say, just as the three of them appear, dishevelled and confused.

"I think the fire might be downstairs," Aunt Katie says. "I heard the alarms first down there, but smoke must be rising to us now. C'mon, let's get out of here."

There is no burning smell inside our apartment as we rush to the door, but when we head out to the landing, there is a faint whiff of smoke. Aunt Katie bangs on the neighbours' door and they too had thrown clothes on to exit the building. We run downstairs and we're near the bottom when I remember.

"Azrael! We've left him up there," I exclaim in horror, and turn back to go find him.

"PJ!" Aunt Katie grabs my arm. "You can't go back—"

"But I can't just leave him, Aunt Katie."

"You'd never find him, even if you do go up. I haven't seen him at all today."

"We saw him in the den last night. I have to go get him." But Aunt Katie is firm.

"Look, anything could happen, PJ, and you can't take the chance. Hopefully, the fire hasn't taken too much hold. The walls are thick and if it's contained in one of the apartments below, it should be OK."

The others are looking on, worriedly.

"She's right, PJ. We need to go. Azrael will be OK." Freya gives me a reassuring nod.

"I sure hope so," is all I can say.

The neighbours from the other occupied apartment on the ground floor are following us outside and tell us the fire brigade is on the way. We quickly establish that the fire doesn't seem to be coming from any of the occupied apartments, so that leaves only one possibility. Mrs Anderson's! *OMG, was it something we did that caused this?*

Freya, Shuggie, Sunny and I huddle in a corner,

shivering, at the bottom of the stoop, away from the adults, who are all talking amongst themselves.

"It has to be Mrs Anderson's apartment," I say. "Do you think we set something off earlier?"

"Nah." Shuggie shakes his head. "We never touched anything, so how could it have been us?"

"It just seems real strange that on the night we go in there, this happens," I whisper, agitated.

Two red fire tenders arrive, blue lights flashing urgently. The occupants of other buildings in the row are now gathering outside too, disturbed by the commotion. The adults from our building speak quickly with the firemen and direct them to the suspected location of the fire. Five of them go in, taking the key from Aunt Katie. A long hose is unwound, which they pull up the stairs behind them. After what seems ages, the firemen emerge from the building.

"OK. All clear now." I think it's the chief fireman that speaks.

"What happened in there?" Aunt Katie is quizzing the fireman, who I notice has a kinda puzzled expression on his face. The others, three guys and a woman look equally confused.

"It's the strangest thing. The fire broke out in the middle of the living-room floor and burned a rug. It was as if a hot ember had come from the fireplace nearby, but that hadn't been used. It was almost like a spontaneous thing as far as we could tell from our investigation." He takes off his helmet and scratches his head. "Never seen anything like it. How long has the flat been empty?"

"About six months, ever since the owner, Mrs Anderson, passed away," Aunt Katie explains.

"Well, we'll come back in the morning and do a full inspection. It was a very small fire and luckily the fire alarms and sprinklers are very sensitive, so there shouldn't be any more danger tonight. You can all go back in now. Goodnight."

Aunt Katie thanks the team of fire fighters and we all trail back into the building. The four of us give each other meaningful glances, but we say nothing that might alert Aunt Katie to any of our activities the night before.

"Hot chocolate, anyone?" Aunt Katie has switched on the kettle in the kitchen where we're warming ourselves near the radiator. "Well, that was weird, huh? I wonder how a fire could start from nothing in the middle of the room. Good thing the place is virtually empty."

"Uh, yeah. Real odd," I agree.

The others nod quietly, still not venturing to speak in case we give ourselves away. We all hug mugs of hot chocolate, yawning and passing each other guilty glances as we sip the creamy drinks. Aunt Katie tidies up a little, and we head back to bed. Sleep is not the first thing on our minds, though.

"What the actual…?" Freya is the first to say anything.

"Weird, man. Dead weird." Shuggie puffs out his cheeks and exhales with a whistle.

Sunny is thinking. "Spontaneous combustion," he says.

"Huh?"

"There is such a phenomenon where things and even people have spontaneously combusted. The fire is usually contained to one place. It doesn't spread, just stays where it is. People have been found partly turned to ashes, with the rest of them intact. It can just stop itself."

"Urgh! Sunny! That's a horrible thing to think of." Freya pulls a disgusted face.

"Well – it would explain what happened down there, wouldn't it?"

"I think we caused it." The others look at me, and in their hearts, I think they believe the same. "I think stirring up the spooks down there might have caused one of them to set the fire. It's too much of a coincidence, isn't it?"

"Aye. Ah think ye're probably spot on there, PJ. It doesnae seem like it really wanted to cause much harm, though, eh? Just maybe wants a wee bit attention, like, eh?"

"Hmm. Possibly. Can't think it was Mrs Anderson who set her house alight, though. Something else, perhaps. Something not as friendly as her." I shiver a little, wondering what on earth we might have conjured up down there.

"Well, how about we get some shuteye? I'm soooo tired." Freya yawns and rubs her eyes, now free of her customary black eyeliner. She looks far prettier without it, and younger.

We agree that there isn't much more we can do for now. It's nearly 6am but at least we can sleep in tomorrow. I'm grateful the fire alarms and sprinklers went off in Mrs Anderson's home, though. Could have been much, much worse.

CHAPTER 14

It's early afternoon before we awaken to the smell of bacon and eggs wafting through the door. I realise that I am ravenous. I call out to the others, "Hey, lazy daisies! I think Aunt Katie's cooking brunch!" Everyone stirs and heave themselves up, still bleary-eyed after the last night's events.

Shuggie lifts his nose in the air. "Aww, that smells pure dead good, by the way. I could eat a scabby horse between two buns right now."

Sunny and I laugh, as we picture the scabby horse looking like a Mickey D's burger.

We roll up sleeping bags and tidy up the room and head off to the kitchen.

"Thought you could all do with a good brunch after last night's adventures." Aunt Katie smiles.

Moments later, our plates are piled high with a full Scottish breakfast.

"Mmmh. Ahh, nom, nom, nom. You make good scran, Auntie Katie," Shuggie declares appreciatively as we all wade in.

After brunch, the others are due to leave and we head back to my room. There is talking coming from behind the door. We look at each other, quizzically. I push open the door, warily standing back and immediately see where the noise is coming from. The TV is on! A collective intake of breath is taken by all of us, particularly when Sunny points to the wall socket.

"Er, PJ? Look at the plug." All our eyes are drawn to the lead, which is dangling from the wall-mounted TV. The plug is not pushed into the wall socket. It's working without any electricity!

"*OMG!*" Freya blurts out in astonishment.

"Get tae France!" Shuggie's standard response for disbelief makes yet another appearance.

Sunny is now inspecting the set, trying to work out how this is possible. He picks up the lead, checks it is the one for the TV, picks up the remote control and scratches his head. Suddenly, the volume increases all by itself and we see the bar across the screen go from thirty per cent to almost ninety per cent so that we can barely hear ourselves think. It's the local news that's on.

"*The residents of Edinburgh are preparing to search for missing schoolgirl Sophie MacGregor, who disappeared early yesterday morning on her way to school. Fears are growing for the eight-year-old, described as a happy, clever girl, who would never go anywhere without telling her parents. A search party is gathering in the city, where police will be directing the proceedings.*"

"Oh dear. That's awful, her parents must be beside themselves with worry." Freya shakes her head sadly. Abruptly, the screen goes black and the TV is silent.

Aunt Katie peers in through the door. "What's going on? I nearly dropped the plates I was rinsing when I heard that racket."

"Er, nothing Aunt Katie. I, er, just stood on the remote when we were picking stuff up and accidentally turned the TV on at full volume." Satisfied with my answer, she leaves us to it.

Shuggie whispers, "Whit was that all aboot, when it's at hame?"

I think I know. "It's connected to all the other funny stuff happening around here, that's for sure," I say uneasily.

"Aye. Ah think ye're right, PJ. Some really weird stuff going on around here."

Freya sits on my bed, pulling at her hair nervously.

"There has to be a rational explanation for all this," Sunny says confidently. "Maybe an electrical surge that powered up the TV. Maybe a piece of glass got caught in the sunlight in Mrs Anderson's house and was slowly smouldering until it burst into flames?"

"But the curtains were shut and it was dark outside," Freya points out.

"Well, maybe cleaners or decorators were in earlier and something happened then. The possibilities are endless. We can't just go jumping to conclusions about ghosts."

I'd like to think that Sunny is right in this instance, but I'm not at all convinced. Freya and Shuggie look doubtful too.

They pack up their things and I see them out. We arrange to be in touch to get a ghost walk organised for Hallowe'en, which is just a short time away.

"I feel bad about leaving you with all this stuff happening

around you, PJ." Freya grasps my shoulder, comfortingly.

"I'll be OK. I hope. Thanks, Freya."

"See ya! Wouldnae wanna be ya!" Shuggie calls helpfully and waves.

"Bye, PJ," says Sunny. "And thanks to you and your aunt for having us. It's been, um, well, interesting. I'll see what I can find out about this stuff. Try not to worry."

I give Sunny a friendly slap on the back as he too heads off in the direction of town.

I shut the external door after seeing everyone off the premises and I feel a blast of cold run down my spine when I accidentally catch sight of Mrs Anderson's door. I find myself speeding up now whenever I pass it, and I try not to look, especially when I'm alone. Azrael is sitting outside her door, cleaning his paw, looking like he hasn't a care in the world.

"Well, hi, stranger! Where do you get to and how come you appear at the oddest of times?" He walks over to me and I stroke his head, and he follows me back to our apartment.

I find Aunt Katie sitting in the den, watching a movie, and plonk down beside her. During the commercial break, I seize the moment to quiz her about the apartment below.

"Aunt Katie?"

"Uh huh?"

"Has anyone by the name of Mackenzie ever lived in Mrs Anderson's apartment?"

Aunt Katie hesitates a moment, creasing her brows in thought. "Not that I can think of. Why d'you ask?"

"Oh, it's just I met a delivery man when I was seeing the guys off. He said he had a delivery for Mackenzie and it had Mrs Anderson's address on it," I lie. "I told him that the home was empty and I didn't know if anyone by that name was connected to it."

"What did he do with the delivery?"

"Oh, I dunno. Took it back with him, I guess. He said it needed a signature and knocked on the door, just to satisfy himself there was no-one there, I think." *Boy, I'm sure telling a lotta lies here.*

"Well, can't say I've ever heard that name. As far as I know it's just been the Andersons for the last fifty-odd years." Aunt Katie shrugs and settles back to watch the movie, while I brood quietly on the strange events of last night.

CHAPTER 15

After all the drama of the day, I need the comfort of something normal and happy, so, after dinner, I head off to my room, checking that the TV isn't doing anything strange before I fully enter. I grab my iPad and connect with the Rosenbaums.

"Hey, PJ! How ya doin'?" It's Mr Rosenbaum who picks up.

"I'm good, thanks. I've been with my new friends that I met at the bereavement counselling group for the last coupla days. It's been fun." I smile broadly, eager not to let any of my uneasiness show. I don't want to worry them. I know if I told the Rosenbaums I had been seeing ghosts and ghost hunting it would freak them out completely. I keep the conversation to my tour of Edinburgh and sleepovers, watching TV. As usual, Mrs Rosenbaum wants to know all about my dietary habits.

"Are you eating enough, PJ? You need to stay strong. Say, has Aunt Katie made you chicken soup? I bet you don't get anything like the Matzoh balls I used to make you! Now, tell your aunt how much you like a nice brisket, why don't you? Do they have hot deli sandwiches like we make in the shop? Oh, PJ, you look like you lost weight. Ezra? Doesn't the boy look like he lost weight?"

Mr Rosenbaum shakes his head in mock impatience and shrugs. "He looks the same to me, Rachael. Stop worrying, why don't you? PJ says he's fine. Tell her yourself, PJ, so that she stops worrying. Day and night, she worries, and I keep telling her: PJ's just fine. He's a strong boy and he's in good hands."

I laugh. They don't change. The familiar friendly bickering between them is something I've grown used to over the years we rented the apartment above the deli.

"I'm *fine*," I assure them. "It's still real hard – you know, with Mom and everything. And I miss Buddy so darn much, I can't even tell you. And of course, I miss you guys. I'm OK, though. Stop worrying! Is Buddy there? Can I say hi?"

Mr Rosenbaum calls Buddy and he comes into view, sniffing at the screen and tilting his head inquisitively. "Hey boy! You're looking great! Are you eating enough? Did you get a nice brisket for dinner?" I joke back at the Rosenbaums' expense. I hear them laughing.

"We love to have him here. Ezra, tell PJ how much we love to have Buddy here with us."

"Yeah, yeah, of course we do. He's a great little guy, aren't ya, boy?" I see Mr Rosenbaum scratching Buddy's face, who licks him back appreciatively. "He keeps trying to go up to your old apartment when we come back from our walks. Still thinks you and Mom are up there and we're trying to trick him. Don't you worry, PJ. He hasn't forgotten you. Funny thing happened yesterday. Buddy ran up the back stairs to the apartment, and I was chasing after him. Something caught his attention, and when I looked up, he was standing with his ears up and his tail wagging as this *huge* white feather sailed down from the ceiling and landed right on his head." Mr Rosenberg shakes his head. "It was the darndest thing. Can't figure out where that could have come from, but Bud was so taken with it, we've kept it."

My heart thuds and I ask, "When was that, Mr Rosenbaum?"

"I can tell you exactly when it was," Mrs Rosenbaum pipes up. "It was just on 3pm when he came back from his second walk of the day. The lunchtime rush was over in the deli, so he and Ezra went out. Isn't that right, Ezra?"

"Ayuh. Sounds about right to me. Why do you ask, PJ?"

Goosebumps are rising on my arms. That would have made it about 8pm UK time, just about when Freya and I were leaving Mrs Anderson's apartment and the feather landed next to us.

"Oh, no reason." I try to sound casual and unconcerned. "I just wondered is all."

Nothing more is said about the feather and we wind up our FaceTime with a bit more chat and reassurances that all is as well as it can be with everyone. Boy, another weird thing. I've given up putting it all down to coincidence. I smile at the thought that Mom is looking out for Buddy and the Rosenbaums too. It really is kinda cool. I open the box where I've begun to store the feathers. *Night, Mom. Love you.*

CHAPTER 16

Aunt Katie has arranged some home-schooling for me to bring me up to speed for when I start at school. She wants to give me time to adjust, she tells me, and also to get a feel for the subjects I am going to study. My tutor will be coming next week, so I'm spending the afternoon flicking through the materials I have to get through. Boy, it's a real drag. I'm not looking forward to going to school here. I didn't like it much back home, and I can't see it's going to be very different here. I sigh miserably. However much I try, I can't take much of this stuff in. I'm pleased with the distraction when a WhatsApp message in the group chat that we've set up for the Paranormal Pursuers arrives from Sunny.

Hey, guys. Can we meet at Starbucks around five? I have some stuff to tell you.

Everyone replies that they can make it and I leap off my bed with enthusiasm for the first time today. I run through to Aunt Katie, who says it's OK with her. I see that Azrael's bowl of food is untouched.

"No sign of Azrael today?" I look around the kitchen, but no cats appear.

"Nope. He sure is a strange critter, PJ. He must be finding a way to get out. I'll need to check the windows to make sure I haven't left one open in the spare rooms."

Azrael is probably stranger than any of us realises, I think, but don't say to Aunt Katie. I head off to get changed and let myself out, calling to Katie that I'll see her later. I speed by Mrs Anderson's door without looking sideways and head off to Princes Street.

As I reach the door at Starbucks, Sunny is just arriving from the other direction. He is flushed and seems excited about something.

"Hi, PJ! I think Freya and Shuggie are inside. They sent me a WhatsApp." I see them sitting in the window, which seems to have become 'our' spot. There are four cups in front of them.

"Hey, you two." Freya beams at us. "Shuggie got the round in today."

"Aye, well, I owe ye's in more ways than one." Shuggie grins and slides a hot chocolate topped with cream and marshmallows to me and Sunny.

"Cool. Thanks, Shuggie." I spoon out some of the cream and marshmallow and savour its sweet deliciousness. "So, what have you two been up to?"

"Och, just having a wee blether between ourselves aboot all the adventures we're having. Ah was just sayin' tae Freya, we'll need to get some proper equipment. I've been lookin' at websites an' that. We can set up a simple one tae start with for free. Only thing is, there'll be pop-up adverts, but we can live with that, eh?"

Sunny looks approvingly at Shuggie. "That's great, Shuggie. Proper equipment and a place we can have a forum to discuss things is a great start."

"So, what was so urgent that you wanted to speak to us, Sunny?" I am delving below the cream and marshmallow now to get to the chocolate drink.

"Well, it might be nothing, but, well, I did some research on local parish records and checked with Edinburgh Council records. I couldn't find anything about anyone called Mackenzie living in your building, PJ."

"No, Aunt Katie didn't recall anyone of that name either. She says Mrs Anderson was there for decades."

"Doesnae mean that there was never a Mackenzie, though," Shuggie adds. "I mean, your bit is over three hun'erd years auld and who knows what was built there before."

"Hmm. True enough." I can't fault his argument.

"Well, anyway, I was up in the Royal Mile earlier and I passed the ghost tour meeting point. You know, the one near St Giles' Cathedral? Where all the posters are? So, I was looking at them to see what we could book onto for Hallowe'en and… well… look for yourselves." Sunny produces his cell and swipes into his photo app. He gives it to me first, so I read what I see.

"'Greyfriars Haunted Graveyard Tour – Home of the Mackenzie Poltergeist'! So, what are you thinking, Sunny? That Mackenzie has left the graveyard to come visit New Town?"

"Well, see, that's not all." Sunny goes to his web browser.

"I did a little bit of reading and look – here." He points to some of the blurb about the tour. This time Shuggie takes the cell phone.

"The Mackenzie poltergeist is one Edinburgh's most malevolent entities, whose activities have included setting fires in the homes of surrounding residents… Aye, but that's miles fae PJ's house, Sunny. Why would he be there?"

"Well, I don't know, but it's a bit of an odd coincidence, isn't it? I mean, that I should be walking along, thinking about Mackenzie, fires, etc. and then, two minutes later, it's there in front of me on a poster! Edinburgh's most famous fire-starting ghost is on the walk we're planning to take."

Freya is poring over the photo and website. "Hmm. It is possible. I mean, didn't you say, PJ, that you saw lots of people in Mrs Anderson's changing face? Some that looked mean, too?"

"Yeah, I did. It was like so many people were coming through her. I guess she might have picked up on anyone in the city, but especially a seemingly powerful and dark entity like this."

"Exactly!" Sunny beams, satisfied that someone is backing up his idea. "Of course, proper research and investigation is needed, but I think this is where we start. There are other ghost tours, but it seems to me that this is one we're being, I don't know, *directed* towards? I know I'm not sounding scientific, but it's a possible lead worth following up." He looks around the table, waiting for us to respond.

"Good with me," I say.

"Me too, sounds a good idea," Freya adds.

"Well, it's as good a place as any to start, Sunny. And ah

think ye're right. It's a sign of some sort. Lead on, Macduff! Ah'm right behind ye!" Shuggie grins.

So, it is settled. We are heading for Greyfriars Kirkyard on Hallowe'en night. As I stroll back to the New Town, hands in my pockets to keep warm, I can't help but wonder what awaits us next. I sure hope Mom is looking out for me, because I have a funny feeling, things are gonna get livelier still.

CHAPTER 17

My cell phone rings in the middle of the night and wakes me up with a start. My heart is beating a little hard because it isn't usually good news when you get a call at this time. All sorts of things run through my head. Aunt Katie is home, so it can't be a problem with her. The Rosenbaums, maybe? Or Buddy? Oh no! What if something happened to Buddy? My hand shakes as I lift the phone and I almost burst with relief when I see Shuggie's name on the screen.

"Shuggie? Wassup? You OK?"

"Aye. Well, naw. No' really." He's hesitant. I've never heard my usually upbeat friend sound this flat. "It's just, well, I couldnae sleep. Thinkin' an' that. Aboot ma maw. Sorry for ringin' so late. Ah just knew ye'd understand."

"That's OK. You gave me a fright is all. Thought something might have happened to someone, it being so late. I do understand, though. You just wake up, going over everything sometimes, huh? Wishing you could change it, hoping it was all a bad dream. And then it hits you all over again."

"Aye." Shuggie's voice quivers a little. I can tell he's been crying. "It's just sometimes, I cannae believe it, ye ken? It's like I try an' imagine ma maw is just away somewhere for a wee while and that she'll be back soon. If I can just keep thinkin' she's just away at a friend's or on a wee holiday, it's OK. But then I cannae pretend forever. I miss her, PJ." He cries openly and unashamedly, his usual bravado giving way to the grief and pain of his loss. I try to comfort him and reassure him that there's no shame in being sad; that I feel the same thing about my own mom. I feel his pain and I share his tears, thinking of Mom and wishing she was here to put her arms around me. I feel closer to Shuggie, us having confided in each other. It's good to have friends who really understand. We say our goodnights and I drift off to sleep.

There's a WhatsApp from Freya on my cell phone next morning when I awaken.

Hey, PJ. Want to meet up after school today? Starbucks, 4.30? ☺

I don't need much persuasion. I'll be in town anyway so a good time for a catch-up. I like Freya's company. She's kinda calm and understanding, although sometimes she too can be a little flaky, especially when she goes all mysterious on us with the witchy stuff.

Sure Freya. See you there.
☺

I head to Starbucks to meet Freya. She's in the usual window booth.

"Hey, PJ!" Freya grins. She's wearing her trademark black skirt and leather jacket, her eyes lined heavily with black kohl. She is wearing black cherry-coloured lipstick.

"Hey, Freya! How ya doin'?" We give each other a hug.

"I'm doing OK, I guess." She sighs a little. "Been missing Alana a lot this week. We were always at school together, so it's really odd with her not being there."

"I know. It's hard. We all seem to hit kinda milestones, don't we? Maybe I shouldn't be saying this, but Shuggie's struggling too. He reached out to me last night." Freya looks at me quizzically.

"Really? He does seem to take things all in his stride usually, doesn't he?"

"Yeah – hides behind the clown mask, I think." I tell Freya about our call. I don't think Shuggie would mind anyone in our group knowing he had bad days and could be sad too. "Have you spoken to Sunny this week?" I wonder if he too is feeling the shared sadness.

"No. I'll give him a call later and see how he is. I've booked the tickets for the ghost walk online, by the way."

"Cool, I'm looking forward to it. Should be fun. Although, well, you saw what I saw at Mrs Anderson's. I think we need to take it seriously."

"Yes – that was so weird, when Mrs Anderson's shadow arrived and turned into Alana and your mum. I wonder if the boys would have seen it if they'd been there?"

"Dunno, but I think they're gonna be determined to find us some ghosts now. Say, I just wondered, Freya. Doesn't your school mind you wearing your goth make-up?" It's a bit of a random question, but I'm curious.

Freya laughs. "Nah. I can't wear my make-up in school.

I slap it on as soon as I'm free of the school gates. Can't stand the way they just want us all to look like clones in our grey uniforms."

I nod in agreement. "Yeah, they seem to think we're all just the same. My mom and I had loads of arguments at my school because I couldn't learn in the way they wanted me to. I couldn't pay attention for long."

"Well, you're not as bad as Shuggie. He has the attention span of a gnat at times." We laugh, recalling the way Shuggie barely sits still for two minutes. "Talking of Shuggie, I brought you these." Freya reaches under the table and produces a plastic sack and hands it to me.

"A present?"

"Sort of." She smiles. "They're a year or two old. I picked them up in the charity shop." I reach inside the bag and pull out two comic books. One is called *Oor Wullie*, the other, *The Broons*. "I thought they'd help you. With the Scots language!" Freya giggles. "Shuggie speaks like them so I thought if you got the lingo from the books I wouldn't need to translate so much."

"That's so cool, thanks, Freya. I'll enjoy reading these – if I can decipher them!"

"Well, they're staple reading in Scotland," Freya explains. "These cartoons are in a newspaper, *The Sunday Post*, each week and then they put all the comic strips in these annuals at Christmas time. Anyway, I'm popping down to my mum's shop to help her with some stocktaking. Wanna come with?"

"Sure!" I'm fascinated to see Freya's mom's witchy shop. We finish our drinks and set off towards the Grassmarket on the old cobbled streets of Edinburgh. We roll up outside the shop which has its name displayed above the door: 'Magickal Moments'. On the way, I'd seen that the Hallowe'en decorations were now appearing in all the shops and a few houses. If I'd been disappointed with the displays so far, this shop sure makes up for it with its window display. There is a witch with a pointy hat and black cloak swinging on her broomstick. Below her is a carpet of leaves, all in red and brown fall colours. On the leaves are pumpkin jack-o'-lanterns, corn dollies, big black hairy spiders, skeletons slumped in each corner, their mouths open in silent screams. There are ghosts in white sheets and a coffin next to a gravestone lies open, revealing a grinning, grey corpse gripping the sides, appearing to rise from the dead. Pinned on the door is a sign that reads, *'Please leave your broomstick at the door!'*

Freya pushes open the door and some chimes tinkle above us. Inside some twinkly, soft music plays, which gives the store a calming feel. I gaze at the strange and colourful things on sale. There are dream catchers swinging from the ceiling and some normal-looking stuff, like candles, incense sticks and aromatic oils that even my mom burned at home sometimes. She used them especially when Buddy had been out in the rain and mud, leaving a pungent 'wet dog' smell in our apartment.

There is some clunky metal and polished stone jewellery (my mom would have called it *bohemian style*, which she quite liked), there are crystals which have explanations for their uses. I read some of them. Bismuth – *to relieve emotional and spiritual isolation*; exotic-sounding stromatolite – *for cleansing the chakras and encouraging you to 'go with the flow'* by removing negativity; kunzite – *to relieve heartache over loss and separation. Boy, could I do with some of these!* I am a little doubtful that a piece of shiny rock could help that much. There are tarot cards, angel cards, pendulums and rune stones to tell the future, and there is a shelf piled with books about Wicca, candle magic, druids, spell-making and feng shui. There are even spell kits that look like packets of herbs but promise users they will help them to find love, make money quickly and bless their homes. This store is a real-life *Harry Potter* place of wizardry!

"Close your mouth, young man!" a woman's voice booms from behind me and makes me jump. "You'll be catching flies in there if you're not careful!" The voice sing-songs with amusement.

I turn and see a woman standing in the doorway that is hung with streamers and dream catchers. She holds them apart as she emerges from the room beyond. Her dark hair is piled up into a messy bun and she wears a long amber, black and yellow floaty skirt and matching jacket which kinda billow around her as she moves. A long necklace dangles over her black T-shirt, the rope glistening with coloured glass and crystals that *clack-clack* as she moves. She wears a matching bracelet and earrings. She comes towards Freya and me, and seems to glide rather than walk. It's as though she is made of air and gossamer. The closer she comes, I can see that her skirt and jacket have symbols on them: five pointed stars, half-moons, an eye, a lotus flower, a wheel and a long stick with two snakes winding around it. She wears heavy eye make-up, similar to Freya's, and bright red lipstick.

"Hi, Mum, this is PJ. He's come to help with the stocktaking."

"Hello, PJ." Freya's mom greets me with a warm smile. "Welcome to Magickal Moments. Freya's told me all about you and the others in your group. I'm sorry for your loss. It's hard for all of us when things like this happen. I only wish we had all met under happier circumstances, but, as I always say, things are meant to happen in the way that they do. Rest assured, PJ, your mum is most certainly still around you, as is our lovely Alana." She seems to be kinda studying me. Not looking directly at me but, around me, as though she's seeing something. She says, "You have a lovely aura about you, PJ."

"Um, yeah. Thanks. Sorry, what's an aura?"

"It's the energy that surround us all, PJ. It allows us to read what a person is like and sometimes what troubles them. It shows up like a coloured halo around the entire body."

"Right." I nod as though I understand what she's talking about. "So, what does my aura say about me?" I inspect my hands but can't see anything around them.

"I see a vibrant shimmering gold, which tells me you have divine protection around you. Angels, if you like. It means that someone is guiding you and helping you to find your way. I also see a deep red colour that tells me you are strong-willed and a survivor. There is also a touch of indigo in there, and that is very special. It gives you an insight into other worlds beyond the veil of life and means you are a seeker, inquisitive." Freya's mom has piercing blue eyes that seem to see right through me. I bite my lip and shuffle a little uncomfortably, wondering what else she might be seeing in me. She smiles, the corners of her eyes crinkling, as though she smiles a lot. "Now then, please call me Cass. Short for Cassandra, a woman who had the gift of prophecy but was cursed never to be believed."

"Uh, sure. Great to meet you, er, Cass." I give her my best smile, unsure what to make of her. She seems to have me all worked out, though. Weird. "So, you can see the future?" I ask hesitantly.

Cass gestures theatrically with her arm around the shop, indicating the stuff she sells. "I should hope so," she replies. "With my wonderful cornucopia of divination goods, I'd be a pretty hopeless witch if I couldn't," she says with a flourish.

"Gee, I hope I didn't offend you. I didn't mean—"

"No, no, PJ. None taken. People often don't understand." She sighs.

I look at Freya, who is clearly enjoying my discomfort. I've never met anyone like Cass before, who unquestionably believes in the mystical arts. I shuffle a bit more, wondering how to get a 'normal' conversation going.

"Why do you spell *Magickal* with a *K*?" I ask because I've never seen that before.

"Ah, well spotted. It distinguishes between what we call true elemental magick of the Wiccan and the rather silly sleight of hand, illusionary magic performed by tricksters on the stage." Her eyes roll a little and she sniffs, turning her nose up as though disgusted. "It has other historical and meaningful associations, which I won't go into now. It is used in ancient texts and has numerical significance," she continues, warming to her subject. "Anyway, it applies to ritual magick, as opposed to stage magic."

My life gets weirder by the minute. Here I am in a twenty-first-century store, run by a woman who believes she is a real-life witch and my reality is turning into a scene from *Harry Potter*!

"Wow! Just wow!" I say, hoping to sound real impressed. I'm half scared and half fascinated but really don't know whether to take any of this seriously, I think, but don't say. Cass's brows knit together as she looks at me again.

"Of course you should take it seriously, PJ." My mouth drops open as Cass admonishes me for my unspoken thoughts. She winks at me, then smiles conspiratorially at Freya, as though they're both in on a secret I have yet to discover. "Now, close your mouth again, PJ. Remember the flies!"

I snap my jaws together and feel pretty freaked. From now on, I will try to keep my thoughts clear by humming a tune in my head. Just in case, you know?

Freya and I spend a couple of hours helping Cass with her stocktaking which is a real education for me in Wiccan magic(k). I ask her what Wicca means.

"Well, it's very different from the usual fairy-tale understanding of witches, PJ. It's a pagan belief that honours nature and sees the divine in all living things and in the universe. Wicca works with the divine for balance and harmony. In mediaeval times, the churches created the idea that witchcraft was evil and then persecuted people, usually older spinster ladies who were simply using herbs and natural remedies for good. Spells and incantations are often used to harness nature and to ask the universe for help, alongside the rituals and herbs. It's always for the greater good, though."

"Wowzers! So, you don't summon up the Devil or demons or anything?"

Cass laughs. "Never! Nor do we turn people into frogs, sacrifice people or animals or try to do bad things, PJ. We have a very strong belief in the power of three, you see. Whatever we do, whether it is good or bad, we believe it will come back to us threefold. So, you can see, doing bad things isn't very appealing to us Wiccans!"

"OK – that's good. No black magic then?" I am feeling a little bit more assured now.

"Well" – Cass stops counting the packs of angel cards on the shelf and ponders for a moment – "just as in every walk of life there are those who aren't good. There are some witches who will try to manipulate their magick for their own gain or for vengeful purposes. I guess you would call them 'black' witches. And then, there are Wiccans who simply make mistakes." She shakes her head and tuts. "Errors can cause havoc as well. Most of us exercise our knowledge carefully and wisely, though."

We work on companionably, counting and recording stock on the computer, chatting about all things witchy and magicky. At the end of the day, Cass gives Freya and me £10 each for our help. We decide to grab a burger. Just as we are leaving the shop and I turn to say bye to Cass, she puts her hand on my shoulder. I feel something like a light electric shock go through my arm. She smiles at me. "Things have been tough on all of us lately," she says. "We might be Wiccans, but we are also human. We feel the same pain as anyone else. There is nothing we can do when it's time for a person to leave us, but we understand that we have to accept it as part of the natural cycle and the will of the universe." She sighs, sadly. "You know that I have lost my other beloved daughter, and I miss her terribly, but she lives on through us. Same with your mum, PJ. It's our memories that keep them alive and our loved ones remain part of this great universe. Their consciousness is still there, all around us. Both you and Freya have strong connections to the other side. Don't despair, PJ. You will find your feet again and find happiness." She pats my shoulder and gives me a smile that seems to show real, heartfelt concern. I return her smile and, in this moment, I can feel the truth of what she says. She turns back to enter the store but stops suddenly and smiles at me again. "Next month, I think, PJ. Yes. Something good. You'll know it when it happens. When it does, remember to give thanks to the universe."

"I will, Cass," I assure her, although I have no idea what she's talking about. "Thanks for today. I've enjoyed it."

She strides purposefully back into the shop and calls behind her, "Good! Freya, bring PJ back soon." She lifts her arm and waves and disappears back inside Magickal Moments.

"Your mom is something else," I say to Freya, who giggles.

"Isn't she just?"

"You don't believe in her Wiccan ways, then?"

"Oh, I believe it. I've seen her work her magick many a time. Just not sure it's for me, that's all. People just think we're weirdos."

"You're not exactly, well, *ordinary* yourself, though, are you?"

"Meh." Freya shrugs her shoulders. "Just individual. Not like my mum. Although, I do seem to have picked up some of her skills," she adds mysteriously. I guess she means the dreams and the telepathy she and her sister shared. She changes the subject rapidly to admire a pair of DMs in a shop window that are colourfully painted with flowers and leaves.

CHAPTER 18

It's Hallowe'en! I'm excited and maybe just a little bit nervous about our ghost walk at Greyfriars Kirkyard tonight, but after our recent adventures with Mrs Anderson, how much scarier can things get? I'm thinking it might just be a bit of fun. As it's a Hallowe'en walk, the tour company is encouraging everyone to dress up. Freya and I are going as modern vampires, like Edward and Bella from the *Twilight* posters.

I head up to Market Street, near the station, where we've arranged to meet up again and at last, Edinburgh seems to have got with the beat for Hallowe'en, with kids all dressed up trick or treating in the streets. Pumpkins with candles light up doorsteps and there are stickers in doors of bats, witches and all sorts of ghoulies and ghosties. Orange lights twinkle in windows and I remember previous years, when Mom and I would dress up and join other families, going to each other's houses and ending up in one big party at the end of the night. I smile, remembering Mom's face all lit up in the orange glow of the charcoal burner when we'd bake potatoes and cook hotdogs over the fire at whoever's house we ended up at for the final party.

I roll up on time outside the Edinburgh Dungeon, where the others are chatting and laughing. Shuggie is woo-hooing and spreading the cloak of his Grim Reaper's outfit at passers-by. The atmosphere is electric with loads of kids and adults in the city, all dressed up, laughing, joking and jumping out of closes, and the older ones heading into bars and clubs where parties are advertised on boards and posters outside.

"Hey, guys, you all look blood-curdlingly ready for a spooky night." I grin and show my fangs, hissing at the others. Freya returns the hissy greeting, her red lips and deathly white face paint matching mine. We've given vampires a cool update with our leather jackets and DMs.

"You suit your black wig, PJ," Freya says admiringly, feeling the spiky texture of the fake hair. She does a turn to show off her own disguise and says, "We really have channelled Edward and Bella. Just like the posters we looked at." She giggles and claps her hands.

"Gee, Sunny, who have you come as? You look awesome!"

"Thanks, PJ. I am Vetala, a Hindu demon. I thought it would be good since we're heading for a graveyard. Vetala are spirits than hang around corpses and abattoirs to enter the dead and make them move around again. I guess they're kind of zombies."

"You sure look like a demon," I say, taking a close look at the sharp devil-like mask Sunny is wearing and the huge papier-mâché wings attached to his back, which he tells us his mom made for him.

"My mum wasn't very happy about me dressing up as Vetala. She's worried it will bring bad luck, but I told her it was just a superstition and she shouldn't get so worked up."

Shuggie is now completely in character as Grim Reaper. For once, he says nothing and gestures dramatically, beckoning people to follow him with his index finger on hands that are covered with grey, wrinkled-skin gloves and long, yellowing nails. He is black-cloaked and hooded, under which he wears the most grotesque skull mask. He carries a menacing plastic scythe. I can't help but laugh as he jumps in front of people who smile but politely decline his invitation to follow him.

Laughing and joking, we climb the steps up to the Royal Mile. I'm sure glad that there are lots of other people with the same idea, although I keep my eyes roaming right and left in case someone jumps out from the nooks and crannies of the ancient close. We reach the top and Freya stops.

"Right, c'mon, guys," she says. "Huddle up together in the archway and I'll take a selfie of us all."

We do as she asks and she takes some hilarious pictures of us in our scariest poses. We're in the party mood now, for sure, as we giggle and scream our way through the crowds, most of whom laugh good-naturedly and join in the fun.

"Hey, look, guys!" I point at the group standing outside St Giles Cathedral, all dressed up and waiting to go on the tour.

"Doesn't everyone look fab?" Freya exclaims, a broad, red smile on her lips. We pitch up to them and everyone says, "Hi," and greets each other like long-lost friends, laughing, whooping and high-fiving.

Sunny whispers, "Isn't it weird how a costume and nerves can make people so much friendlier?" He's grinning broadly and entering into all the fun. It's good to see him less serious and enjoying himself. Freya winks at me. I think she's glad to see this new, laidback Sunny, who beams at the group now admiring the detail and handiwork in his costume. He's busy telling them all about Vetala. Shuggie, meanwhile, starts whooshing around the crowd, holding out the cape at either side as he tries to 'catch' people for the underworld, like a warm-up guy before the main entertainment.

"Look!" Freya points at a man striding purposefully and confidently towards us. He's tall, wearing a top hat and a leather coat that reaches the ground. He kinda sweeps around the corner of the cathedral. He pitches up, takes off his hat, which he flourishes while taking a bow.

"Good evening, ladies and gentlemen. My name is Rory and I shall be accompanying you on this tour of majestic Edinburgh, which will culminate…" He pauses and looks at each of us in turn before dramatically continuing, "…in meeting your DESTINY!" He bellows the last word as we all stand listening to this showy guy, who's gripped our attention. "Yes, my friends. We are about to embark upon a tour that will serve as a sharp reminder that we are here on this earth but a short time." He swivels around the group, lowering his voice now. "Or maybe… maybe you will discover that we are here for longer than you might think. Perhaps, indeed, we are here, FOREVER! That is the mystique of Greyfriars Kirkyard, ladies and gentlemen, our destination on this special night, when ghoulies and ghosties walk the earth and whom you are most likely to meet as we explore one of the most haunted locations in Scotland!" Rory spins on his heels, his long leather coat flowing out behind him. "Come! Follow me!"

Shuggie, for the first time since meeting tonight, breaks his Grim Reaper silence. Must have been a real strain on him, I think. "Man! He's amazing." Shuggie can barely hide his admiration for our very theatrical tour guide and his vibrant story-telling.

"Actually, Shuggie," Sunny chirps up, "he reminds me of you."

"Really, Sunny?" Shuggie's voice is bright and he is clearly thrilled. "D'ye think so? Ah'd luv tae dae this sort of thing. Ye can be a real showman and entertain people doin' this, eh? Must be braw fun!"

Rory stops and the group gathers around him. "So, ladies and gentlemen, the Romans breezed into Scotland from England, like a warm knife through butter…" Shuggie snorts his amusement, interrupting Rory. "Aha! The Grim Reaper is among us and amused by the tale! It must have been a good year for you when our Picts met the Romans and made their, shall we say, *ill-tempered* and violent introductions. The Picts of Scotland were not impressed with the Romans bringing their new-fangled engineering – roads, viaducts and worse still… *bathhouses* – to our country. In fact, the Picts said, *Not on your nelly shall we scrub ourselves clean, you bunch of mini-skirted fashionistas from Rome! No! We shall continue to wander naked and dirty, and paint ourselves blue and we shall ROAR at you to scare you back to the catwalks of Milan!*" Everyone giggles at Rory's tale, as he demonstrates with a deep, throaty, loud roar which makes some of the party jump back in shock.

"Now your turn," Rory challenges us. Unselfconsciously, everyone bellows back a roar. "Not bad. Probably better if you strip yourselves naked and paint yourselves blue, though. Anyone up for it?" Laughter ripples through the group, but no-one takes him up on it.

The bants from Rory are great fun and I'm enjoying myself as we all happily scuttle along the streets of Edinburgh as he gives us his unique spin on local history, encouraging us all to participate light-heartedly. After about fifteen minutes, we arrive outside Greyfriars Kirkyard and I start to feel just a little twitchy, wondering what might lie in wait for us behind the gates.

"Aww, look," Freya says, pointing to a statue of a little dog on a plinth. "That's Greyfriars Bobby. He's famous because his master died and he sat at his grave every night for the rest of his life, faithfully keeping watch over him."

"Wow. That's so sad," I say. "Buddy is probably pining for me while I'm here having a good time. It makes me feel bad and guilty that I'm doing stuff while he's been left behind." Just then, a white feather floats down and lands on my shoe. No-one but Freya notices and I bend to pick it up.

"That's your mum telling you everything is OK, PJ." Freya winks. "I think she's telling you Buddy is OK too." She rests a hand on my arm. I nod and smile. Maybe it's true. Seems like it. I feel a little better anyhow.

"Now then, young Bella." Rory appears in a *swoosh* of his leather coat in front of us. "I heard you telling Edward here the popular myth of Greyfriars Bobby! Ladies and gentlemen, this little mutt is perhaps the most famous resident of Greyfriars, apart from *Bluidy Mackenzie*, whom we may have the extreme displeasure of meeting later. The story as you've heard it, though, isn't quite the truth. Bobby was a Skye Terrier, owned by shepherd John Gray, who sadly died when Bobby was a pup. The touchingly sad tale of Bobby spending sixteen years sleeping faithfully on his master's grave, whilst lovely, isn't quite correct. If you don't want your illusions shattered, cover your ears, because the truth is this. John Gray is not buried in Greyfriars Kirkyard and is in fact buried over a mile away in a different graveyard. Bobby, however, regularly accompanied his master to a local hostelry and restaurant here in Candlemaker Row before he died. Their habit was to go there as the one o'clock gun went off. After Gray's death, Bobby continued to dine there for the next fourteen years on the dot of one o'clock! The restaurant's owner spun the sad tale about Bobby, never letting on he was really there for the promise of daily sausages. People came from far and wide to see the famously faithful dog, making the restaurant owner, Mr Traill, a steady income. When Edinburgh Council introduced dog licensing, Mr Traill, the cad, refused to pay the seven shillings. Bobby's bacon – or sausage – was saved by the kind intervention of the Lord Provost, however, who paid it on his behalf. I'm sure Bobby would never have hung around Greyfriars Kirkyard in any case, my friends. As we are about to find out, no living creature survives for long here."

"Clever Bobby." I laugh. "Dogs always remember where their next meal is likely to come from. Say, why is the statue's nose all shiny and brassy compared to the rest of him?"

"People are told to rub his nose for luck, but it started to wear out," Sunny tells me. "It's been mended, but they still do it." Sunny shakes his head in disgust.

Rory is now striding towards the gates of the Kirkyard. "So, this is the focus of our tour tonight," he announces. "This beautiful, sombre and terrifying cemetery is the last resting place of the great, the good and, quite frankly, the bad of Edinburgh. See these five-storey buildings? You can see only two storeys, I hear you say? Well, that is because only two storeys remain above ground. Centuries of dead bodies have been piled higher and higher to create a mountainous terrain… OF DEATH! Yes indeed, the bodies are buried so close to the ground, that on a dank and rainy day, you might just glimpse a stray limb, seeping from the wet earth, to grab you by the ankles!"

"OMG!" Freya exclaims, her hand covering her mouth.

"Gross!" says Sunny.

"Cool." Shuggie grins with relish. I shake my head in mock despair of him.

We are confronted with ancient tombstones, memorials and mausoleums, all closely packed together.

Freya, who's treading warily along the path, checking every step she makes, says, "Ooch, I'm scared a bony hand is going to come up from the ground and grab me, like he said."

"Don't be afraid, Freya. He just tells that story to get everyone in the mood for the scary stuff. It's just theatre," I say. "Hey, don't all these gravestones and statues look like a big mouth of crooked teeth, though?"

"Hmmm. They do a bit," Freya replies, not distracted from picking her way along the path. She links arms with me and Sunny, who is on her other side. Shuggie has abandoned us and is following his new leather-coated, top-hatted guide, hanging on his every word.

"LOLs," says Freya. "How funny does that look? A huge man, in top hat and leather, followed by a mini-me Grim Reaper?" It does look real comical, I have to agree.

"Now, dear friends." Rory has stopped and is facing the audience. He points to the headstones with a flourish. "Look carefully at the ancient tombstones, for they will remind you how fleeting our existence is, here on earth. Take note of the warnings written on them, to live the best life we can, lest we be judged badly in the afterlife. See the angels, skull and crossbones, and the worn faces carved into the stones? This is the home of many famous and pioneering Edinburgh folk, including the worst poet Scotland, and probably the world, has ever produced, William McGonagall. Who else could have created the immortal lines:

> '*On yonder hill there stood a coo,*
> *It's no' there noo…*
> *It must have shifted.*'"

"Well, it's aye better than anythin' I ever had to read at school," says Shuggie with obvious glee, as he bounces from foot to foot. Imitating Rory's theatrical delivery, Shuggie steps in front of the surprised tour guide to address the audience himself. "How about this, then?" Shuggie steams in.

> "'*Here lies William McGonagall in Greyfriars Kirk,*
> *Where ghosties and ghoulies are said tae lurk!*
> *We all agree he was a berk,*
> *Cos ye cannae put his lines tae music 'n' twerk.*
> *Which is a cryin' shame.*'"

There is a collective groan from the group, followed by laughter and clapping, as the Grim Reaper takes his bow.

"You'll be trying to take my job, Grim Reaper," Rory says.

"Aye, well, if ye're hirin' any time, let me know," says Shuggie, cheekily. Freya, Sunny and I clap him on the back as he decides to join us again. We continue until we reach a great black vault, topped with a massive dome.

"So, we've arrived at the tomb of 'Bluidy Mackenzie,'" Rory tells us in sombre, quiet tones, as though he doesn't want the occupant to hear him. "This is the site of terror and hauntings by the poltergeist George Mackenzie, one-time Advocate to King Charles II and slaughterer of the Covenanters, who fought against the English trying to impose their church on the Scots. Those staunch Presbyterians said, '*Nae chance!*', with thousands putting their names to the National Covenant in protest. They were defeated in bloody battle and our man here, Bluidy Mackenzie, authorised 1,200 of them to be imprisoned at the back of this very Kirkyard, where they were tortured, starved, hanged and beheaded, their heads displayed on spikes and their hands sent to relatives as a warning."

"I think I just puked a little in my mouth," Freya says. "It's no wonder they're restless spirits."

I nod, trying not to think of the bloody massacre and torture. Shuggie and Sunny are listening intently, fascinated. The darkness seems to envelop us and I feel the air kinda thicken around us, making it harder to breathe. I glance at Freya and see that she's wrapped her arms around herself protectively. She catches my eye and grimaces.

"Before we venture further, my fearless friends, I must

now give you a health and safety warning. This Kirkyard is thought to be a portal between this life and the next. When the circumstances are right, the portal opens and the dead come out to torment us." I glance around at my buddies as I catch myself swallowing hard. *This guy really sounds serious! A portal that dead people come out of.* I'm shivering just a little. Sunny looks in deep thought, frown lines etched in his forehead as he concentrates. Shuggie is awestruck, his mouth gaping. He can't get enough of the gory tales or his admiration for his new hero, Rory. Freya gives me a sideways look, biting her lower lip. She raises a concerned eyebrow.

"Consider this" – I tune back into Rory's tale – "Bluidy Mackenzie is interred in this, the Black Mausoleum, a mere twenty feet from those he menaced and brutalised in the Covenanters' Prison, behind these gates. We believe this is why there is unrest in these grounds. People say this Kirkyard gives off bad energy." Rory's voice is sombre, his Scottish enunciation precise, intimidating. "The Mackenzie Poltergeist can be very active, particularly when 'sensitives' are with us, those who can channel the dead. If you are such a person, you might become unbearably cold as the temperature drops suddenly by several degrees. If you feel this, move away from it. It means a spirit is near and could attach to you. Others have felt heat and have been burned, bruised and scratched. If you do genuinely feel something strange, tell me and we will move away from it. In fact, I will move faster than you because I am the biggest coward. You'll find me in the pub outside with a wee dram to calm my nerves. Those of you old enough can join me. The rest of you, well, there's a chippy round the corner where you can buy a Coke. If you make it out, I hope to see you on the outside and hear your tales!"

The group laughs uncertainly, but Rory's light-hearted comment breaks the tension a little and I feel a little relieved. *It's just theatre.* I'm not convincing myself, though.

Our group huddles together and I rub my hands, blowing into them for warmth as the night chill deepens. A sudden breeze kicks up from nowhere in the otherwise still Kirkyard and rustles the trees as we stand in the shadow of the Black Mausoleum. I'm uneasy. I feel that something bad is near me, lurking in the gloom, ready to pounce, and my breathing gets faster and shallower as the air feels thick with menace. My hands shake and I thrust them in my pockets so no-one can see.

"*Help me!*"

I swirl around, surprised, expecting to see a small child beside me. I look every which way, but there is no-one around from whom that voice could possibly have come – unless one of the gang is playing a joke? I check everyone out, but as far as I can tell, they're all engrossed with Rory's spiel. No-one else appears to have heard the voice, otherwise, surely there would have been questions?

"What is it, PJ?" Sunny has noticed my agitation.

"Um, dunno, Sunny. Could've sworn I heard something. A child's voice, calling for help. Did you hear it?"

"No, I didn't hear a thing," he says, stealing a glance around and shining his flashlight to see if there are any little kids hanging around. "Maybe someone is playing a prank. Perhaps a set-up, by the tour company?"

"Hmm, maybe," I say doubtfully.

"I didn't see anyone else react if they did hear it," Sunny says.

"Oh, maybe it's just my imagination. It sure is creepy in here."

"Probably," Sunny whispers. "Maybe an animal, or a bird? Cats and foxes can sound like babies crying in the night," he suggests. I'm unconvinced.

"Now, my young friends." Rory turns his attention to me and Sunny. "Did I hear you speaking about animals and birds a moment ago?"

"Uh, yeah." I nod. "I thought I heard something. Might have been an animal, we thought."

Rory shakes his head dismissively. "Everyone, will you be silent for a moment and listen carefully?"

The group stands still. Faces are turned upwards and tilted sideways as everyone listens intently. Freya and Shuggie (who has removed his mask) look at me and Sunny, puzzled expressions on their faces. Shuggie, palms up, shrugs. Moments later, Rory asks, "Well, what did you hear?" The members of the group all look at each other, kinda expectantly, but they all seem reluctant to speak. I guess none of us is certain what the answer is meant to be.

Finally, a young woman raises her hand, her index finger pointing upwards. "Nothing," she says. "I didn't hear anything." A murmur of agreement breaks out around the group.

"EXACTLY!" Rory proclaims. "Let me explain. There is no birdsong in the Kirkyard. You will hear no fluttering wings or mewling cats in here. Quite simply, no living creature chooses to be here. Creatures that venture into the Kirkyard have been regularly found dead as the proverbial dodo! Now, THAT should tell you something about the energy in this place. Be under no illusion, it is bad energy and most of it appears to emanate from this very mausoleum. This is where most of the dead animals are found. Stories of ghosts have been circulating for many years in the Kirkyard, but in recent years, the poltergeist activity has intensified. Gather round!" Rory shines his flashlight upwards, illuminating his face, making him look ghostly, sinister and skeletal as the shadows play around and contort his features. Freya hooks her arm into mine.

"In 1998, a tramp, looking for a 'hospitable' place to take shelter from the rain, decided that Mackenzie's tomb looked a cosy option! He stumbled around in the darkness and found the coffin of Bluidy Mackenzie. The tramp apparently fancied his chances of finding something valuable in the coffin and broke the seal, searching for treasures. Meanwhile, the warden was outside walking his dog when they heard banging coming from the mausoleum as the tramp battered his way into the coffin with a piece of wood. Suddenly, an other-worldly scream cut through the darkness and the terrified warden shone his torch into the mausoleum. Seconds later, a figure emerged from the shadows of the crypt and the warden was met with a terrifying vision." Rory's voice becomes urgent and he gesticulates wildly. "The tramp stumbled out, features contorted, his mouth open in a terrifying maw, eyes rolling in his skull. He was covered in slime and loped off into the darkness, never to be seen again. The warden, at first, was convinced he had seen a terrifying apparition and only later learned of the break-in. It was discovered that the tramp had fallen through a hole into another burial chamber, where bodies had been piled one on top of the other during the plague. The bodies were intact and remarkably well preserved, due to lack of exposure to the air in the sealed chamber. They were still covered with skin, hair and their eyes stared glassily into space. The whole place was covered in green, stinking slime that oozed from the bodies; noxious substances exploded as the tramp fell upon the corpses. It's no wonder he screamed in horror, scaring the warden, as he emerged from the tomb looking like one of the bodies he had disturbed."

The group looks disgusted and groans of horror break out as people 'yuk' and 'bleurgh' around Rory.

"Aye, right enough, it would gie' ye the boak just thinkin' aboot it," Shuggie says helpfully.

"Nice," Freya says, wrinkling her nose. "Imagine falling into all those bodies and being covered in gunk. I wonder where the tramp went to clean up. I bet he was vomming until he found a way to get rid of the goo."

"Why would a homeless person choose to break into a mausoleum, though? It's the last place I'd go," says Sunny.

"He must have been desperate," says Freya sadly. "It must be awful having nowhere to go in bad Edinburgh weather."

We're now walking through iron gates that Rory has unlocked, which he tells us is the Covenanters' Prison. We walk along a wide pathway, bordered each side with doorways leading into dark musty rooms floored with compacted soil and brick. Rory gathers us inside one of the rooms and tells us to stand around him in the pitch black, murky darkness. He shines his torch around to make sure no-one trips and tells us to stand in a semi-circle around the walls.

"Now, stay exactly where you are, even if you feel something touch you," he advises. It feels hard to breathe in this musty, stuffy room, where the walls seem to close in on you. We all huddle together, and I feel slightly comforted by having companions nearby. Rory stands with his back to the entrance.

"Shortly after Mackenzie's mausoleum was desecrated, people regularly began to report strange happenings. Strange noises, smells and cold spots were common. Visitors to the tomb would feel icy blasts of air, pushing them inside. Reports extended to this very area in which you are standing: the Covenanters' Prison. They heard strange rapping noises, someone breathing next to them, a child's tearful cries. People often felt sick and fainted."

A child's tearful cries? Is that what I heard? I shudder at the thought of what might have caused the misery.

"Nowadays," Rory continues, "the mausoleum itself is kept locked, as is the Covenanters' Prison. In 2004, however, teenagers broke into the tomb and stole Mackenzie's skull and played around with it. Kids for years had played dare at the mausoleum and it is common even today. Visitors often peek inside and recite the old children's rhyme:

'*Bluidy Mackingie, come oot if ye daur,*
Lift the sneck and draw the bar.'

"I wouldn't recommend poking the bear, so to speak. Taunting the spirits is never a good idea. Even more activity has been experienced in surrounding houses, where inexplicable noises and voices have been heard, shadows lurking in corners, a report of a blood-like substance oozing from the walls of one house and unexplained fires breaking out."

I shine my cell phone on my buddies, who are looking wide-eyed at me. I think we're all on the same page as we're reminded of the night in Mrs Anderson's. Could there really be a link between the fire in Mrs Anderson's house and Bluidy Mackenzie? It was the name we'd heard on the digital recording that had brought us here! Could he have been looking for a way to communicate through her? Or is this just a series of clues that's brought us here for a reason? Was Mrs Anderson trying to warn us that Mackenzie was going to set her apartment alight, I wonder? But for what purpose?

Freya jumps clean up in the air and lets out a blood-curdling shriek of horror.

"Whaat the…? Freya?" I grab her arm to support her, her breathing fast and panicky.

"Are you OK?" Rory is making his way towards us.

"I-I'm not sure," Freya says. "A sharp pain on my arm. It felt like I was scratched. Sorry. I'm feeling a little sick."

"Can you show me?" Rory shines the torch on Freya's arms. She pulls up the sleeve of her coat and everyone gasps at the three deep and bleeding scratch marks just above her wrist.

"Oh. My. Gosh," is all I can say.

Shuggie is carefully inspecting the scratches and shakes his head, whistling as he exhales. "It's a sign of demonic activity," he says knowledgably. I look at him disapprovingly as Freya's face takes on a look of even more terror. Sunny now takes her arm and gives the wound his own forensic examination, when someone else screams at the back of the room, followed by a flop and a thud as she hits the floor, out cold.

"OK, everyone, keep calm," Rory commands, more serious than he has been at any time during the tour. "You'll all be fine, but we need to make an orderly exit now. Can I please ask you all to walk calmly from the room and gather on the path outside? Would two of the adults please remain behind to help me with the lady who's fainted?"

We stumble out of the chamber, shocked and horrified. What the heck just happened? Freya is holding a Kleenex to her arm to stem the bleeding when suddenly I feel a tap on my shoulder, followed by an evil, growling laugh behind me.

"Did you guys hear that?" I'm freaking out now, as a chill runs through me so deep I feel like my limbs will crack and fall off if I move.

"What?" Freya looks nervously around her, eyes wide.

"That horrible laugh! Shuggie, was that you tapping my shoulder and making that noise? Because if it was, I swear, I—"

"I didnae dae anythin', PJ. Not after last time. I gie ye ma' word," Shuggie replies seriously. "But… look! Guys! Can ye see that next tae PJ's shoulder?" He shines his flashlight on me as the others look intently into the darkness.

"It's like Tinkerbell," Freya says.

"Huh?" I jump to the side, brushing my shoulder. Shuggie is holding his cell up, following something.

"It's no' Tinkerbell, Freya, it's a freakin' orb!"

"An orb? What's that?" I am officially terrified. I snap my head over each shoulder, trying to see what the others see, and turn in a circle, not wanting to stay still for a moment, in case the orbs try to go through my body.

"Ooch, did ye no' watch the telly the other night?" Shuggie sounds a bit exasperated. "An orb is a ball of light. Spirit energy as it tries to materialise. I think I've caught it on ma video. It's gone now."

"Did you see it, Sunny?"

"I saw something. Could have been an insect, caught in some of the lights from our phones," he says, ever-logical.

This can't be happening, I think. Disembodied voices, laughter and an inexplicable three-pronged, claw-like injury on Freya that appeared underneath her leather jacket. I could just about cope with the gentle, if weird, happenings at Mrs Anderson's, but this is taking a much darker turn.

Freya is trembling and clearly shaken. I whisper we ought to stay with the larger group, thinking it will be safer than venturing off into the darkness of the Kirkyard on our own. The others agree. Rory emerges from the chamber and, along with another member of the group, supports the girl who fainted. I'm relieved to see she is conscious and is walking out, unsteadily, her face deathly pale.

"What happened to her?" A woman, clutching her husband's arm, is desperate to know the details.

"Sharon here felt someone push her and thinks she saw a dark shape right next to her. She felt dizzy and sick, then fainted."

The fearful girl looks up and speaks to Freya: "That's right. I remember now. You cried out and Rory went over to see you. It was then I felt something thud into me from behind and then I-I saw this dark shadow thing coming towards me." She is tearful now, her breath coming in short gasps. "It seemed to wrap itself around me and then go through me. It was icy cold as it went through my body. I felt sick and then the next thing I knew was when Rory was speaking to me and helping me up."

Freya lets the group, which has gathered around us, see the scratches on her arm. Amid shrieks and sharp intakes of breath, Freya asks the girl, Sharon, "Did you feel anything scratching you too?"

"Not so much scratching. I felt as though something punched me in the back. Come to think of it, it feels a bit sore. Do you have a torch?" Freya nods and switches her cell phone flashlight on again.

"Would you like me to have a look?"

The girl nods warily and points to the middle of her back where she said she had felt the assault.

Freya lifts the girl's sweater and exclaims, "OhmyGod! Look at this!" She gently turns the girl so that her back is exposed to the group.

I go closer and shine my flashlight on her skin. There, quite clearly, is the beginning of a humungous bruise and it's shaped like a hand! I glance at Freya, who throws me a look of concern, her brows furrowed. I don't understand what's happening here, but that one look at Freya tells me it's nothing good. Murmuring breaks out among the group and several say they've had enough and want to leave now. Rory raises his hand to quieten everyone.

"OK, everyone, we've come to the end of the tour now, anyway, and I think you've experienced the very worst of what the Kirkyard is famous for. Let's wrap things up now and head back. Keep together and follow me."

The group is subdued now. All the fun and nervous

laughter is replaced by fearful faces, clinging together and walking quickly to the exit. Sharon starts to cry. She's really disturbed by what's happened. Freya stoically puts a comforting arm around the girl.

"S-sorry. I'm just so scared the ghost will follow me." She's getting a little hysterical now, crying hard. "Can that happen, Rory?"

I can't wait to hear the answer to this one, and listen intently for his answer.

He frowns thoughtfully. "Look, it can sometimes happen that these things can attach themselves to visitors, but it's really unusual. I've only heard of it once in fifteen years of running the tours."

Sharon, who is shaking uncontrollably, wails and sobs. I can't blame her. This is becoming one freakfest of a night. Freya puts one hand on each of the girl's shoulders and whispers something to her. After speaking quietly together, the girl miraculously calms down. Freya lifts her hand and circles the air around Sharon, whispering something as she does so. She hands her something and Sharon smiles feebly.

"Thank you," Sharon says to Freya. To Rory she says, "I think I'll be OK now." Relieved, Rory signals for us all to move on, and we pick our way through the roots and stones of Kirkyard.

"What did you do? She seems to be much calmer," I say to Freya as the four of us huddle together to hear what had happened.

"I just did a little ritual to put a protective light around her and said an incantation my mum taught me to keep bad stuff away," she explains, as though it was the most normal thing in the world. "I gave her a crystal to ward off evil spirits. She'll be OK now. It won't follow her."

"Eh? And what aboot you? If you gave her the crystal are you protected?"

Freya smiles. "I'll be fine, Shuggie. Just another day for we everyday witchy folk!"

"Well, you certainly cheered her up," I say, mystified. Sunny appears less impressed.

"It's just the power of suggestion," he states, matter-of-factly. "What we just observed was mass hysteria. When the girl heard you cry out, she scared herself silly and convinced herself there were ghosts attacking her."

Freya raises a knowing eyebrow but says nothing.

"Aye, but that disnae explain the scratches, or the hand mark on the girl's back," Shuggie comments quite reasonably.

Sunny just sighs as though we're all a bunch of looney tunes. "It's psychosomatic," he replies, as though the big word explains everything.

"Well, what does that mean?" I ask irritably. He can't just say something and leave us hanging.

"Well, I was reading about it before we came here. Sometimes you can have something appear physically because of stress. It's the mind that actually causes the physical reaction, nothing more."

"Nah, nah, nah." Shuggie shakes his head emphatically. "I dinnae buy that, Sunny. Marks like those just don't appear from nowhere."

"Well, I agree, they are a bit odd," Sunny concedes reluctantly. "But my guess is that you, Freya, probably scratched yourself earlier and you noticed it only because it was being discussed. Sharon probably bumped into something sticking out from the wall and, focusing on the spooky atmosphere, she thought it was something else. Then she scared herself silly. We all just saw what we expected to see. It was a bruise that just happened to have a shape a bit like a hand."

I don't think any of us are really buying Sunny's explanation.

"Nope." Freya is emphatic. "I can assure you all, those scratches weren't there before I came out."

"Aye, and there are three clear scratches, like claw marks. A sign that the Holy Trinity is being mocked." Shuggie is not deterred from his own explanation. "They happen when there is really bad spirit energy around."

"Aren't you afraid this could happen again, Freya?" I'm concerned for her now.

"No. It just caught me off guard, is all. I was kinda caught up in the fun side of things and I didn't really think anything would happen on the tour. I just forgot to keep my protection going. It'll be fine. Mum taught me how to deal with these things."

"You sure are brave, Freya." I whistle admiringly. I would have been squealing like a baby if it was me.

"There was de-fin-*ately* activity going on there," Shuggie says. "I saw the orb. A sure sign of spirits."

"Oh, gee! With all the excitement, we didn't look at your video, Shuggie! Lemme see it," I say, terrified but intrigued. Shuggie switches his video onto replay and we all gather behind him. The light isn't great, but I can see a hazy image of me, brushing my shoulder, as Shuggie tells me there's an orb next to me. Sure enough, there is a round, shimmering, blueish white ball, hovering above my right shoulder. We look at it several times. It lingers a few moments and moves off in a straight line before disappearing through the mausoleum wall. Shuggie captured it perfectly.

"Well, that sure was strange," I say, scratching my head.

Sunny sighs. "Maybe. I guess that's what we aim to find out with our paranormal investigations. I think it's really important we don't jump to conclusions, though, guys. We should keep an open mind but always look for a rational explanation. *Occam's Razor*," he says smugly.

"Whit's that when it's at hame, Sunny? Ye dinnae half speak in riddles sometimes," says Shuggie.

"It just means the simplest explanation is probably the correct one. It was an English Friar, William of Ockham, who said that in the fourteenth century."

"Jeez, you're a walking encyclopaedia, Sunny," I say, admiringly. *Is there nothing this guy can't explain?*

Sunny is dismissive of my praise. "Not really, PJ." He smiles bashfully. "I just think we have to be objective and do things properly. I've been reading up on the science of paranormality and if we are to be taken seriously and investigate properly, it's important we eliminate the obvious before reaching an opinion."

"He's absolutely right," Freya says supportively. "What do you think the light was, Sunny?"

"Hard to be certain. It could, as I said, just have been an insect caught in the lights, but it seemed to move *purposefully* rather than erratically, as an insect would. You know, it didn't circle or move around in the way you would expect an insect to do. It appeared to want to hang around next to PJ, and it moved straight and smoothly to the mausoleum. Odd."

"So ye're sayin' there is no obvious explanation, Sunny?"

"Yes, I guess so. Maybe there's a way we can slow down the video. I'll get a package for the computer and we can try to analyse it better."

"Aye! He's right," Shuggie agrees, surprisingly. "They always look to debunk stuff on *Ghost Hunters* and *Ghost Adventures* and often there's a rational explanation. It's braw having someone like you, Sunny, who can think things through."

"We could maybe pick Aunt Katie's brains. She knows a lot about this stuff," I suggest.

"Yes, good idea." Sunny smiles. I think he'll love a conversation with Aunt Katie.

We've almost reached the gates, having caught up with the group, when Rory points us towards a small building nearby.

"So, ladies and gentlemen, you haven't been disappointed tonight. You've seen the perils the Kirkyard can throw upon the unwary visitor. I hope that despite the evening's events, you have enjoyed your sojourn with Bluidy Mackenzie and those who wish to make their presence known to you. In here" – he gestures to the large shed-type building – "we have a shop that might interest you. It contains all things historical and spooky about the Kirkyard and Edinburgh City. I invite you to take a browse before you leave. I shall be in the hostelry outside, should anyone wish to join me for that much-needed wee dram."

With a last flourish of his long coat, he opens the door and we clamber in gratefully to the light and normality of the shop. There are books and souvenirs inside, so I decide to treat myself and buy a book about paranormal Edinburgh. It might give us some ideas for other investigations, but I'll be sure to keep the lights on when reading it.

At last, the night is over, and the group disappears into the night, with several adults commenting that they'd join Rory in the bar. As we exit the gates, I take one last look back and what do I see? That darn cat, Azrael, cleaning his paws, as usual. He gives me a knowing look, turns and runs off into the Kirkyard. *You'd better be a special kind of cat, li'l guy*, I think, recalling the tales of doomed animals. But then, I don't think there's any doubt about that.

CHAPTER 19

"That wis some night, eh, guys?" Shuggie is slumped like roadkill on the couch in his house where we're all staying tonight. He shakes his head and whistles. "Awesome activity in the Kirkyard. Ah've been thinkin'. How aboot we make the Kirkyard our first proper investigation? We could get some braw evidence of poltergeists and ghosts if we did a real vigil there."

"I guess so," I chip in. "I'm thinking it's what we're meant to do. Like we've been led to this in some way. The voice on the EVP back at Mrs Anderson's hinted at Mackenzie and then the fire breaking out in her apartment later. It's got to be more than coincidence, surely?"

"Yes, that's right," Freya agrees. "And remember Mrs Anderson's voice asking for help."

I frown, remembering that EVP. It said, *Help needed. Danger… Mackenzie. Beware…* I shiver a little, but something inside me is saying we have to go back to the Kirkyard. Mrs Anderson was trying to tell us that. I can't explain why I am so certain, but I am.

"Aww, pure dead brilliant! Settled then. Let's get back there soon as we can and find oot whit's goin' on, eh?"

Sunny has been quiet but now adds, "I think it will be an excellent location for our first investigation, but the Covenanters' Prison is kept locked. Rory had a key for the gates, remember?"

"Aye, that's right. So he did," Shuggie concedes, a little deflated.

"Well, maybe we can get permission from whoever is in charge of it? Or maybe we could even get Rory to come with? We could go up to the Royal Mile and ask him?"

"Ach, I dinnae think anyone is gonnae let a bunch o' kids loose on their own inside the prison and I cannae see Rory wanting to come with us. He's up there just aboot every night anyway."

"I'll ask Aunt Katie if she'll come with us," I suggest. "Or maybe she'll have some idea about how we could organise it. You know – with her connections and everything?"

"Great idea, PJ." Shuggie brightens now.

"I think it's a very haunted place," Freya says, rolling up the sleeve of her jacket. "It's not just haunted, but it has a very dark side to it. It could be dangerous, you know," she says, scrutinising her arm. Shuggie leans over the couch and peers over Freya's shoulder.

"Help ma boab, Freya!" Shuggie is wide-eyed as he grabs her wrist. "They scratches are sure fading fast!" We all gather round her and sure enough, although there are still visible marks, they're no longer the angry red bloody welts that were there earlier. As we gaze at them, they gradually fade even more, and in moments, they disappear completely!

"Jeez, Freya, what just happened?" I'm stunned.

"I'm not sure exactly, but I think the psychic energy has probably faded, now we're away from the Kirkyard." She shrugs.

Shuggie draws out his cell. "As a matter of fact, I took a coupla wee sneaky pictures on ma phone of Freya's scratches and that girl's back. Look! I still have the evidence." He gives a self-satisfied grin. We pass the cell phone around, each of us inspecting the images carefully. There's no doubt about it. Those scratches on Freya's arm were livid and raw. Three evenly spaced swollen welts. How could they just disappear before our eyes, I wonder?

I check out the picture of the bruise on Sharon's back, zooming in for a better view. It's certainly large enough to be a handprint, but it's not totally distinct as such. "Shuggie, can you email these to me?"

"Aye, nae problem? Why, like?"

"I'll show them to Aunt Katie. Maybe she'll have some explanation for them."

"Excellent idea, PJ." Sunny perks up, always looking for alternative explanations.

"I definitely heard a child calling for help in the Kirkyard," I remind the others. "It was real creepy. So, we've got scratches, bruising, fainting, disembodied voices and orbs. The Kirkyard is a serious place to be investigating. It could be dangerous, as Freya said. Just say weird stuff follows us? Not gonna lie – I'm a bit scared."

"Och, dinnae be such a fearty, PJ." Shuggie looks at me with mock disdain.

"Well, I can get some really strong protection," Freya says. "There are lots of things we can do, like special meditation before we start to surround ourselves in a protective shield of light. It stops the spirits attaching to us."

"Or maybe just stay calm and not let our imaginations get the better of us," Sunny offers. "The mind is really powerful. I've read that you can sometimes make things happen just by believing it, or see things that aren't there. We should keep Occam's Razor in mind and look for the obvious before jumping to conclusions."

Everyone has had their say and we all sit quietly thinking our own thoughts for a few moments. It's me who breaks the silence. "So, in principle are we all in favour of investigating Greyfriars Kirkyard? Hands up and say, 'Aye,' if yes.

"Aye!" Shuggie and Sunny's hands shoot up without hesitation. Freya and I are a little more hesitant, but we put our hands up.

"I think we should make this as professional as we can," I say. "I'll create a website, where I can write up a history of the places we investigate and tell the stories of what happened. We can put up photos and videos of what we find. Shuggie, I think you should be the frontman for the videos. We could get a YouTube channel for our films."

Shuggie is beaming from ear to ear. "Aw, pure dead brill idea, PJ. Ah'm well up for that. Ah can bring a wee bit levity and entertainment tae it."

"Yeah, and you know what? Vloggers can make a lot of money if they get famous. If we go viral, it could help us fund our investigations and equipment."

"Aye – yer right there, PJ," says Shuggie. "We might even get famous and rich frae this! It's a really popular subject.

I watched some videos on YouTube and I reckon we could dae it better. They get a shed-load o' hits and likes."

"Maybe I could start my own Insta fashion line for ghost hunters." Freya is now warming up to the possibilities too.

"Right then, so I'll be the lead investigator then, with Sunny as the scientific sceptic. Shuggie, you're the 'face' of the vlogging, as well as one of the investigating team, and Freya, you are the spiritual one, who can bring some insight into what's happening. Is everyone happy with that then?" Everyone says, "Aye."

"And our name, how about the 'Paranormal Pursuers'?"

"*PJ* and the Paranormal Pursuers," Shuggie exclaims.

"Bit of a mouthful, isn't it?" I frown doubtfully.

"A wee bit of alliteration goes a long way, PJ." Shuggie laughs. "Ah mean, we could call ourselves 'Sunny and the Scary Spirits' or 'Freya and the Frightening Fiends', but they're no' very slick. We want tae sound professional, dynamic. We do what it says on the tin, eh?"

We all agree that 'PJ and the Paranormal Pursuers' has a ring to it. Shuggie gets the Irn Bru out and fills up our glasses so that we can toast our newly founded group. I'm nervous but also excited. Investigating, writing a website and vlogging. It's everything I'm interested in. I wonder if Mom has a hand in all this. I wouldn't mind betting she's up to something behind the scenes.

CHAPTER 20

It's pitch black in the Greyfriars Kirkyard as I stumble over headstones and crash into monuments, desperately trying to escape the unknown horror that's close behind. I shake my head and put my hands to my ears, trying to block out the relentlessly pleading voice that cries, *Help me! Help me!* A terrifying growl bellows out and I run faster, faster, knowing that I am doomed for all eternity if the thing behind catches me. The darkness engulfs me and I truly fear that my heart is about to rip through my chest as I run without any sense of direction.

I hear that other-worldly, low menacing growl again, closer this time, and my flesh feels icy as the creature's breath blasts my neck. I squeal out in shock and horror as I feel sudden burning on my back, as though razor blades are cutting through my flesh. I know, without having to look, that its claws have slashed my skin. I run faster, and out of the darkness, the domed roof of the Mackenzie tomb looms, illuminated against the sky that has miraculously cleared to reveal the silver light of a full moon. Onwards

I run, with the thing in close pursuit. I am being herded towards the door of the tomb. I try to veer away from it, but the looming mass that has been toying with me pushes me forcefully through the door that gapes open like a giant mouth waiting to devour me. I am no match for the creature as it hurls me through the door into the blackness beyond and my screams cut through the silence of the Kirkyard.

I land in soft mulch, wet and stinking, and as my eyes adjust to the darkness, I look down to the floor that appears to undulate. *No! No! Please, not this!* I scream inwardly as I realise I am surrounded by inexplicably live corpses, horrifying in their appearance, their bony limbs reaching out for me, opaque, lidless eyes staring at me blindly. I thrash and scream, fighting off every bony hand that touches me.

"PJ? PJ, are you OK?" Relief floods through me when I hear the voice and I push myself upwards, away from the corpses, finally escaping the suffocating depths of that noxious crypt. Gasping for breath, I find myself sitting bolt upright, confused and terrified. I hear a wailing sound, that I realise is coming from me. I am still thrashing my arms around, until I jolt out of the horror when someone grabs them and holds them still, and I hear Freya's voice commanding, "PJ! Stop it! Speak to me! You're having a bad dream. Wake up!" I almost hug her with joy as I see that I am still in Shuggie's house, my sleeping bag tangled around me and my face damp with perspiration.

I stutter weakly, gulping for air, "I-I'm OK, Freya." I laugh hysterically, recalling the worst, most vivid nightmare I have ever had.

"Sshhh, calm down, PJ." Freya is rubbing my arms

comfortingly, but warily, no doubt eager to avoid the danger my flailing arms might have posed moments before. She smiles. "It's OK. It's over now," she murmurs soothingly, and strokes my hair that is plastered to my head. It's a nice feeling; like my mom is here, comforting me as she did whenever I was sick or upset.

My breathing is less rapid now and I'm able to speak. "I'm cool, Freya. Fine now," I assure her, still only able to manage short sentences. "Wow! That was some nightmare. It felt so real. I fell down the hole in the Mackenzie tomb. I think he was chasing me. Someone, a child, I think, was crying out for help. When I fell into the crypt, there were corpses, just like the tramp saw, but they were alive and squirming and trying to drown me in gloop." I shudder at the memory.

Freya switches on the light and I see that Shuggie and Sunny are both sitting upright in their sleeping bags, open-mouthed, hair dishevelled, eyes wide, shocked at their sudden awakening by a screaming madman.

Shuggie whistles in amazement. "Jeez, PJ. Ye dinnae dae things by hauf, dae ye?" He yawns widely and scratches his head and armpits. "Ye must have a wild imagination in that heid o' yours!"

"Uh, yeah, I guess," I reply, still struggling to shake off the confusion and terror of my dream.

"Would you like a glass of water?" Sunny asks.

"Yeah, that'd be cool, thanks, Sunny," I manage. It sure feels good to know I'm with my friends and it had all been a nightmare. The ghost walk must have made some impression on me.

"Here you go." Sunny kneels on the floor and solicitously

hands me the water, which I drink deeply. "All better now?" he asks.

I nod appreciatively. "Think so, thanks, Sunny." I untangle myself from the sleeping bag and stretch out, checking out my surroundings, just to be doubly sure I really am back in the waking world. The dream hangs over me and I still feel uneasy.

"You were totes tangled up in that sleeping bag." Freya nods to where I had been sleeping. "Your head was completely covered and I thought you were suffocating in there. Then you started screaming, so I came over to find out what was going on."

"Gee, Freya, I'm sure glad you did." I laugh uncertainly. "I think I was gonna be drowned in bodies in the crypt. Don't they say, if you die in your dreams, you die in real life?"

"I have heard that said, but I dunno if it's true." Freya shrugs. "You did give me the fright of my life, though."

"Well, I think after PJ's Oscar-winning horror movie performance, sleep is over for the night. Cuppie tea, anyone?" Shuggie emerges from his sleeping bag and smooths down his *Teenage Mutant Ninja Turtle* pyjamas.

"Tea sounds good. Lots of sugars, please, Shuggie." The normality of tea is a wonderful thing. No wonder the British love it so much.

I shuffle to the kitchen, behind Shuggie, Freya and Sunny following. Shuggie slams on the light and puts bread in the toaster as the kettle boils comfortingly. As I settle myself at the breakfast bar, I feel something stinging on my back and rub it absently. My blood runs cold as I remember the nightmare.

"Shuggie?" I beckon him over uncertainly.

"That's me. Whassup?"

"Take a look at my back, would you? It feels kinda sore and burning." Shuggie obliges and I feel him push up my sweatshirt and his hand, cool on my back. He gasps.

"Freya, Sunny," he calls the others, for once urgency in his voice. "Quick! Take a swatch at this!"

"What is it?" I ask fearfully, already anticipating the answer to my own question.

"Oh my," Freya says.

"My goodness," Sunny adds helpfully.

My patience is wearing thin. "Look, will y'all stop *oh my-ing* and *my goodness-ing* and tell me what you see?"

"Three deep scratches." Freya confirms my worst fears.

"Red and swollen," Sunny tells me.

"A wee bit blood there, too," Shuggie observes.

"OMG, PJ! The ghost from last night – Mackenzie. It must have followed you. Stupid me! I should have given us all protection last night." Freya facepalms in self-anger.

Shuggie meanwhile has his cell out and I hear the click of a photo being taken. He passes it round the table and we peer at it, zooming in and out, trying to get a better view of my injury.

"Defo similar to Freya's scratches," Shuggie says.

"I felt it happen in the nightmare."

"I think you've had a psychic attack alright," Freya says worriedly, her face pinched in concern. "It's too much of a coincidence, what with the nightmare and the scratches," she continues. She gives me a serious look. "OK, so we need to do some protection now, to make sure it doesn't happen again, or to any of us." I'm sure not gonna argue with her.

"Shuggie – will you send me a copy of the photo? I want to talk to my aunt about this."

"Aye, nae probs, PJ," he replies, already forwarding the picture via WhatsApp.

My hands are shaking as I take a gulp of steaming tea. "So, what do we do now, Freya?"

"Stand up. Shuggie, Sunny, over here," she commands. We stand in a circle. "Now, close your eyes. I'm going to pass a crystal around your body, top to toe, and it's going to create a shield against the bad stuff. You all have to do your part as well. First and foremost, you must have absolute faith in what I'm doing. If you show fear, or waver in any way in that belief, then dark spirits can get through. OK?" Freya looks solemnly from one to the other of us and we nod our agreement. "Right then." Freya produces a long crystal that's attached to some thread. "As I pass this crystal around you, I'm going to seek protection from the angels for each of us. Now, close your eyes and imagine you're entirely surrounded by white light. Picture yourselves as completely enclosed by the light, like an aura, or protective shield. No gaps in it, mind. Now, it's glowing white and it comes from a good source. You are encircled by the white light and we banish any evil entities so that they can no longer touch us. Guys? Do you feel the heat?"

Oddly, I do feel a kind of energy around me. It kinda tingles and feels warm and safe. "I feel it, Freya."

"So do I," says Sunny.

"Aye, me too," Shuggie confirms.

"Good. OK, so the light is now protecting you. Keep it around you and believe that nothing can get beyond it. You won't come to harm as long as you keep on believing.

Always think of the light if you feel uneasy or afraid. It'll be with you as long as you use it properly."

Freya murmurs some sort of incantation and we're done; the ritual is over. "How do you feel?" she asks.

"OK, I think. Better," I reassure her. Sunny and Shuggie seem a little less certain, but I guess they haven't come quite as close as me to the danger. The scratches really worry me.

"Ah suppose it's just possible you scratched yourself when you were fightin' aff the ghoulies in yer nightmare," Shuggie suggests.

"Good, Shuggie." Sunny beams at him. "As I said earlier—"

"Occam's Razor," we chime in unison and laugh.

Sunny grins. "Exactly. Always look for the simplest explanation. It's usually the right one. I mean, which one of us hasn't woken up in the morning with random scratches on us from time to time?"

"Yeah, that's a good point, Sunny," I agree. "It's happened a few times and I've never even considered the scratches were put there by an evil spirit. I was so tangled up in the sleeping bag, thrashing around, who knows? I could have scratched myself easily."

Dug comes scampering through the kitchen door, sliding on the laminate floor, and pulls up abruptly, like a cartoon dog putting the brakes on.

"Whit's wrang, pal?" Shuggie kneels down to rub the dog's head and ears which are clamped tight to his head. He's shaking and eyeing me suspiciously. I go over to him, but he draws back, his hackles rising. He is rigid and still, his little legs apart and braced on the floor. After a moment or so, he relaxes and allows me to rub his face.

Whatever had spooked him was gone. I glance at Freya, who shrugs.

"Maybe some residual bad energy that he sensed," she suggests. I shiver at the possibility of evil spirits still following me around. Still, Dug seems happy enough around me now and he's scampering off to find his ball for a game.

Aunt Katie is due to come for me soon, so, at Shuggie's suggestion, we have a pow-wow about next steps. We agree that Sunny will source some simple equipment on eBay, I'll speak to Aunt Katie to get some helpful tips on paranormal research, Freya will do some meditation for spiritual contact and get more protection for us, and Shuggie is going to borrow his sister's camera for vlogging. It's agreed we'll do a daytime recce of the Kirkyard first of all, to familiarise ourselves with its layout. We'll also record a history of the Kirkyard's dark and bloody history, for which I am tasked with the research. I'm also going to ask Aunt Katie about how we might get access to the Kirkyard at night for the real deal.

CHAPTER 21

"You're very subdued, PJ," Aunt Katie says as we ride home together in the car.

"I'm OK," I say more brightly than I am actually feeling. "Just thinking about stuff that happened on the ghost walk last night."

"Interesting evening, then? Did you have fun?" Katie is all ears, waiting to hear what we got up to.

"Yeah, you could say that. Some real creepy stuff went down at the Kirkyard last night and I'm still trying to process it."

"Like what?"

"Well… first of all, one of the women in the group fainted and when she came round, she was convinced she'd been touched by a ghost."

"Easy to explain, PJ. She just got taken up by the atmosphere and scared herself. Just panic, is all."

"But that wasn't all. She had a handprint on her back. And then Freya got scratched by something. It was like three scratches in a row on her arm that was covered by a thick leather jacket. I heard a disembodied voice crying out for help and then there were sort of twinkly lights floating around my shoulder at the same time. I have pictures to show you."

Aunt Katie frowns thoughtfully. "Hmm, well, I have come across this type of phenomena quite a few times, but it can be explained, PJ. You shouldn't get too wrapped up in thinking it's definitely paranormal. Let me look at your photos when we get home and we'll talk it through."

"OK. Just one other thing, Aunt Katie…" I say gingerly, not quite sure how she's going to react to my next nugget of information.

"Uh huh?" She eyes me warily.

"So, you know we're all interested in ghosty stuff? Well, we've decided we're going to set up our own group of paranormal investigators and see what we can find out."

"Okaay… I would just caution you all, PJ. You're all at a really vulnerable time in your lives and that makes you susceptible and impressionable. I'm a little worried that this could be dangerous for you guys right now."

"Dangerous? What do you mean, Aunt Katie?" She's starting to spook me a little – *as if I'm not already all spooked out*.

"Oh, I don't mean *physically* dangerous, necessarily, but, you know, you could scare yourselves and persuade yourselves of all sorts of things when you're too ready to believe in stuff. Like, if you think you're seeing ghosts, you might get disappointed and sad if you're hoping someone particular might show, then doesn't…" She leaves that kinda hanging in the air for a moment. I know what she's saying: that if I was looking for Mom to appear, but she doesn't, how am I gonna feel. Truly? I do want to see Mom again and I'm hoping for that more than anything. The thought that she might not is devastating and I disguise a sob with a cough. Aunt Katie knows she's made her point but carries on. "Or what if something bad happens and you associate it with any of the paranormal things you're studying; you could scare yourselves and cause all sorts of psychological damage. The power of suggestion is strong at the best of times. It's a complex area of study and not something you should just dabble with."

"I think we'll be OK, Aunt Katie. We have Sunny, who is a super-sceptic! He won't believe anything until it's been tried, tested, twisted, chewed up and thrown out the other side. His by-line is *Occam's Razor.*" I laugh, more assuredly than I'm feeling.

"How clever of him to know about that!" Aunt Katie smiles in admiration. "It's good that you're looking into things in that way. Heck, don't mind me. I'm just being a Debbie Downer, as usual. Look, I know you've had a few odd experiences, and I'm interested from a professional point of view in possibly paranormal things that happen, so how about I help you? From a distance, of course, but just to make sure you're all doing things safely, huh?"

I beam at my aunt. She's real cool. "That would be great, Aunt Katie. In fact, we thought we'd like to go back and investigate Greyfriars Kirkyard for ourselves. Properly, I mean, not just as part of a tourist group. Wondered if maybe you could find a way of getting us in there?" I haven't plucked up the courage to tell her about our visit to Mrs Anderson's yet. I'll get round to it, when I work out how to confess we trespassed and possibly caused the fire in there. That's for another time, I'm thinking.

Aunt Katie suggests I invite the Paranormal Pursuers over and meantime, she'll see what she can do to help us.

I head off to my room when we get home and switch on the TV, having done a quick check to see if it's still plugged in. As I am flicking through the channels, I stop at the Scottish news. There is another story about the missing schoolgirl. Her photograph is flashed on screen and the newsreader says that despite a thorough search by loads of local people, she still hasn't been found. It gets me thinking. This story was on when the TV took on a life of its own. I facepalm. *Wow, why didn't I think of it before? This* has *to be something significant!* I think back to the voices on the tape and the voice I heard at the Kirkyard, calling for help. *Can it be? Is it this kid, Sophie MacGregor, who's been calling to me? And if so? Ohmygod. Does it mean she's dead?* Suddenly, the next investigation at the Kirkyard is imperative. I WhatsApp the gang and tell them to come over this evening and let Aunt Katie know when they've all confirmed.

As ever, Katie has prepared goodies for us, and she's busy warming up sausage rolls and quiche as we wait for the Pursuers to arrive. The buzzer goes off on the entry phone and it's Shuggie on the other side. "Hey, PJ, we're all here. Beam us up, Scottie!" I smile and press the release for the external door and wait for the gang at the door to our apartment. They all roll in and I usher them into the kitchen.

"Hey, guys! How y'all doin'?" Aunt Katie greets my friends with a welcoming grin. They reply that all is good with them and as we tuck into the food, Katie sits at the table with us.

"PJ's been telling me all about your plans to investigate ghostly phenomena," she says. Everyone looks wide-eyed at her. I'm wondering if we're gonna get the Debbie Downer, shouldn't do this, should do that stuff again, but she says, "I think I have a couple of surprises for you. To help with your new hobby. So, you all know where I work, right? I am a parapsychologist at the university. And it just so happens" – Aunt Katie reaches under her chair and pulls out a big cardboard carton with a lid on it – "that I have some equipment right here, that you could borrow – if you'd like, that is." We all jump up excitedly to examine the contents. To a chorus of ooohhhs and ahhhs, Aunt Katie delves into the box and pulls out a video recorder with infra-red lighting and night vision, a couple of digital recorders and motion sensors, including, most extraordinarily, a teddy bear that lights up when it detects motion. Freya squeals in delight as she picks up the bear for a hug and it lights up. Shuggie is thrilled to be holding a K2 meter.

"Aww *get tae France*," he says excitedly. "It's only yer actual K2 meter like yer actual Jason Hawes and Grant Wilson, of yer actual *Ghost Hunters*, use!" Freya, Sunny and I glance at each other and smile, while Shuggie turns the K2 meter reverently, this way and that, admiring it from every angle. "Ah'm a *real* ghost hunter wi' this electromagnetic field detector in ma' pocket. Awesome, Aunt Katie. Ah've always said it and ah dinnae care whit anyone else says aboot ye! Ye'r a right bobby dazzler in my eyes and ye'll always be pure barry in ma opinion."

Katie shakes her head and laughs, secretly enjoying Shuggie's compliments, I suspect. We finish emptying the box and find that there are a couple of cameras and lenses that we can 'lock off' at locations and film activity while we're away investigating elsewhere.

"Now, one final surprise for you," Aunt Katie says, as we tidy up the gadgets and settle back down at the table. "I have a contact, a friend of mine, who runs one of the Greyfriars tours. He's agreed to allow you full access to the Covenanters' Prison for your investigation. There's only one condition. You have to take walkie talkies and keep in constant contact with him throughout the night, OK?"

"Sure, Aunt Katie." I am almost speechless at the lengths she's gone to help us.

"So, tomorrow night OK for y'all?" she asks. "You can go along in the morning, stay all day to familiarise yourselves with the layout of the Kirkyard, and then carry out your investigation through the night, if that suits?"

"If that suits? Aunt Katie, you're a miracle worker!" I forget myself and throw my arms around her in appreciation. It feels good. Like hugging Mom. We stay like that a moment, each of us reluctant to let go. Eventually, we draw apart and Aunt Katie holds my shoulders, her face flushed with happiness. She looks at me earnestly and says, "PJ, you're my only family," and she looks at each of the others, in turn, "and you're my only family's dearest friends, so I want each and every one of you to promise me you will take care of yourselves and each other. If you feel in any danger, or even just a little afraid, remember, *there is nothing to fear but fear itself.* In my experience most paranormal activity is entirely explicable and can't really hurt you as long as you don't let it get to you in here." Aunt Katie points her finger to her temple and taps it.

"I'm not so sure ghosts can't hurt us, Aunt Katie," Freya pipes up, her face frowning and perplexed. "Did PJ tell you anything about what happened in the Kirkyard?"

Aunt Katie nods. "He did, Freya. Say, why don't we grab ourselves an Irn Bru each, and I'll explain just a little of what might have happened to you." I smile. Aunt Katie has become quite the Irn Bru fan in the last coupla weeks!

There's a popping and fizzing of cans and Aunt Katie throws herself open for questions. Sunny is first. "What does a parapsychologist do, Aunt Katie?"

Taking a sip from her can, Aunt Katie explains what she had told me. "Well, it's just the study of people who experience things in their mind and behaviour that is beyond the usual, or normal, do you see?"

Sunny nods seriously. "Like people who claim to move things just by thinking, or can read minds, that sort of thing?"

"Exactly, Sunny. We scientifically test these seemingly extraordinary mental abilities and behaviour. We also look at people who claim to see ghosts, speak to the dead, poltergeist activity. One way or another, we've found that most of this can be explained as happening through the human mind. And that, in itself, is fascinating, because who knew that the human mind could have so many potential abilities?"

Sunny whistles in admiration, while Shuggie's face is a picture of consternation.

"I keep telling the others, Aunt Katie, the simplest explanation is most likely to be the likeliest explanation," says Sunny proudly.

"And that is very true, although sometimes, very

occasionally, we find no rational explanation, and for us parapsychologists, it's very exciting."

Shuggie perks up. "So that suggests that there's something going on, then, Aunt Katie, that maybe ghosts do exist, for example?"

Aunt Katie nods, but says, "Yeah, but just because we can't explain something away scientifically, we can't just make assumptions about ghosts and other worlds. I mean, take rainbows, for example. What d'you think primitive man might have though at the sudden appearance of a glorious colourful rainbow in the sky?"

"I guess they might say it came from the gods," I suggest, shrugging.

"Exactly, PJ. And Shuggie, what if primitive man saw a volcano erupting? What do you think he might have made of that?"

"Well, ah suppose, they might've thought that their gods were angry with them and punishing them?"

"Well done! Yes. So, Shuggie, would you think that either of those things were something strange, abnormal or even supernatural today?"

"Naw, Aunt Katie. They're just natural things that occur," Shuggie has to concede.

"And why do you think that's how they're perceived now?" Aunt Katie puts the question out there to no-one in particular. Sunny is the one who answers.

"Well, because scientific study has eliminated the paranormal and found that these are just normal events. It's just that primitive man didn't have the knowledge at the time to prove it."

"Good! You got it, Sunny. As man became more

knowledgeable, they relied less on superstition and taking things at face value and looked at patterns in circumstances. So, a rainbow often appears after rain because the effect of sunlight shining through the water reflects all the beautiful colours in the spectrum. Scientists know that there is molten rock deep within the earth's core and when it heats up, gas bubbles form in the magma. That in turn creates huge pressure and causes the volcano to erupt. All perfectly natural and not signs of supernatural activity, d'you see?"

We all nod, but Freya looks pensive and unconvinced.

"Yes, but Aunt Katie, surely without some sort of supernatural involvement, rainbows and volcanoes wouldn't be part of life in the first place? I mean, *something*, or *someone*, must have created them?"

"Ah, well, that leads us into very different discussions about science and belief, Freya," Aunt Katie concedes.

"So, science can't explain everything, can it?" Freya is persistent in her objections.

"Nope, it can't, Freya, and it can be difficult to convince anyone who holds certain beliefs that science has explained many things. So, who's to say anyone is wrong? All we can do is look at patterns, analyse unknowns and come up with the most probable explanation."

"Well, I have a question, Aunt Katie," Freya says.

"Sure, Freya, shoot."

Freya turns to me. "Do you have the pictures Shuggie sent you on WhatsApp, PJ?" I nod and take out my cell and show Aunt Katie the scratches on Freya and me and also the handprint on the girl's back at the Kirkyard. "So, how do you explain these, Aunt Katie?" Freya's expression is serious as she eyes Katie intently. Aunt Katie, meanwhile, scrutinises the pictures, zooming in and out to get a better view.

"OK, so you guys have been watching ghost-hunting programmes that will suggest that these scratches are signs of evil supernatural being attacking humans, right?"

Shuggie, warily now, says, "Aye…"

"But the most likely explanation is they are examples of *dermatographia*. Quite common, nothing supernatural."

"So, what is this dermatographia, then?" Sunny is eager to learn.

"OK, so *derma* is Latin, for skin, in broad terms, anyway. *Graphia* also has Latin and Greek origin, meaning writing, or sometimes, a field of study. Put the two together and what do you have?"

"Writing on skin!" Sunny exclaims.

"Huhhh? Yeah, but Aunt Katie," I say, getting more perplexed by the moment, "that doesn't explain *how* the writing got on the skin, does it? I mean, *who* is writing on our skin and, more to the point, *how* and *why*?"

"Och, c'mon, Aunt Katie! They scratches were something else! We saw them develop an' then almost disappear before our eyes!" Shuggie is still sceptical of any rational explanation.

"I'm getting to that, guys," Aunt Katie says, scrolling through some pictures she's found on her iPad. "Take a look at these."

We gather round Aunt Katie and peer at the screen. The first set of pictures show people with deep red welts just like the ones we had. Aunt Katie pulls up some newspaper articles showing people with actual words and pictures etched on their skin in raised bumps and lines. There are intricate patterns that look like body art.

"Dermatographia is a recognised medical condition, guys. Sometimes known as *urticaria*. The lightest scratch can cause the effects you see in the pictures. Kinda like hives that cause the skin to redden, become itchy and inflamed, and come up in red welts. Sometimes it's due to allergy, but here's the thing. Often it can happen when you're anxious or upset. A sort of nervous reaction. They generally disappear within thirty minutes or so. These are commonly reported when people think they are being haunted, so *of course* they're abnormally anxious and upset."

"But that doesn't explain those pictures with real writing and pictures on the skin, Aunt Katie. How could that happen?" I am still unconvinced.

"Those are people who suffer with the condition all the time and very acutely. They just have to stroke the skin lightly, in the patterns they want to create, and their skin reacts by swelling in the shape they traced out. Nothing paranormal, guys. Just a stress reaction when histamines are produced in enough quantity to create an allergic reaction. You know what hay fever is, right?"

"Yeah, I get that," Freya says. "Eyes all streamy, itchy and sore. Can't stop sneezing in the summer. It's murder."

"Me too," I say.

Shuggie and Sunny say they have never had hay fever.

"Well, that's telling us something, isn't it?" Aunt Katie waits to see if any of us work it out. As usual, it's Sunny who gets it.

"Course. Both Freya and PJ came out in allergic hives because they're prone to hay fever. Their histamines must have overloaded with anxiety that night! We didn't get scratched because we don't have allergies!"

Gee, is there anything that stumps this guy? I wonder. *He's like a walking computer, processing everything quickly and coming up with answers!*

"Okaaay." I'm ready to challenge Aunt Katie again. "What about the handprint on the girl's back?"

Aunt Katie, as usual, has an explanation. "She's the one who fainted, right? So, she just panicked and got overwhelmed, is my theory. She was susceptible to the scary stories, and maybe it got a bit claustrophobic and she fainted. We don't know that she didn't just have a strange bruise on her before that, or if she maybe hit something hard as she fell. Nothing to say it was a ghost that did it."

"But the hand shape, Aunt Katie. That's not usual. And what about faces of ghosts caught in pictures?" I'm not sure if I'm relieved by her explanations or annoyed that nothing seems to convince her that there is anything supernatural out there. That would mean my mom appearing would have a natural explanation and I'm not sure I want to believe that.

"Pareidolia," Katie says. I glance at Shuggie. He's rolling his eyes in disbelief. "Have you ever looked at the clouds and seen faces or shapes you recognise?"

"Well, duh-uh," I retort, slightly cheekily. Aunt Katie just gives me a wry, *told you I could explain it* sorta smile.

"Well, it's just another example of how we're wired to see faces or familiar objects in random shapes. Theory goes it helped stone age man to be aware of danger. Like, if you think you see a sabre-toothed tiger in the bushes, even though it's really only just a bunch of leaves arranged in a particular way, it's better to assume it's the tiger and get the heck outta there." Aunt Katie laughs at her own brilliance, as I catch her eye and shake my head with a grin.

"Right then, ah've got one for ye, Aunt Katie. How about when things move around, like when poltergeists move things, or like on *Most Haunted* when the table tips, or the glass skites along on the spirit board?"

"Ideomotor movement, Shuggie." He looks at Aunt Katie disdainfully. "It's when people, even lightly touching something, have miniscule reflexive movements that they're not even aware of, cause something like a glass or table to move, seemingly on their own. They're not really moving independently; it's just people moving them unconsciously. Of course, it could be an example of telekinetic energy too – mind moving matter."

Shuggie sighs. "Aye, right, next ye'll be tellin' us the Easter Bunny doesnae exist!" He slumps down on the chair, defeated. "Well, Aunt Katie, ye've well an' truly peed on ma chips an' ripped ma' knittin' oot," he says despondently.

"Not at all," Sunny says brightly. "Shuggie, you've always said we need to do this properly, so we have to be aware of all the things we have to consider so that we can debunk stuff when we're investigating and keep it credible. There would be no point in investigating if every time something a bit out of the ordinary happened, we just decided it was paranormal, would it? We'd be no further forward in knowing whether there was life after death, or grounded spirits, would we? And that's the whole point. We want to prove something, if we can."

"Yeah, he's right, Shuggie," I say. "It's more important when we've eliminated the obvious and we still can't explain things." Sunny is nodding.

"Occam's—"

"Aye, we know – Razor," says Shuggie.

"Aunt Katie, that's been a great chat," says Freya. "I'm certainly going to take on board all you've told us. Although… I still believe that some things just can't be explained away by science. We just have to balance it all, guys."

"Thank you, Freya. Look, guys, I didn't want to burst your bubbles today, but Shuggie, rest assured, there is much we can't explain yet with science and if you play things straight and carry out your investigations sensibly and safely, who knows, you might come up with something we can look at further at the university. How about that?"

We retreat to my room for a debriefing and a closer look at all the equipment Aunt Katie brought for us.

"She's something else," Sunny says admiringly about Aunt Katie. "She's so clever."

"Aye, she has an answer for everything," Shuggie adds ruefully.

I laugh. "In a coupla thousand years, they'll probably regard us as primitive man, chasing rainbows, after there's an explanation for ghosts."

"Aye, or runnin' away frae sabre-toothed tigers that aren't there," Shuggie hoots. "Talkin' o' which, I had tae run away frae ma sister, who was defo there this morning. She was pure radge, man!"

"Why?" Freya wants to know. "What did you do to her?"

"Ah was practisin' ma YouTube presentation skills wi' her camcorder. Didnae realise I'd recorded over her graduation video," he says miserably. "Man, she's gonna make ma life a misery. She'll get over it, though. In time.

That pareidolia did make her look a bit like a sabre-toothed tiger right enough…"

We giggle at that and set about planning our visit to the Kirkyard next day. I also tell my friends about the hunch I have that Sophie MacGregor is in some way involved in all this. Freya looks aghast. "In what way? Do you think she might be dead and she's been trying to contact us?"

"Maybe," I say. "I sure hope not, but it has to be a possibility, doesn't it? I mean, it was the story on the TV when it came on by itself. And then, I heard the voice calling for help. It sure sounded like a little girl. I just have this strong feeling, Freya – I think the answer is at Greyfriars Kirkyard."

"Good thing we'll be there tomorrow, then," says Freya, her voice quiet and solemn. "We need to call out and let the spirits guide us, I guess. I just hope we're not too late."

It's a subdued group that says our goodbyes, each of us mulling over what we've learned and wondering what, if anything, tomorrow is going to bring.

CHAPTER 22

When I arrive at Greyfriars Kirkyard next day, Shuggie is delivering pieces to camera with a GoPro he's borrowed from a school friend. Freya, meanwhile, is meandering around the Kirkyard, deep in conversation with a tall, serious-looking man dressed in, I think, a tweed suit. Sunny holds a digital recorder to his mouth, noting details of the Kirkyard and checking things off on a clipboard.

"Hey, everybody," I call out. Each of my friends waves back and I head over to Freya and the man she's with. Her face lights up with a welcoming, black-cherry-lipped smile, her kohl-lined eyes crinkling warmly.

"Hey, PJ!" she calls. "I want to introduce you to my Uncle Hamish."

I saunter over and Uncle Hamish absently nods in brief acknowledgement before leaving Freya and me moments later.

"Uncle Hamish is my mum's brother, PJ. I told him we were coming here to do a recce this morning and he offered to come with."

Hamish is striding purposefully towards an ancient-looking tree. I gaze bemusedly, as he approaches and plants his hand firmly on its trunk. He seems to be concentrating real hard, his forehead drawn into a deep frown, his head cocked to one side, as though listening intently to something. Moments later, he flings both his arms around the tree and mutters something into the bark. He swirls around, strides back over to us and promptly grabs my hand in a vice-like grip, shaking it vigorously.

"PJ! I am so sorry – didn't mean to be rude there – something, errrrr, drew my attention, don't you know? Anyway! A veritable pleasure, nay, *joy* to meet you, dear boy! I've heard a lot of good things about you and the others from Freya," he booms heartily in a well-spoken Scots burr.

"Back at ya," I reply. "It's a pleasure to meet you too, sir."

"Hamish is a druid, PJ." I don't have a clue what a druid is, but it sounds kinda mystical. *They're some family*, I think, recalling my visit with Cass at Magickal Moments. Hamish momentarily loses interest in me and again, he seems to be listening intently to something I can't hear. Freya pulls me aside and whispers, "He's listening to the trees talking, PJ."

"Umm, yeah, sure," *said nobody ever...* "Say what, Freya?! He's talking to the trees, like – that's a normal thing?" I try not to laugh as I turn to see Hamish standing next to the same gnarled old tree, tapping his chin with his fingers and nodding as though receiving information in a very deep, meaningful conversation. He smiles, seemingly in understanding and acknowledgement of what Mr Tree appears to be telling him.

"So, he's talking to the tree, you say. Freya, have I just

gone completely mad, or is it just the world around me that seems a little offbeat these days?"

Freya giggles. "As I say, he's a druid, and druids fully connect with nature. It's a very spiritual philosophy with roots in pagan tradition," she adds helpfully.

"And roots in the trees, I guess." I throw that in there, trying to make a funny.

"Uh huh," Freya says, either choosing to ignore my quip or taking what I'd said at face value. "Druids work with ancient spirits and practise healing with herbs and trees. I asked him to come along this morning, to see if he could shed any light on what's happening in the Kirkyard. He's also really good at protection rituals, but he needs to understand the nature of things here to give us the right one."

It's a stunningly beautiful fall day and the sun shines through the near-naked tree branches, giving light and warmth to a place that is also dark, grim and foreboding. There is a bitingly cold breeze accompanying the sunshine and I shiver a little as the chill gnaws at my bones. Hamish sees me pull my hoodie closed and hunch up against the wind.

"Embrrrrrace it, my boy!" Hamish grins, opening his arms wide and enthusiastically. "Isn't Motherrr Naturrrre a most wonderrrrrous goddess?" Hamish muses, and says this more to himself than us. "Ah yes – she gives light to warm us, rainwater to drink and to nourrrish the earrrth; thunder and lightning when she's angry and snow to remind us to appreciate the burgeoning of a new spring that gives way to the warming joy of the summer sunshine."

I raise a quizzical eyebrow in Freya's direction and she

smiles, enjoying my discomfort. *Uncle Hamish seems a little bit like primitive man, chasing rainbows and tree gods*, but I don't say it to her. Hamish looks a little dazed, as though he's coming out of a trance, and realises that Freya and I are transfixed. He lowers his arms, brushes his sleeves and clears his throat, somewhat self-consciously. Seems he was so absorbed in praising Mother Nature, he's forgotten we are there.

"Forgive me," Hamish says. "I become so excited when I meet new trees and they tell me about their lives, that everything else pales into insignificance. You cannot imagine the secrets they hold and impart to me."

I'm eyeing Uncle Hamish, wondering if he needs medication, but say, "Uh, yeah, sure, totally see where you're coming from," as though he just said the most normal thing in the world. *But really? Talking to trees? They cannot be serious.*

Hamish beckons me over to the tree, his index finger wagging impatiently, as I hesitate and throw Freya a pleading look. She nods, encouraging me to follow. *OK, so this is a joke. I'm gonna play along and join the fun.*

"Now, PJ, I perceive that you're a little – *sceptical*, shall we say? Do you know what that means?"

"Yessir." I nod. "Someone who is doubtful and questioning of what they see." I'm holding back from approaching the tree.

"Good. Well, come, come. Come, come, come," Hamish says, impatiently, his words increasing in pitch and speed. Hands in pockets, I stroll up casually. The tree is slap-bang in the centre of a group of tombstones, which I step over, gingerly, fearing I might disturb those resting below.

My stomach lurches at the thought of a hand smashing through the earth and grabbing my ankle, like I've seen in a horror movie.

"Good, good. Good, good, good," Hamish says in that same rapid, rhythmical tone. "Now, touch the trunk of this tree." I give him a questioning look. "Well, go on. What are you waiting for, dear boy? It won't bite, you know."

I humour him and tentatively stretch out my arm and lay my palm on the tree that looks as though it has been through the wars. The branches are like gnarled, arthritic arms, twisting in pain towards the sky, its knobbly trunk contorted and stretched into an impossible angle.

"Now concentrate," Hamish orders. I close my eyes and dutifully try to focus on the feeling of the rough, knuckled bark beneath my palm. "Now wrap your arms around the trunk as far as you can. Tell me what you feel from this tree, PJ."

I stand ever so quietly, trying hard to feel something. For a moment, I think I will have to create a story, just to please Freya's very odd uncle, but now – *I feel darkness. And sadness – no, worse. Despair!* It feels like the tree is crying! Pictures are flashing in my head. Funerals. People standing at the graves, sobbing. The tree starts to tremble and I snatch my hands from the trunk, stumbling backwards to the ground, my head narrowly missing a tombstone.

"Ah! Dear boy! Careful. Trees have powerful emotions and reactions." He turns to the tree and says, "Forgive us, Spirit of the Tree. The boy is a novice. May you be gentle on him as he learns the lore of nature." Uncle Hamish pats the trunk comfortingly. "Now, PJ, do tell us what happened."

What did just happen? Surely just my imagination?

I take a deep breath and clear my throat, my cheeks blazing hot. "Well, I guess I felt like maybe the tree seems… um… kinda sad? Like it sees the funerals and feels the unhappiness. The tree didn't like it."

Hamish gives a nod of satisfaction, a thin smile on his lips. "Quite so, PJ. Quite so. This tree is indeed a troubled spirit. It is in a location filled with deep sorrow and it has seen things that would horrify us. It's over three hundred years old. It goes against the grain, if you'll pardon the expression, for a living thing, that represents birth and renewal of life to have death taint its psyche." Uncle Hamish strokes the tree sadly, as though comforting it. I wrap my arms around myself, remembering how the tree seemed to vibrate. Weird!

Satisfied now, Uncle Hamish stretches out his hand and pulls me up from my still seated position, next to the tombstone.

"The trees are friends, PJ. Connect with them wisely and they will guide you. They have the wisdom and experience of the ages." Losing interest in me, Uncle Hamish strides off to a group of trees in the corner and appears to have a discussion with them, gesticulating, nodding and smiling, as though he's chatting with old friends in a coffee shop. He sure looks cray cray from here.

"Gee, Freya," I say, turning my attention back to my friend. "You sure do have a bunch of strange people in your family."

"Yes, but it makes life interesting, doesn't it?" She giggles. "Did you really feel all that from the tree?"

"Yeah. Really strange. I thought you were both playing a joke on me. Were you? Was it just my imagination playing tricks on me?"

"No jokes, PJ. Uncle Hamish truly believes in it. Although…" Freya glances over in Shuggie's direction. "Didn't want to say so at the time, but Shuggie was over there with his GoPro having a great time filming you while you were hugging the tree." She laughs.

I groan. No doubt that'll be used against me sometime in the future. Freya joins her uncle and I go to find Sunny, wandering through the carpet of red, yellow and brown leaves. The Kirkyard doesn't feel very intimidating in daylight.

Sunny is at the Mackenzie Mausoleum, where he is studiously using the various instruments supplied by Aunt Katie. He has a clipboard with a pad covered in scrawls and diagrams. As I approach him, my stomach leaps. There is a definite change of atmosphere here. The sky seems darker and the silence is heavy. There is no birdsong from the trees and I feel my good mood is being sucked from me.

"Whaddup, Sunny?" I try to sound brighter than I feel. Sunny's brows are furrowed together in concentration.

"Hey, PJ. I'm doing some base readings to give us a starting point for our investigation. Checking the K2 meters to see if there is anything causing electromagnetic fluctuations."

"Cool. You found anything yet?"

"Nope. Nothing that's generating electricity just now. If anything shows up later, I think we can safely say there's no obvious or natural source that would cause the K2 lights to flash. There's nothing around that might cause electrical surges. Look. No power lines, certainly no power sockets or anything else that could interfere with the meters."

I look up and around and sure enough, there doesn't seem to be anything obvious.

"I was reading on my iPad that there is some evidence of infrasound near the mausoleum that might be causing some of the activity here," I tell Sunny. "It might explain some of the feelings people get because when sound vibrations go below a certain level, twenty hertz, it can cause a feeling of pressure in the chest, fear and anxiety."

Sunny looks pleased. "Wow, PJ, that's really interesting. I'm sure there's a gadget for measuring sound in the box. I'll check that out."

"Yeah, infrasound can also cause hallucinations when the vibrations hit the eye. It affects the vision so you can see things that aren't actually there."

"That could explain a lot of what's been going on here, PJ. Especially if there is any evidence of infrasound. We can check it out later."

"Have you spoken to Shuggie lately?" I ask. "I saw him a few minutes ago with his digital video recorder."

"Yeah, he was here just before you arrived. He interviewed me to explain how we would be doing the investigation. He's having a great time, I think." Sunny grins.

"OK, well, I guess I'll go see him. I have a bone to pick with him!"

"You sure have plenty of bones to pick from around here."

I laugh at Sunny's grisly joke. He sure is coming out of himself these days. I wave to him as I head off. Shuggie is near the Kirkyard gates, walking towards me as I round the path.

"PJ, pal!" he calls, waving. "I never had you down as one o' they tree-huggin' types!" Shuggie smirks, enjoying his little joke.

"Oh, very funny, Shuggie," I retaliate. "I was just being polite and humouring Freya's Uncle Hamish. Did Freya tell you about him? He's a druid."

"Aye, she did. Are they no' the ones who wear white robes and meet up for the Summer Solstice at Stonehenge?"

I shrug. "Dunno."

"Aye, something like that. Worshipping nature and the changing o' the seasons, I think. Freya seems to think he's not as nutty as he looks, so I just went along with it too. What have you been up tae?"

"Been doing some research on the history of the Covenanters and reading up on ghostly activities that have happened here and I'm going to check out infrasound readings by the mausoleum with Sunny. How about you?"

"Well, I've been doing some daylight shots to let our YouTube viewers get a feel for the place before we go to darkness an' I'm interviewing the Pursuers. Ye've just arrived in time. How aboot we film ye in front o' the Covenanters' Prison?"

"Sure," I say as we head off back in the direction I just came from. We decide that I'll just ad lib my piece, rather than Shuggie asking me questions. We decide it should be a short bio, rather than too much about the investigation, which will come later.

"OK, you stand there, next to the gate." Shuggie moves me around until he has the angle he wants. "Ready… Lights! Camera! And… action!" He points when he's ready for me to start.

"Hi, everyone. I'm PJ. I recently landed here from New York City and I'm gonna be your lead investigator as we search out the ghosts that haunt this famous Greyfriars Kirkyard in Edinburgh. Using scientific means, we aim to find out whether Bluidy Mackenzie, enemy of the Covenanters, is really frightening and attacking the visitors to the Kirkyard. As you see, in daylight, it's a beautiful, serene location. By night, though, it takes on a whole different feeling and we invite you to share in our adventure.

Why are we doing this, you might ask? All of us on the team – me, Shuggie, Sunny and Freya – all lost loved ones this year and this is our tribute to them. We're on a quest, hoping to find out what happens when we die. I know that if we do find evidence of the afterlife, I sure will feel better that maybe my mom is still around and happy in a different place – unlike some of the folks that are said to roam this Kirkyard.

Maybe, just maybe, our time on earth doesn't immediately end. Maybe we'll meet again, when our time here is done. We'll leave you to decide…"

"Brill, PJ! Got it in the can!" Shuggie grins. "You looked quite the presenter daein' that piece tae camera. Well done! Ah'm thinkin' you might be the team heartthrob like Zak Bagans on *Ghost Adventures*. Ye've got that *exotic* American touch the lassies will love."

I blush from the soles of my feet to the top of my head, which, of course, Shuggie sees, and teases me mercilessly. Shuggie has the format all outlined in his head. After the interviews and the filmed tour around the Kirkyard in daylight, I'll outline the history of the place. After that, he wants Sunny to explain the science stuff and Freya to explain the phenomena that we might find. He is going to film and narrate the investigation and then interview us at the end as we analyse the evidence caught. He's real excited. I have no doubt he'll present in true Shuggie comic style.

The afternoon draws into evening and the sun gives way to a darkening sky. The Kirkyard feels less welcoming. We all meet up at the shop, where Hamish is preparing to give us protection for the night's vigil.

"Firrrst," Hamish announces, "I'm going to give you a variation on the white light protection Freya taught you. Now, close your eyes and picture the same white light surrounding you like a wide bubble. OK, you with me?" We all murmur, yes, we can see the light. "Good. Instead of hugging it around your body, let it surround you and enclose you in the bubble."

I'm taking no chances and visualise the bubble of light as Hamish instructs us.

"Now, imagine the light is coming closer to your body, closer, closer still. It's now touching every part of your outline. It's touching your skin and still glowing. Now it's turning blue. It's like an electric fence protecting you from all harm. Anything bad that tries to hurt you won't be able to get through. Got it?"

Strangely, I do feel something. It's like a heat shield and I'm no longer shivering in the chilly late-afternoon air.

"OK. Open your eyes now." Hamish looks at us earnestly and solemnly. "Make sure you carry out that ritual before you start the vigil. Good! Now you're going to become *superheroes*!" he announces.

Okaayyyy, bring it on. I catch Shuggie's eye and we stifle a giggle.

"This technique can be directed at anything evil that

comes your way. It's like having your own light sword in your hand. OK, ready?" Hamish looks at each of us as we nod our readiness.

"Right, then. Imagine that one of the baddies from a film is coming after you, or the school bully wants your sweeties. You can immobilise and deflect anyone with this technique. It won't harm them, but believe me, they'll feel a force that will stop them in their tracks. No-one will mess with you, least of all anything that is psychically attacking you. Now, the bully is coming for you and your sweeties are at risk. Thrust out your arm and point at him, picturing the bright white light, burning hot, fizzing out and through your fingertips. Bam! He's thrown backwards with force and shock and you've put the fear of his worst nightmare into him. Got it?"

I look round at my buddies and they're eye-rolling, smirking and stifling giggles.

"Hey, can we test this out, Hamish?" I smirk back at the others in solidarity. There's no way this can work and we all know it.

Undeterred, Hamish strides off. "Come, come. Come, come, come." He beckons us towards the external gate of the Kirkyard and finds a murder of magpies on the pavement outside. He gestures towards them.

"We're going to send the magpies on their way. Now, silently, concentrate. The white light is travelling from within you, through your arms to your fingertips. When I tell you, point at the magpies and direct the light at them. Ready? Now!"

We point our arms like magicians with wands and aim at the birds, who are minding their own business, scavenging for food. I visualise the light zapping through me and into the birds. As soon as we point, to my amazement, the birds flap their wings and begin cawing and squawking and screeching. They rise noisily and panicked into the sky, their glassy eyes looking shocked.

"Awesome, man!" Shuggie exclaims in disbelief. "That cannae have just been down tae us pointing at they burds!"

Hamish is examining his nails nonchalantly. "Oh, believe me, they felt the full force of your superhuman power. Use it wisely, though. Never use the power to attack; only with reasonable force in self-defence and protection. Remember, *with great power comes great responsibility.*"

"Aye! In the great words of Spider-man's dad," Shuggie points out.

Hamish merely rolls his eyebrows and says, coolly, "Voltaire, actually, Shuggie, was the first to coin the phrase."

"Wuz he in *Harry Potter*, then?" Shuggie is bemused.

Freya laughs. "No, silly! Voltaire was in *Les Miserables*!"

Hamish sighs audibly. "No, no. No, no, no. We are talking neither of Voldemort nor Valjean. *Voltaire* was a great philosopher. Dear me, what *do* they teach you these days?"

We look at each other sheepishly and shrug. I'm not convinced at what happened with the birds. Probably just saw a bunch of lively kids and decided to make a sharp exit.

It's time to meet Aunt Katie's friend, Donald, who runs one of the tour companies. He's agreed to monitor the investigation and run base camp for the night. Hamish heads off home and we chatter noisily as we head back to the meeting point at the shop which will be our base this evening.

CHAPTER 23

"Hi, guys." Donald Logan rises from the seat in the shop as we enter and has to stoop to avoid brushing the roof beam with his mop of fair hair. He offers his hand and I am the first to take it, squirming just a little at the force of his enthusiastic grip 'n' shake.

"I'm PJ, Mr Logan. And these are my friends, the other Paranormal Pursuers, Freya, Sunny and Shuggie." He shakes each of their hands in turn and smiles broadly, white teeth gleaming.

"He's really handsome, PJ," Freya whispers coyly in my ear, keeping one eye on Donald. "Did you say he and Aunt Katie are friends?"

"Um, yeah. I think so," I say. "She just told me she knows him through her work and he runs one of the tour companies."

"So, it's great to meet you all," Donald says. "Katie's told me all about your plans and I think it's terrific to have a young team aboard. Maybe you'll come up with a new perspective on what, if anything, is going on here. Now,

I'm not going to interfere too much with your investigation tonight, but I'll just stay here at base camp in case you need me." Donald hands us a walkie talkie each. "These will let you keep in direct contact with me at all times. I've set up the computer, so we can enhance any EVPs you might get, and transfer any video evidence you pick up so that we can look at it more closely on the big screen."

The computer looks impressive, with an audio mixing desk and big speakers attached to it.

"So, before you set off, I have a couple of rules, OK?"

"Sure," I say, feeling slightly relieved to have him close by.

"Good. OK. First rule is that you stay in twos at all times, so that you can cover each other. No wandering off for solo vigils." We all agree that's a good idea. "Secondly, if I feel it's necessary to wind up the investigation for any reason, you make your way back here immediately." Again, there is no argument from any of us.

Shuggie's cell phone beeps with an incoming text and he excuses himself. "Just be two seconds, guys. Just gotta step ootside a wee second." He returns moments later and there is a scuffling behind him as Dug scampers into the shop. He greets us all in turn, shoving his head into our legs and sniffing around the shop enthusiastically. I bend down to scratch his ears, thrilled to see the cute little guy.

"I thought he might be good company for us tonight," Shuggie explains. "Ma dad just brought him over, cos he's out working tonight."

"I'm kinda surprised you've brought him, Shuggie," I say. "After all we've been told about animals visiting the Kirkyard?" I feel worried for Dug and don't want him to be in danger.

"Ach, dinnae worry. He'll be fine wi' me. I brought him because dugs can often sense things we cannae. He'll mebbes be our *first responder*, like a wee alarm dug. Yvette from *Most Haunted* has Watson, the bulldog. Well, we've got Dug!"

"He's more like Scrappy Doo!" I laugh, watching his antics as his claws slide along the laminate floor.

"Aye." Shuggie grins. "Hopefully more Scrappy than Scooby or I'll be carrying him back shakin' in ma arms wi' his teeth chatterin.'"

We all laugh and I picture the cowardly cartoon mutt who is usually outdone by his naughty nephew.

Freya says, "And we have Shuggie, instead of Shaggy! Same applies to you, cos none of us are carrying you back with *your* teeth chattering." She grins.

Dug has lost interest in us and is now sniffing around the Edinburgh Rock and fudge shelf. Donald stands and looks out of the window.

"OK, so we're just about ready to start. The last tour is about to leave, guys. Let's have a look at these walkie talkies, and I'll show you how to use them."

We each grab one of the walkie talkies and Donald shows us which button to press whenever we hear someone trying to contact us. They're looped so we can all hear what's happening. Moments later, voices come from the pathway running by the shop and there is lots of giggling and chatter going on. Donald pokes his head out and calls to the guide with the group.

"Hey, Andy," he says. "All quiet tonight?"

"Ooft, Donald! Quiet? You've got to be joking. One thing after another up there tonight. Someone heard a voice coming from the mausoleum, another was pushed over and felt sick. Feels quite active up there just now."

It knows we're here! My heart pummels wildly against my chest. I'm not sure if this is good or bad news.

"Great!" Shuggie says excitedly. "We might get some good footage tonight, then."

"Aye, you'll need to tread warily, though," says Donald. "We don't want anything too dramatic."

I gulp loudly, but though I'm scared, I do really want to get out there and find out what's going on. It's decided that Shuggie and Sunny will team up together and Freya and I will buddy each other.

"OK, guys, so let's do this properly," I say. "Shuggie and Sunny, you two check out the readings on the K2 meters and the infrasound meters and see if there's anything different from the base readings Sunny and I got earlier. Then you head off into the Covenanters' Prison, while Freya and I do a vigil at the mausoleum. That cool with everyone?"

"Awesome," says Sunny. Shuggie is twitching and shuffling around, eager to get out there.

"We'll each do a while at the two points of interest and then we'll swap over. How about we meet back here in about ninety minutes to compare notes and decide what's next?"

It's all agreed. Flashlights are checked, new batteries and bulbs are inserted into the equipment, and everything is working well. Everyone wraps up against the cold night air with gloves and scarves over our coats as we bid farewell to Donald to begin the walk along the pathway towards the mausoleum and the Covenanters' Prison, which the tour guide had been instructed to leave unlocked. We fall silent and the mood becomes sombre as the light and warmth of the shop recedes into the distance. I tread carefully to avoid slabs of tombstones, jutting crookedly upwards from the earth, trying not to think about what lies in the murky depths below. I hear our breathing, the pitter patter of Dug's paws as he skips alongside, sniffing selected spots every so often, and the crunch of leaves and bark beneath us.

"Sure is spooky out here tonight," I say, shining my flashlight every which way to reassure myself that there's no-one other than the four of us here.

"Ach, no' really," says Shuggie, confident as usual. "Ah'm no seein' or feelin' much happenin' in this part of the Kirkyard. Ah wuz talkin' tae Donald earlier and he told me that for the most part, graveyards dinnae have much activity. Most people didnae die here, except the ones who might have been buried alive, cos medical science wisnae up tae much in the old days. Some got mistakenly buried when they were only in a coma or unconscious. Some coffins were found later with scratch marks inside where the person tried to claw themselves oot."

"Oh, well, that alright, then. I don't need to worry," I say, with just a touch of sarcasm. On we trudge until we reach the sad, quivering tree.

"Are ye no' gonnae say hello, then, PJ? Tae yer new pal? I hear his bark is worse than his bite!"

"Oh, ha, ha!" I say. "Very funny. You know what? I'm gonna do just that," I say, leaving the group and walking through the gravestones, towards the tree.

I feel the others' eyes boring into my back as I stride purposefully to the tree, feeling just a tad silly now and wishing I hadn't bothered. I lay my hands squarely on the trunk of the tree, lean into it and close my eyes, concentrating hard. I hear a faint whisper in the air that might just be a breeze through the leaves. I look up. Not a movement. The night is as still as it can be. I concentrate again, the rough bark scratching my palms. Images flood my thoughts. A line of people, beaten and bloodied, limping, dragging themselves along the pathway towards the prison. I hear wails of terror and despair as they are pushed roughly and mercilessly through iron gates into the empty fields beyond, by guards who surround them, like evil sheepdogs, rounding them up. I take a sharp intake of breath as I see the great, dark, imposing outline of a man, wearing a long horsehair wig and black gown, standing to the side, watching in grim satisfaction, his thin mouth drawn into a humourless grin as the trail of people pile through the doom-laden gates. I feel the tree breathe in, as though venting its sorrow, and it vibrates as if shaking with tears. I stumble backwards as the depth of the vision and the tree's emotion threatens to engulf me. I am reminded of how I had felt at Mom's funeral. Instinctively, I know the tree is sad, but it is our friend. It just wants to share its sorrows. I know it is looking out for us.

"Are you OK, PJ?" Sunny runs over to me, Freya following behind, just as I hurl backwards from the tree.

"Yeah, um, I think so. I just had a vivid picture of the Covenanters when I touched the tree. I felt it, I dunno, kinda breathe? It sure was weird, but just like what happened last time. I saw *him* as well."

Shuggie has now joined us. "Him?" he queries.

"Mackenzie," I say. "He sure is evil. I could see his face and how he really enjoyed the suffering of all those poor people he tortured. It was sickening." I shake my head in disbelief and rub my arms, trying to throw off the tingling in them.

Freya smiles and hugs me. "You see, PJ? Uncle Hamish isn't such a duffus after all. He really knows stuff. Listen, we should do our protection ritual before going any further. Here, I have a crystal for each of us." She hands the crystals round and tells us to put them around our necks. "Right, now for the visualisation." Freya carries out the ritual, just as Hamish had shown her, and I swear I feel the heat of the light enveloping me again.

"OK," Freya continues thoughtfully. "I think we're good to go. Remember, guys, if you feel like something is attacking you, direct the light sword against the attacker, OK?"

We head off to our agreed destinations. My body trembles as the black dome of the mausoleum comes into view, silhouetted against the moonlight. The tremble turns to a violent shudder as we near the looming monstrosity.

A beep from the walkie talkies, followed by a crackling hiss, causes us all to jump and dissolve into giggles as we realise it's Donald calling.

"Hi, team, come in, please. Can you hear me OK? Over." Donald's voice cuts through the static.

I press the button and say, "Hi, Donald, we can hear you. Over."

"That's good. Whereabouts are you now? Over."

"We're still together, just approaching the Mackenzie tomb. All quiet for now. Over."

"OK, I'll check in with you in about fifteen minutes. When you split up, one member from each team to confirm all is well, OK? Over."

"Roger, Wilco and out!" I am relishing my chance to sound like I'm in a movie.

"What exactly does that mean?" Freya asks.

"Roger means *message received in full* and Wilco and out means *we'll comply*, I think," Sunny explains.

If I'm honest, I'm not entirely sure myself, but it sounds about right and I agree with Sunny. "Yeah." I nod knowledgeably. "What he said."

Freya and I pitch up abruptly at the mausoleum while Sunny and Shuggie continue the short walk to the Covenanters' Prison gates. We watch them, both of us holding our breath as they walk through, the gate groaning and squealing as they push it open. Seconds later, they disappear.

"Right then," I say with more confidence than I feel, as I shine my flashlight over the external walls of the mausoleum. It's scary enough by day, but the grey/black walls of the rounded building radiate doom in the darkness. We inspect it thoroughly. It has a panelled door, with inlaid wrought-iron grates. I hesitate before shining my flashlight through them to look inside. There is a column on either side of the door, bordering arches on either side. The whole structure is intimidating and seems built to warn off intruders. "Can't imagine why a tramp would choose to use this place to sleep in, no matter the weather," I say to Freya.

"Guess if you're homeless, you'll go anywhere that's dry," she says sadly.

We tiptoe around the mausoleum, circling it, shining the flashlight this way and that. Relieved, I say, "Doesn't seem to be anything out of the ordinary about it."

Freya gasps and grabs my arm tight.

"Oww! What was that for?"

"Did you not hear that?" she asks urgently, a tremor in her voice.

"Uh, no. What?" I ask, going closer to her while scanning every direction with the flashlight.

"It was like a sigh. It sounded right beside my ear."

"Nope. Didn't hear a thing. Hang on a minute, I'll get the camcorder on and you set up the EVP. You do a call out, while I film it."

"OK, here goes." Freya flips the switch of the digital voice recorder. "Hello," she says. "My name is Freya, and this is my friend, PJ. We come in friendship and mean you no harm. Is anyone here with us now?" She pauses to allow a response. We don't hear anything with our own ears and she carries on. "Can anyone hear me? Would you like to communicate with us? If so, you can speak into this machine that I'm holding. Is there a Sir George Mackenzie with us by any chance?"

Still nothing. I film Freya as she speaks and pan the camcorder round the mausoleum, when suddenly, from nowhere, I hear a deep, throaty growl and jump thirty thousand feet into the air. Well, maybe a couple of centimetres, anyway. I almost drop the camcorder and my breathing comes in short sharp gasps.

"I heard that! Surely you heard it too, Freya?" She is frozen to the spot, her eyes wide, mouth clamped shut. "Freya? Are you breathing? Speak to me!" I give her a gentle shake.

"Y-yes, sorry. I was holding my breath to hear better. I did hear something. It was terrifying. It sounded like a wild animal, but not like any animal I've ever heard. It was like a really, really angry person roaring. I wonder if the recorders picked it up?"

"Dunno, but let's carry on for now. We can check back at base camp later," I say with more conviction than I feel. Base camp sounds like a good option right now, if I'm honest.

Freya tries another EVP. "Did you just growl at us?" Her voice quivers.

I try to hold still as the ground quakes violently beneath us and the door of the mausoleum rattles noisily. I turn the camcorder to home in on it and sure enough, I can see it gently vibrating at first, building violently to a full-throttled shake. I don't dare to blink or breathe. A scraping sound, followed by a massive thud, resonates from behind the door. That's it! I've had enough! Freya and I wordlessly glance at each other and I see terror in her eyes. We flee in the direction of the Covenanters' Prison, and as we put some distance between us and the mausoleum, we stop to catch our breath. We're panting more in fear than exertion.

"Oh, boy. Oh, boy," I say. "Holy moly. What just happened?"

Freya is bent over, hands on her knees. "Dunno, but it scared the life out of me. We probably shouldn't have run away. Doesn't say much for us as investigators." Freya unbends as her breathing eases.

"Um, yeah. I guess that's true. But we can go back a bit later. I'll get Sunny to check the infrasound again," I say, hoping for a rational explanation.

"OK – let's see if we can find the guys and then maybe we can go back to base camp and play the recordings back.

Maybe there'll be something on them that will give us a clue."

"Good idea. Time to regroup and rethink our strategy," I say. We head through the groaning gate of the Covenanters' Prison and I can just make out the flashlights at the opposite end. Freya and I hurry along the pathway, swinging our flashlights right and left. After what just happened, I shudder as we pass the vaults on either side, wondering what is behind the doors and whether it will stay there.

We catch up with the boys and Shuggie is just doing a piece to camera, recounting the horrors of the Covenanters' Prison, as Sunny is simultaneously calling out for EVPs.

"The vaults you see here on either side of the path did not exist when the prisoners were here and all that stood was a cold, miserable field where the prisoners would huddle together for warmth and meagre comfort." Shuggie is indicating to the doors either side of us as he sees us approaching. He switches off the camcorder.

He turns the camera off and waves us forward.

"Hey, guys – you didnae take long. Anything doing?"

"Well, something's going on at the mausoleum. We thought we'd go to base and review it and then head back," I tell him. "Much happened here?"

"Nah, nothing really yet. Sunny's been taking some readings. Temperature seems steady, no interaction with the K2 meter or any sign of infrasound. Dead as a dodo here at the moment, if ye'll pardon the expression!"

Dug, who's been inspecting the perimeter and marking the territory, so to speak, stands still, his little ears alert and cocked high on his head, which is tilted as though he is listening intently.

"Look!" I whisper. "What's Dug up to?"

"Hmm." Shuggie frowns. "He's heard something that's caught his attention. Doesn't necessarily mean much, though. He's aye daein' that. Could by anythin' – a cat on a windowsill up at the tenements or just some random noise that's startled him."

We watch Dug, still standing rigid and motionless, but his hackles now raised as he growls at some unseen (at least to us) foe.

"Now that's no' like him unless he's seen a cat in oor garden. He hates cats wi' a passion. Shhh then. Let's just keep still so we can listen and watch what he does."

Our cameras are trained in all directions to monitor where Dug goes.

We remain silent, listening for any disembodied voices or growls such as Freya and I heard at the mausoleum. It is Shuggie who breaks the silence.

"Oh, ma days…" he says.

"What? Whassup?" I ask as cold pierces my bones and I cross my arms around my chest and slap my back.

"Over there." Shuggie points. "Two figures. They're kinda shining. Over by the vault on the left. Aboot five doon."

Sure enough, as I peer ahead in the darkness, there are two shimmering outlines. They are indistinct but seem to be people-sized. We silently watch to see them fade, apparently through the wall of the vault. Cameras trained on the area, we remain still and quiet. I'm unsure what to do next, afraid to break the spell.

Eventually, Shuggie breaks the silence. "Did ye's all see that?"

Freya and I both say yes, we saw it. Dug, legs splayed

and standing braced to the ground, begins to bark.

Sunny says, "There was a strange light anomaly over by the vault, but look where the moon is. The light could just have reflected on something and created the illusion we just saw. I'll go down and take some readings."

Sunny bravely wanders down to the vault where we saw the shape-shifting lights and turns on the K2 meter. The lights all illuminate, green to red.

"Hmm," he says. "That's a bit odd. Nothing from the base readings suggest there was any electrical interference before."

"Let's try asking questions an' see if we can get it to interact," Shuggie suggests, and switches on his digital recorder. "Right, spirits of the Kirkyard, are ye with us? Make the lights shine once for naw and two for yes."

"Uh, Shuggie," I say, catching Sunny's eye, both of us stifling a giggle.

"Aye, what?" We can't hold in the guffaws of laughter anymore. "What are ye's both laughing at?"

"Didn't you hear what you just did there?" I am doubled over with laughter, my eyes streaming, barely able to speak. Shuggie just looks at me and Sunny as though we've gone mad. "Y-you s-said…" I struggle to catch my breath through the giggles. "You said, '*Are you with us? Make the lights shine once for no.*'" Shuggie still doesn't get it. I roll my eyes upwards. "So, if they're not with us, how can they shine the lights?" I splurt out another belly laugh and see Sunny shaking his head, overcome with the silliness of it. It breaks the tension.

Shuggie shrugs and can't help grinning himself. "Ah was just testin' ye's, that's all. I knew that!" He bursts into laughter himself. "Aye, fair cop," he admits. "Ah wasnae thinking there! Classic schoolboy ghost-huntin' error there. Ye's got me bang tae rights. Ach, ye've given me a beamer now!" His face has reddened with embarrassment. "Right, let's get on. Pull yerselves together now."

I take a deep breath.

"We're here in friendship if anyone can hear us," Shuggie says. "We mean ye's nae harm. We think we just saw ye's ootside this here vault. Can ye light up the K2 meter in ma pal Sunny's hand. See? It has green and red lights. Can ye light it up if yer here?" We all wait; I realise I am holding my breath.

Bam! The K2 fully lights up in response to Shuggie. I gulp. *OMG, this is more than I'd bargained for. And we've only been here half an hour!*

"OK, thanks for daein' that. Can ye light it up once for each of you here right now so we know how many of you there are?"

My legs feel weak as the K2 fully lights up and off once, twice. I'm filming Sunny and Shuggie, still holding my breath in case the slightest noise distracts the spirits.

"Thanks. So, there are twa of ye's here, is that right?"

The K2 fully lights up again, and once more.

"Are ye women?"

We wait, watching the K2. Nothing. It lays dormant in Sunny's hand for a minute.

"Were ye prisoners here? Covenanters? Please make the lights come on twice for yes, once for naw."

The lights come on twice in quick succession.

"Did ye's die here in the prison? Once for naw, twice for aye."

The K2 lights up in direct response just once.

"Were ye taken frae here an' executed? Once for naw, twice for aye."

The K2 goes crazy this time, the lights coming on repeatedly and in quick succession.

"I think they're angry," says Freya, who is holding her temples and concentrating hard. "I feel like they're really fuming."

"Cos we disturbed them?" I wonder.

"No." Freya shakes her head. "Because it was unjust, the way they were treated. They want revenge. I definitely feel that."

"Are ye's angry?" Shuggie takes his cue from Freya.

The K2 goes mad again and there's a thud right next to us in the darkness that makes us all jump. I clunk my teeth together. "Owww! Shoot!" I exclaim. "What in the heck was that?" I shine my flashlight on the floor and see a large stone lying next to us where it's just landed.

"I think they want us to go," said Freya. "They're not happy with us being here. I think they're trying to warn us. That's the feeling I'm getting. We could be in actual danger here."

Suddenly the lights of the K2 flash on as though agreeing with Freya and an ear-piercing howl cuts through the air. I cover mine with my hands.

"Ah, right, OK," says Shuggie. "Guys, ah've got ma EVP recorder on so hopefully we've caught all this on there and on camera. Anyone else want to ask anything?"

"Let me try," I say. Shuggie hands me the K2 meter. "Say, we'd like to thank you for speaking with us. Are you trying to warn us about something? Freya here thinks you are."

The K2 lights up twice, the lights strong and bright.

"Thank you. Who are you warning us about? Is it Mackenzie?"

Again – two for yes. The lights remain lit for longer than usual. A prickling sensation runs up my arms as every hair stands to attention.

"Would you like us to leave now?" I ask.

Again, the lights flash on strong and long.

"We'd like tae come back a wee bit later just tae see how ye's are daein'. Is that fine wi' ye both?" Shuggie can't help himself from adding a question.

After a slight hesitation, the K2 lights up a weak two flash, yes.

"Time for a break and a debriefing, guys. What do you think? Shall we head back to the shop?" I ask. The others agree that's a good idea. Some hot tea would be a welcome sight. The walkie talkies blip and Donald's voice booms out: "That's about forty-five minutes, guys. All OK? Over."

Sunny flips the switch on his as it crackles to life.

"Yes, Donald – we're all together and heading your way to review some footage and regroup. Over."

"Roger. Wilco and out."

We all hurry back to the shop, Dug scampering ahead, sniffing around but otherwise now appearing unperturbed back in the main part of the Kirkyard. He was as spooked as us in the prison. I feel happier to see him back to his jaunty self. Shuggie and Sunny walk slightly ahead of Freya and me, deep in conversation about the night's goings on.

"So how did you know those guys were angry?" I ask her.

"I felt Alana close by. She came through to me; I'm

certain I heard her voice. She said they were angry but not at us. She told me to be careful, though, because they were worried that we might get harmed. The rock they threw was to warn us off, not to hit us. If they'd wanted it to hit one of us, believe me, it would have."

As much as I am scared, I'm also intrigued. I certainly won't be the first of us to wuss out.

We troop into the welcoming lights of the shop and grab our flasks. Donald listens intently as I recount what happened, raising his eyebrows as I get to the part where the rock was thrown and the spirits told us to leave.

Sunny remains a little more reserved about the night's events. He is determined to remain objective but even he has to admit that the K2 meter's responses were so on cue that it really did seem like something was making direct contact with us in answer to our questions. He sits at the computer as we pour tea and assorted other hot drinks from the thermos bottles we brought with us.

"OK, guys," I say. "I think after Sunny has taken some readings at the mausoleum, Shuggie and I should stay there and do a vigil since we've already had some activity there. Sunny and Freya, you go back to the prison and see what else happens there. It'll be around 2am by the time we've finished here so I say we should stay a couple of hours in each area, then come back here for a debriefing. That should give us all enough time to see what's going on."

Everyone agrees to the plan although I'm real wary of the mausoleum. The Covenanters' Prison is spooky, but it felt a lot less scary there than at the mausoleum. I have a real bad feeling about that place.

Sunny gasps. "Listen to this!" he calls, pulling off his

headphones. He is listening to the audio from our EVP recorder when we'd been at the Mackenzie Mausoleum. Soundwaves are on the screen and he highlights a section for us to listen to. Suddenly, from the speakers there is a **ROARRRRR** and **HOWLLLLLL**, the first, deep and dangerous, the second high-pitched and pained-sounding. I leap back, instinctively, in case whatever is making that noise jumps out from the computer to grab me. One thing is sure; it isn't just angry. It's raging.

"And that's not all," Sunny says, winding the audio backwards, stopping to highlight another section where Freya had been calling out and asking if anyone wanted to communicate with us. He presses play and we listen. In reply to her questions a voice, as horrible as the growl, yells, "*Get OUT! Not WELCOME!*" A second voice startles me as it comes through the speaker. It's softer and sounds like the child's voice I'd heard on the ghost walk. Through heart wrenching sobs, it gasps, "*Help me, please, help me. bad. It's bad.*" My stomach churns as a thought hits me. Sophie MacGregor? Next, Sunny plays back the footage from our cameras. The door can be seen shaking, just as we'd seen with our own eyes, and the scraping sound cuts through the night. A tall, dense, very black shadow passes over the doorway, something we didn't see at the time.

"Ohmygod. Go back, Sunny," I say. "Play that bit again." Sunny presses rewind and stops just at the point the shadow makes its appearance. My mouth is dry, but I manage to splutter, "That's truly freaky. I never saw that. Did you, Freya?"

"No, I didn't." Freya is ashen-faced. "I think it's dangerous. But judging from the audio, I also think that we're needed. Something, or someone, needs our help and thinks we can give it. We have to go back, PJ."

I agree and I'm almost certain I know who needs us. I'm not so sure, though, how we can help. I just hope we're not too late. I voice my concerns to Freya, who asks, "Would you like me to come with you to the mausoleum?"

Before I can answer, Shuggie interrupts: "Naw, after seein' that footage, I'd like to see what's happening there for myself, Freya. Anyway, you made a connection with the Covenanter Prisoners and it might be dangerous at the mausoleum. Whatever, or whoever's lurking at the mausoleum might try to attack you, being a girl an' that. Dinnae forget he's frae the olden days, when girls were regarded as weaker than boys. He might think ye're fair game, Freya."

"Well, how very dare you, Shuggie," Freya barks back. "Number one, I'm from the here and now and girls are made of stronger stuff, these days. Number two, I don't think that just because I'm a girl I'm in any more danger than you. And anyway, I'm more experienced with using the protection rituals, so I'd be safer."

Shuggie reddens. "Sorry, Freya, I didnae mean tae offend ye. Mebbes the truth is, I'm just eager to see some o' that amazin' activity for myself than I think ye cannae handle yerself. It's OK. You go with PJ."

Freya glares at him. She's real mad with Shuggie. She hesitates. "No, Shuggie. You go. But only because you're right about the Covenanters. I think I did strike up some empathy with them, and I felt close to Alana there. Maybe she'll come through if I go back. I think whatever is at the mausoleum was blocking our connection earlier." Shuggie looks sheepish. "But don't think you've heard the last of this, Shuggie." Freya's eyes flash angrily. "I might be a girl, but I can do anything any of you guys can and more! You'd do well to remember that."

"Aye, Freya. I know that. Ah wus just bein' stupid, that's all. Sorry."

We decide to leave the review of the Covenanters' Prison until later and gather up our flashlights and rucksacks to head off to our vigil areas. My heart is thudding. I'm not looking forward to being back at the mausoleum and I recall the terrible nightmare I had after our first visit. I sure hope it wasn't a premonition. It's even colder outside now, and I shiver in the moonlight. We split off from Freya and Sunny heading to the prison while Shuggie and I approach the mausoleum, with Dug scampering ahead. As soon as we reach it, Dug braces his paws to the ground and raises his hackles, tail tucked firmly between his legs. He doesn't like the place at all and starts to whimper and shake as Shuggie tries to encourage him closer with a doggy treat. Even that doesn't persuade him to come nearer. Instead, he lies in a crouched position, poised to attack, his ears standing straight up as he stares intently at the forbidding mausoleum that I sense is waiting for us.

"Right," says Shuggie, too brightly, "let's get some action goin' here."

Uh oh, what's he planning? Shuggie stands, slap-bang in front of the doorway and begins to recite, "*Bluidy Mackingie, come oot if ye daur, lift the sneck and draw the bar.*"

That's not good. Nope, no good is going to come of this. No siree.

Shuggie keeps his camera trained on the door and says, "Come oan, PJ, this is gonnae take the two o' us tae get it tae work. Say the rhyme with me. We need to provoke him if we're gonnae get some action here."

"OK, how about we say it three times, getting louder each time? That should provoke him, if anything's gonna."

It goes against my better judgement to anger an already unpleasant spirit, but I stand next to Shuggie at the door in readiness to lure the nasty poltergeist out to show himself.

"Ah'll count us in. Ready… One, two, three, GO!"

"*Bluidy Mackingie, come oot if ye daur, lift the sneck and draw the bar,*" we chime in unison. Nothing. So far so good.

"*Bluidy Mackingie, come oot if ye daur, lift the sneck and draw the bar.*" Louder this time. Still nothing.

"*Bluidy Mackingie, come oot if ye daur, lift the sneck and draw the bar.*" Loud and confident this time. The children's nursery rhyme hasn't produced the ghost and I relax my guard a little.

SNAP! BANG! Shuggie and I both lurch backwards in fright. The unmistakable sound of the latch bar drawing back from the door rings out into the night. Dug whimpers and howls and takes off into the darkness behind us. Shuggie and I gape at each other.

"Whit in the name o' watsit wis that?" he shrieks, his voice unusually high-pitched.

I am rigid, unable to move, frozen in horror. If I move, whatever is behind that door might just decide to move as well.

"Dunno. Sounded horribly like the 'sneck' drawing backwards," I whisper, every inch of me trembling.

We hear Dug squealing and barking in terror, for all the world as though he is being attacked.

"Oh naw, Dug! Listen, wait here, dinnae move. Ah'm just gonnae find Dug. Sounds like he might be in trouble. Ah cannae leave him, PJ. Just keep filmin'. I'll be back in a minute, OK? He disnae sound far awa.'"

Before I can object, Shuggie has turned tail and rushes off amongst the tombstones in the direction of Dug's yelps. I sure hope Dug is OK. I can't bear the thought that anything bad has happened to the li'l guy. I debate whether to just get the heck outta here myself but before I can do anything there is a rumbling from the direction of the tomb as the heavy door pulls slowly inwards, creaking, scraping and groaning. I can't move. Sheer terror makes my limbs jelly-like as they quiver wildly and the hairs on my arms rise. My mouth is dry and I can see the steam forming from my breath as the air around me becomes icy cold, far colder than it was just moments ago. A smoky fog forms around the base of the mausoleum and rises slowly upwards and all around it, obscuring the building from view. I am freezing now. My fingers feel stiff as I try to press the button on the walkie talkie to call for help. I find it but my attempt to make contact is futile. My heart feels as though it drops right into my boots when all I hear is the crackling sound of static.

"C-come in, guys? Can any of you hear me? I… I think I'm in a bit of trouble here? SOS?" I mutter weakly. The dreadful realisation hits home that no-one can hear me. It is as though time has stopped as I wait expectantly for something to come out of that ominous black maw of the open doorway. I press the button again and again, my finger jabbing urgently, my mouth drying up in fear. More static, but I almost drop the walkie talkie with a jolt when within that white noise a voice booms, "YOU. HAVE. DISTURBED. ME. REVENGE…!" It is the most terrifying thing I ever heard and it most definitely isn't human. It sounds like a *Doctor Who* Dalek, real freaky. Now I do drop the walkie talkie. I don't want to hold on to that thing that was speaking. The EVP recorder is running and I have the camera pointing at the doorway. Suddenly, the camera light goes off and it whirrs as it shuts down. The red recording light on the digital recorder shuts off too and my flashlight dies. I stand there, alone, without any means of communication, in the blackness of the night. Even the moon has disappeared behind a big black cloud. I blink helplessly in the dark, hoping my eyes will adjust so that I can see something. The mausoleum door creaks again and I feel an almighty push from behind. I fall hard, straight through the door. It slams – *BANG!* – behind me and I hear the latch draw across it, locking me in. My stomach falls into my boots.

The smell inside is intense. The stench of mould, musty stuff and dead things assaults my nose. I don't need to be told that there are ancient bodies in here. I sit, winded and petrified, on the floor where I landed. Jeez, that had been some thwack to get me over the doorway. I'm still holding my flashlight and I frantically untwist the battery housing, hoping that if I move the cells around, maybe they'll spring into life. My hands shake frantically, making it difficult to work. I try again, but there is still nothing but the dense, dark, stifling air that feels like a suffocating cloak gathering around me. Although it's pitch dark, I moan in terror, as out of the corner of my eye, I see an even blacker shadow forming on the far side of the circular building. I inhale sharply and loudly, my mouth parched. The shadow grows from the ground upwards, elongating into a straight column at first, which stretches out on either side as it grows arms then legs. I see a face forming, contorting and screaming in rage, black holes where its eyes should be. As the head forms, I can make out long curly hair, like the wigs of olden days, and just like the vision I'd seen of Mackenzie earlier.

I gulp, but my throat feels constricted and I choke a little. This is really, really happening. I scramble backwards as the figure moves – no, *glides* – towards me and I know, if it gets close, it's gonna smother me, for sure. Instinctively, I move away and try to stand. I stumble again in the darkness just as the moon makes a brief reappearance and I see its silvery glow through the iron grates in the door. The light illuminates the figure of a man lying on top of a stone plinth. I stifle a scream but it's just a sculpted figure. That must be his actual tomb! I lose my footing, dislodging a metal grate and fall straight through, finally landing with a crunch. *Owww!* My butt takes another battering and I feel sharp jabs from unidentified shards on the ground. I don't even want to think about what they might be.

"Help me? Please don't hurt me," a weak little voice whimpers.

I swallow hard. *What the…? It's the voice I heard on the ghost walk and the one we heard on the EVP at Mrs Anderson's.* I feel like I want to puke. What new horror is this?

CHAPTER 24

"Who… who are you?" I call out. Timidly, my voice weak, fearing the answer, I ask, "Are you a ghost?"

A deep roar of wicked laughter rings out in the darkness, shaking the building. I gulp loudly. *What the heck is THAT?* The smell of rot fills my nostrils as the shadow begins to form again, having followed me to whatever hell hole I've fallen into. I hear a swish followed by stinging heat across my cheek. I recognise that sensation! Oh. My. God. I am living the nightmare! This is just like when the scratches appeared on my back. Bluidy Mackenzie is doing his worst.

I hear the whimpering again. It seems to be falling away into the distance. I look every which way, but there is no light in this stinking hole.

"Please help. Please. I want to go ho-o-o-me…!" The voice is weeping and echoes eerily around me.

I back away from the swirling black mass that is still trying to form. Its evil voice fills my head, snarling, laughing, roaring. It's trying to speak to me, random words are being spat out as though the thing is trying to remember how to articulate a sentence. It succeeds and as its booming voice fills the space around me, it drowns out the weak cries for help.

"For centuries, my tomb has been disturbed, first by the treasonous spirits of the Covenanters who trouble my peace for bringing them to justice and then the pestilence of bairns like you who taunt me to lift the sneck and let you in! Well, your request is granted. If you cannot respect a great advocate and protector of the Crown and you deny him his rest, then you can join me for eternity. I will not have my bones taken and played with like a puppet! DO. YOU. HEAR. ME?" the voice roars.

I nod frantically and utter a pathetic, "Yessir. I'm sorry, sir."

"Aye, sorry now, eh? Well, let me assure you, young sir, YOU WILL BE SORRY!"

I sob in horror, my breath coming in short, sharp gasps, as the shadow swirls around me, its own terrible features alternately forming and disappearing.

"I'm over here. Please. Help me," the other haunting voice cries out from across this stinking cavern.

I try to gather myself, hoping beyond hope that the others have realised I've disappeared and will be searching the tomb any minute. *Surely, they'll alert Donald when they can't find me?* The thought reassures and gives me strength.

"Who is it? Who are you?" I call back.

"Sophie MacGregor. My name is Sophie MacGregor. I want my mum."

I knew it! We were being led here. All the clues that were given at Mrs Anderson's and by the switched-off TV playing the news report now make sense!

"Um, Sophie?" I call, my voice quivering. "Are you alive, or a ghost?"

"I'm alive, but he wants to keep me here. He wants me to die of cold and hunger like his prisoners. He wants to frighten and scratch me to death. Please help me."

"I can't see you. Where are you?"

"He's shoved me behind some loose bricks in the wall. I'm stuck."

"My flashlight isn't working and he's attacking me. I can't see. Keep talking. I'll try to reach you, OK?"

"OK. I'll sing, shall I? I like to sing when I'm afraid."

"Great idea." I squint in the darkness. The shadow seems to be losing strength for the moment. Maybe speaking to me has drained its energy. Suddenly, it dawns on me. It's using the energy from my electronic equipment. Yes! That's it! Perhaps when it's all used up it won't have the strength to materialise again. I can't be sure it won't find some way of energising itself again, so I have to work quickly. It's impossible as the darkness is so thick, wrapping around me like a cloak. I can't tell which way to go to reach Sophie. She sings, "*Ring a ring of roses, a pocket full of posies…*"

I shudder. Children's rhymes are all full of horror, and after tonight's experience I don't want her summoning up the plague victims who supposedly lie in this tomb as well. I know the rhyme she's reciting is all about the plague.

"Uh, Sophie, can you maybe sing something else? Maybe something from the radio?"

"OK," the reedy little voice comes back. "Taylor Swift OK for you?"

Tbh, I'd prefer Ed Sheeran or Rag 'n' Bone Man but this is no time for requests.

"Um, yeah, go for it," I respond, and Sophie breaks into her version of 'Shake It Off'. Apt choice, I think. Yeah, let's shake it off and get outta here. But how? The shadow is still thinning and swirling like smoke in the corner. I turn in the direction I think the voice is coming from and crawl towards it, muck and mulch oozing over my knees and fingers, a dreadful odour filling the air. Suddenly I have the feeling of bony hands clawing at my back, pulling me as though trying to stop me getting to my destination. They grip me hard, harder still, and I feel my whole body lifting into the air. I try to scream, but no sound comes out of my mouth as I gasp in terror. My legs and arms flail wildly, held by this unseen horror that swings me back, then forwards, gathering momentum, until finally, I am hurled forcefully into the wall. My skull cracks against it with an almighty thud that leaves me winded and disorientated. My head throbs and I see flashing lights in the darkness, but I can't decide if it's a concussion or a manifestation of spirits. I sit still, so weakened, I can't bring myself to move.

It's gone ominously quiet. I rest against the wall and examine my head, squeamishly wondering if my skull has cracked. It sure feels like it. Miraculously, I can't feel anything oozing out; no blood, but *ouch,* I can feel a lump the size of an egg at the back of my head. I stifle a wave of nausea and my stomach lurches wildly. The silence is broken by piercing screams. Ohmygod! I suddenly remember what I was doing before I was assaulted by that thing! "Sophie! What's happening? Are you OK?" I heave myself up and once more try to follow the direction of her voice.

"PJ?" Sophie is sobbing and howling, and I fear whatever fresh terror Mackenzie is committing to scare her so much.

"Sophie – what's happening? Stay strong. I'm coming for ya. Keep talking – I need to follow the sound of your voice."

"He's here, PJ." Sophie sounds like she's gasping for air. "His hands are grabbing at me. I can't breathe!" She coughs and her voice rasps, "PJ, he's going to kill me! Owwww! Now he's scratching me, PJ." She wails and cries inconsolably. "He's not going to let us go!" She is sobbing hard now.

I summon every last ounce of strength I have and use the concave wall to guide myself around the mausoleum, navigating towards Sophie. The air is thick and heavy as I recoil in horror, feeling dozens of hands grasping my ankles, grappling with my arms and poking my face, doing all in their power to keep me from Sophie. My breathing is laboured and my head throbs. I feel sick, but there's no way I can stop trying to help Sophie.

Suddenly, from nowhere, a bright column of light forms and a white feather falls to the floor in front of me. The column of light moves forward, another feather falling. Four or five times this happens until the column of light stops near the concave wall, revealing loose brickwork. I sit on my haunches, hope filling me now. "Mom?" I whisper. "Is that you?"

"Shh, PJ. Hurry. I'm here, but I can't stay for long. Find Sophie now."

I breathe a sigh of relief, and with Mom's words, a feeling of peace and strength washes over me. I push off the hands and will them to lay off me. They weaken and I am finally able to manoeuvre myself to the source of Sophie's cries. She is whimpering miserably, but I'm relieved that she's still breathing.

Desperately, I begin to pull out the heavy bricks, heaving at them with all my might, straining and panting, until a crawl space is revealed behind them. The air is thick and heavy and a black shadow, blacker than the darkness, hovers menacingly in front of me. It's Mackenzie! I know it, even though I can't see his face. I feel his evil presence, chilling my bones, squeezing my chest, intent on attacking me, his interest in Sophie diverted. I summon up every bit of strength I can muster and picture Mom, encouraging me to fight. I lash out at Mackenzie. "I'm not afraid of you. I'm not! You're just an evil bully and I WILL NOT LET YOU BEAT ME!" I push against the black mass with all the physical energy I have left in me. In my head I chant, *Ya don't scare me, Bluidy Mackenzie*. I swipe the air, arms flailing in all directions. *Take that, you bully. That's for all the people whose lives you ruined. And this is for Mom!* I thwack the air wildly. I'm real mad now; so mad I forget to be scared, and with that realisation, the shadow's grip on me loosens. I have to be quick! I reach out and find Sophie, covered in dirt, her hair matted, scratches and bruises etched into her skin. She is huddled, terrified, cold and shivering inside the cramped space. I hold my hand out to her and she gazes in awe at the white light that now illuminates the space around us. She grabs my hand and I pull her out of her tiny prison. She can barely move, her limbs stiff and sore from sitting in the cold, damp and dank crawl space.

"Hurry – we need to get outta here now."

"How? Is he gone?" she whimpers.

"For now. My mom is here. She'll help us but we have to be quick."

"Your mum? Where? How did she get here?"

"Long story. I'll explain later. See the light, though? The white light? We have to follow it, OK? Don't be scared."

"OK."

I remember the protection ritual and the crystal. I slap my forehead. *How could I have been so dumb! I should have used it earlier!* Before moving off, I visualise the white light and the blue light, and I grasp the crystal Freya gave me. I feel power surge through me and with it comes renewed strength. I can do this. I grasp Sophie's hand and together, we crawl along the floor, following the column of light from which feathers continue to fall. I pick each one up and pocket them. We reach the iron grate above us but my stomach lurches as the swirling black mist is hovering over it. I can see it's trying to take shape and gather energy again. It's waiting for us!

Sophie whimpers fearfully.

"He's here! The boogey man! It's Bluidy Mackenzie, look!"

"Yeah, just keep calm, Sophie, keep watching the light. It's gonna protect us."

I have to get the swirling fog to move so that I can pull myself up through the grate. I remember my 'superhero' protection. Will it work? I wonder. Although my urge is to just try to reach up through the mist, my instinct tells me that will be dangerous, so instead, I take a deep breath, squeeze my eyes shut and summon up all the concentration I can muster to picture the energy building up inside me.

When I feel ready, I sling my arm straight out in front of me and point at the black mist.

"Begone, Bluidy Mackenzie," I yell. "Let us through!"

Suddenly, I feel a crackling of static as a burst of lightning shoots out of my arm straight into the shadow. To my amazement the shadow shatters into pieces, drifts into the air and disappears. I laugh almost maniacally. It works! For now, anyway. Quickly, I heave myself up through the grate in the floor and manage to scrabble up to the ground floor level. I reach down to see Sophie, tear-stained and stunned, below me.

"Give me your hand. I'll pull but you need to push yourself up. Steady yourself by putting your feet on the wall."

Sophie is remarkably light and I manage to haul her, without too much difficulty, through the grate. We lunge for the door. I take a deep breath, lift the latch and pull. Nothing! It's stuck! *Jeez, what now?* Sophie is getting restless behind me. I try again. Still, it won't move. To my enormous relief, I hear barking. Dug! He's outside. I see flashlights through the grate in the door and voices are calling my name.

"Thank goodness!" I say to Sophie. "Don't worry, my friends are outside. Hey, guys! In here! The door is stuck fast."

I glance behind me and the white light has grown stronger. It lights up the whole room and I am able to gaze upon the stony figure of Sir George Mackenzie lying on top of his marble bed. I watch the light intently as it forms into a shape. Inside the light, there is Mom! She's smiling and I well up with love and warmth.

"Go now, PJ. You're safe. Well done. I sure did raise one brave, strong boy and I'm so proud of you for what you've done. Get outta here, kiddo. You've made sure Mackenzie won't bother you again tonight. But beware – there's more to be done yet."

I want to reach out to her, run and hug her, but I know we have to go. All the emotions in the world run through me as I take one last, lingering look. I grin and say, "Thanks, Mom. I miss you. Love you."

She smiles her beautiful smile and says, "I'm never far away, PJ. It's all going to be OK. Love you too."

The door of the tomb flies open and in sweeps Donald, followed by Shuggie. Mom has disappeared.

"What the…?" Donald exclaims as he sees me, with Sophie gripping tightly on to my hand.

Relief washes over me but as I emerge from the claustrophobic and cloying tomb into the freezing cold night air, I feel dizzy and the black cloak descends over me as I am drawn once more into darkness.

CHAPTER 25

I come round to find myself propped in the chair in the shop, a blanket wrapped round me and an electric heater nearby. I blink my eyes open, and at first, think I've woken after another nightmare like the one I'd had the other night. As my eyes focus, however, I see all my friends and Donald surrounding me, looking worried. I know it's all too real when I see Sophie, dirt-streaked and mussed up on the seat next to me. She's grasping a steaming mug of hot chocolate in both her hands and grins as I gradually inch back to life.

"PJ!" She beams. "Thank goodness you're OK! You're my hero!" She puts the mug on the table and leaps up to hug me.

"Whoa, Sophie! Say – did all that really happen? The black shadow? The white light and the feathers?" I whisper. Following my cue, she whispers back that yes, it all happened and that the shadow had been tormenting her and had kept her trapped for days. She'd been terrified, thinking that she was going to die there, alone in that crawl space.

"Did you call out while you were in there?"

"Only in my head," she confirms. "I was too frightened to really shout in case it made him mad."

I wonder how I heard her? Telepathy, like Freya, maybe? The others all clamour around me, asking if I am OK and what happened so I don't have much time to think about it now. I can barely string my words together so I just say I will tell them everything later. Unfortunately, I don't have any real evidence to show them of all that had happened in the mausoleum.

"The police are on their way," Donald says. "They'll want to interview you about Sophie. Her parents are coming with them. I think you're going to be a very popular young man, PJ." He grins.

I smile weakly. How am I ever going to answer all the questions that will be coming my way, I wonder?

"Sorry ah left ye, PJ," Shuggie says sheepishly. "Ah wis so worried that Dug might be hurt that ah just had tae find him. Ah just didnae stop tae think aboot it."

"That's OK, Shuggie. I'd have done the same if it had been Buddy. You weren't to know what would happen. I take it Dug was OK, then?"

"Aye, right as rain. He'd got his collar caught on a raggedy bit o' stone between the gravestones and panicked, cos he wis stuck. He was spooked as well."

Our chat is interrupted as the police arrive with Mr and Mrs MacGregor. Mrs MacGregor lunges towards Sophie and scoops her up in her arms. She's tearful and looks as though she hasn't slept for days.

"I... *we*," she corrects herself, "can't thank you enough, PJ. We thought we'd lost Sophie for good," she says, hugging on to Sophie for dear life and sobbing into the little girl's hair.

"Amazing, young man," Mr MacGregor says as he grasps my shoulder and shakes my hand. "Anything we can do in return for you and your team – *anything*, you've got it."

"Ah, it was nothing, Mr MacGregor. Just happy that Sophie is OK and back with her mom and dad," I say weakly.

Donald, who's been speaking to the police, comes over to tell me they'll delay interviewing me it until I am feeling better. Aunt Katie arrives, ashen-faced and desperate to know what on earth has been going on. I assure her all is well, and when I've downed a cup of that very welcome hot chocolate and we say our goodbyes to Donald, Sophie and her parents, she takes us all back to our place where we will spend the rest of the night. On the way home, I pinch myself, still wondering how real it had all been and how I'll explain it to the police. As all my equipment failed in the mausoleum, I won't be able to show them what really happened in there, which is probably for the best. That would be some explanation! I'll just tell them I heard Sophie calling and went in to investigate. They'll just think we're a bunch of kids playing at ghost hunting anyway, I'm sure. They won't take any of that stuff seriously. I plunge my hand into my pocket and there, just where I'd put them, are at least a dozen white feathers. I smile happily. "Love you, Mom," I mouth silently.

In my bedroom, we don't talk much. We're shattered and I'm shell-shocked. Before I drift off to sleep, I take comfort from the steady, companionable breathing of my buddies bedded down in their sleeping bags on the floor, Dug snoring contentedly. What a night it's been.

We sleep until late in the afternoon when the police come to see me.

"Well, young man," the senior police officer says to me. "You're a very brave laddie, by all accounts." I wonder what Sophie has been telling them.

"I'm sure you'll want to know how Sophie came to be in the Mackenzie Mausoleum in the first place," the police officer says.

"Yeah, I sure would, sir," I say, deciding not to give any information from my side just yet.

"Sophie was missing for three days and we were beginning to think the worst," the police officer tells us. "Apparently some other girls at her school had dared her to enter the mausoleum and when she refused, they wouldn't let her into their group and taunted her for being a coward. It got so bad that she decided, without telling anyone, that she would go to the mausoleum and video her experience to prove that she had done it. There's an old nursery rhyme that kids have recited for years. Something about Sir George Mackenzie drawing the latch to let them in. Anyway, Sophie tells us that she recited the rhyme and when she approached the door, it was, very unusually, open. We think it must have been the warden that left it unlatched. She went inside and fell down the grating into the floor below and I think, from there, her imagination must have run wild. She had hallucinations, thinking that the ghost of Mackenzie terrorised her and shoved her into the crawl space in which she'd become stuck."

The police officer smiles indulgently. "Of course, that

would just be a frightened child's imagination playing tricks on her."

"Um, yeah, probably," I agree. "It's real scary and claustrophobic in there and knowing you're surrounded by dead bodies would frighten anyone. Poor kid."

"Funny thing is, she said that when you arrived, you fought off the ghost and that your mother helped."

"Oh, uh, well, no. Our group, the Paranormal Pursuers, were investigating there, as I guess you know. I was checking the place out on my own and when I touched the door it opened and I got stuck in there. She probably thought my yelling and roaring was me fighting off that old ghost. You can think a lot of strange stuff when you're stuck in the dark, alone."

Freya, Sunny and Shuggie sit quietly listening to my story and don't interrupt. I know that they know there is much more to it. Aunt Katie grips my shoulder and whispers, "Well done, PJ. You're some guy. Mom would be so proud of you."

Satisfied, the police leave it at that. Sophie is home safe and for them, Occam's Razor is the best outcome. Leave it as the simplest explanation being the right one!

The team and I are settling into an afternoon of stuffing our faces with food (Tunnock's Teacakes and Irn Bru included, of course) and we're about to start the debrief, when Aunt Katie takes a call from one of the Scottish daily newspapers. They want to interview me about finding Sophie and to hear the full story. I am reluctant at first, but Shuggie gets real excited.

"Ye've got tae dae it, PJ. Think o' the publicity it'll generate. We can discuss what tae tell them aboot the

Pursuers, but this could get the group and the vlog well an' truly on the map, eh?"

I think about it and yeah, there doesn't seem any harm in it. I don't have any proof of what happened inside the tomb so it isn't like there would be anything to contradict what I told the police. Only Sophie and I really know the truth which I am about to tell the team.

"OK," I say to Aunt Katie. "You can tell them I'll do it, but only as long as they include all of us. After all, it was a team effort and I only found Sophie because of what we were doing as a group."

Aunt Katie speaks with the reporter, who is more than happy to see the team and hear all about our adventures. Aunt Katie arranges for him to come over the next evening when we agree the others will come by after school.

Eager to hear what I've missed of their investigation and the team desperate to hear my story, we head back to my room and sprawl on cushions on the floor.

I am excited to tell everyone what had happened and how I'd come across Sophie. I explain how after Shuggie had gone, all the electrical equipment had shut down, including my flashlight.

"It was real weird, you know? I mean, *everything* just going at the same time."

"Really typical paranormal phenomena, PJ," Shuggie says. Even Sunny finds it hard to come up with a reasonable explanation for all the equipment failing at the same time.

"I did get something, though, just as you'd run after Dug." Having charged the battery, I press play on the camcorder. First is the moment before Shuggie chases after Dug and I've recorded us saying the Bluidy Mackenzie rhyme. Then there is the loud dragging sound coming from the mausoleum that sounds like the latch being drawn back. Shuggie disappears after Dug, and I'd been so rigid with fright, without realising it, I'd just stood with the recorder trained on the mausoleum as the door slowly groaned open and the mist formed from nowhere and swirled around it. The really exciting bit is what happened next when I tried to contact the others with the walkie talkie before it died and the voice, clear as anything, on camera booms out from the static, "YOU. HAVE. DISTURBED. ME. REVENGE...!"

Everyone gapes, open-mouthed.

"That's a 'class A' EVP ye've got there, PJ. It's awesome!" Freya shudders. "He's a piece of work, that Mackenzie."

Sunny is quiet. He has no explanation at the moment.

I tell the guys what happened in the tomb, all about the black shadow that formed into a human shape with a horrible face, then about me stumbling through the grate in the floor and how Sophie had called out.

"It was the same voice I heard on the ghost walk," I say. "Sophie told me she had been too frightened to actually shout out in case it drew Mackenzie to her. I don't think anyone would have heard her anyway from behind that brickwork."

"You must have connected with her psychically or telepathically, just like me and Alana," says Freya. "Perhaps things just came together in some way and Sophie's terrified energy tuned into your own heightened awareness."

Sunny nods. He seems impressed with Freya's explanation.

"So Bluidy Mackenzie has you two cornered and he's

swirling aboot in the tomb. How did ye's get back out?" Shuggie wants to know.

"My mom helped us," I say simply.

"Yer ma?" Shuggie exclaims. "Whit did she dae?"

I recount how Mom had guided me and Sophie with her light and feathers. I dig deep in my pocket and pull out all the feathers she had used to guide me to Sophie. I stand up to fetch the trinket box from my bedside table that contains all the other feathers and place the new ones inside.

"I used my protection ritual and the crystal too," I say to Freya. "And oh! I almost forgot, as we got to the grate where Mackenzie was trying to re-form, I zapped him with the superhuman finger shot and guess what? The black form just split into tiny bits and disappeared into the air! That's how we got out. Anyway, when we got to the doorway and it wouldn't open, I looked back and, in the light, Mom had actually taken shape and she spoke to me. She told me it would all be OK and that she was always there, looking after me. Then you guys all arrived to let us out."

"Oh, that's so wonderful," Freya says. "You see. I *knew* they were all around us. It really doesn't take an EVP or a camcorder just to know it. It's common for loved ones who've passed over to leave feathers, PJ. They join your guardian angels and let you know that they're still there for us. That was your mum's particular way of telling you."

"It could, of course, just have been a hallucination brought on by stress," Sunny said.

"Sunny!" we all groan.

"That doesn't explain the feathers, though," I add as we start throwing jellybeans at him from a jar Aunt Katie had picked up for us earlier.

"Nor PJ's equipment dyin' on him," says Shuggie.

"Or the EVPs," says Freya.

"Steady!" Sunny laughs and shields himself from the onslaught. "I'm just saying. OK, I accept the feathers are difficult to explain except, duh-uh – birds? We have to keep an open mind, you know." He seems suddenly sad and says, "How come all of you have experiences like this and I'm the only one who hasn't? I'd love to see my dad again."

"I think you have to totes believe and be prepared to let them in," Freya suggests. "At the moment, you're concentrating more on proving that there's nothing there. You're convincing yourself there always has to be a rational explanation. Maybe, in time, as we do more investigations, you'll start to believe it yourself, Sunny." She puts a comforting hand over his.

"Hm. Maybe you're right. Maybe when I look through all of the evidence, I'll be convinced," Sunny says doubtfully.

"You should take it to Aunt Katie," I suggest. "She can maybe run some tests on what we have?"

"Yeah." Sunny brightens. "I'll ask her later."

"So, guys, that's my story. What happened to you while I was fighting off a malevolent poltergeist single-handed?"

"Oh, wow! Of course, we haven't told you about the Covenanters' Prison, have we?" says Freya. "Well, Sunny and I headed back there. You remember we saw the figures earlier and got all the K2 readings and responses? So, this time I decided to do some EVP work to find out why they were still there." She picks up the EVP recorder and presses the play button. "So, have a listen to this."

FREYA –	"We come in peace and with great respect to you all. Can you please tell us why you are still here?"
EVP –	"Revenge. Mackenzie. Torment him."
FREYA –	"OK, thank you. I think I understand. So, because of what he did to you, is it that why you don't want him to rest in peace?"
EVP –	(whispered) "Ye-e-sssss."
FREYA –	"Is it you who attacks people when they visit your prison?"
EVP –	"MacKenziiiiie!"
FREYA –	"Thank you, so it's Mackenzie that does everything bad, then?"
EVP –	"Dangerous. Warn. People."
FREYA –	"OK, am I correct then, that sometimes maybe you do push people and make them sick, then? To make them go away from the danger?"
EVP –	(a chorus of voices) "Ye-e-ssss."
FREYA –	"If we could stop Mackenzie doing the really bad stuff, would you want to cross over and leave this place?"
EVP –	(sadly whispered) "Y-e-sss. Sleep. Peace."
FREYA –	"We will see what we can do. Thank you."

Something comes back to me as I listen to the EVP and the story that's unfolding from the Covenanters' perspective.

"Guys! That's it!" I say.

"What?" Shuggie asks.

"I remember now, when I was in the mausoleum,

Mackenzie told me why he was doing all the bad stuff. He's really sore that the Covenanters are getting their own back on him and disturbing him, but what's also making him real mad is when kids show their disrespect to him and taunt him to let them in!"

Freya is deep in thought. "So, if we could persuade the Covenanters to let go of the bad and sad memories that aren't good for them, then perhaps we could get them to cross over and find happiness with their families instead. They just want to be heard and to tell their story. They've done that now and we can document it with our footage."

"Hmm, maybe, Freya. I don't think that would be quite enough, though. We'd have to find a way of appeasing Mackenzie and stop people from saying the rhyme. It set him off big time when Shuggie and I said it, and look what happened to poor Sophie. He was gonna make an example of her if I hadn't got there in time, that's for sure."

"OK, let's ponder that one," Freya agrees. "But I think we can stop all this nasty stuff from happening if we can just persuade the Covenanters to cross over and work out how to stop people winding up old Mackenzie."

We all agree it's worth a try and we'll see what ideas we come up with.

"If we stop the ghostly activity, we're sure gonna upset all the tour companies," I say. "Although, I kinda think Mackenzie will continue to make his presence known from time to time, even if we do appease him somehow," I say doubtfully. I know just how strong that spirit is and how much he likes to intimidate people. Still, we can but try.

CHAPTER 26

Aunt Katie is poring over the morning newspapers when I head to the kitchen for breakfast. I sit at the table and pick them up, one by one. Every one of them is headlined with Sophie's discovery at the mausoleum by a bunch of teenage ghost hunters and me, PJ Wilson, hailed as the hero of the night. There are pictures of Sophie with her mom and pop all grinning happily into the camera. Sophie hasn't held back on the story about the dare and her torment by the evil ghost Mackenzie who was vanquished by me, her rescuer. It is all there, right down to my mom coming in to light the way for us. Some of the newspapers disregard her tale as one told by an overwrought child with an overactive imagination brought on by her entrapment in the grim black tomb with no food or water for days. One or two, however, take great interest in the supernatural tales of the Kirkyard and speculate over Sophie's story.

"I took several calls from the papers this morning, all wanting to speak to you and to hear your side of the story,

PJ. They're taking a real interest in your night of ghost hunting and what really happened in the tomb. I told them you'd already agreed an exclusive and couldn't speak with them, though."

"Cool," I say, absorbed by the story unfolding in just about every newspaper.

"So, PJ. What about Sophie's story? What *did* happen in the mausoleum?"

I push aside the papers and take a deep breath. "Well, it's true, Aunt Katie. Everything Sophie said did happen." I sigh. "I can't prove any of it, though, apart from the stuff I had on audio and video just before I went in the tomb. I think you might be impressed by that when you see it. Shuggie's editing it all together for our YouTube vlog."

"Well, I'd sure love to see that when it's ready," Aunt Katie says. "Um, Sophie says your mom came to visit in the mausoleum and that she saw her? Is that true?"

"It sure is, Aunt Katie. She lit up the tomb and sent feathers to guide me to Sophie. Then I saw her. A full-bodied apparition." I smile, remembering how serene and beautiful she looked. Just like an angel.

"Oh, PJ. It would be wonderful to think your mom was really there with you," she says wistfully.

"Well, we've got some other stuff recorded that's pretty amazing and I'm certain we were led there by the stuff we captured at Mrs Anders… uh… n's." I bite my bottom lip, realising that I'm gonna have to confess everything now.

Aunt Katie raises an eyebrow suspiciously and pours herself a coffee. "You were saying, PJ?"

"Um, well, you know the night you were out and the Pursuers stayed over?"

"Yeah, the night the fire broke out in Mrs Anderson's?" My face feels hot as Aunt Katie's eyes bore into me.

"OK, so I'm really sorry, Aunt Katie, I was gonna tell you before, but I thought you might be mad at me." I tell her everything that happened and about the EVPs we got and how Mom and Alana had appeared after the ruckus between Sunny and Shuggie.

"PJ, you should have asked me. I mean, if you'd all been caught by someone suspecting you were breaking in, you'd have been in terrible trouble. Bad enough the fire broke out." Aunt Katie's brow furrows. "You have some EVPs, you say?"

"Yeah, I have everyone's stored on my cell. You wanna hear them?"

Aunt Katie says she would like to hear them, so I fetch my cell phone and she puts in the headphones to hear more clearly. She plays the voices over and over, her eyes widening and her eyebrows disappearing higher into her fringe. Eventually, she takes off the headphones.

"They really are clear EVPs you have there. I'd like to analyse them in the lab, if that's OK with you guys?"

"Sure," I say, breathing a sigh of relief that she's forgotten to be mad.

"So, from what I can hear, someone bellows out Mackenzie, and there's a warning from a woman – who, I have to say, does sound like Mrs Anderson – telling you that help is needed. And later, the fire breaks out, which I know from Donald is a common feature of the Mackenzie poltergeist activity."

"That's not all, Aunt Katie. The same night, do you remember when you came into my room because the TV was on full volume?"

"Yeah, I remember. What was that all about?"

"Well, when we went in, the TV was on, but it wasn't plugged in at the wall. It was a news report about Sophie MacGregor and as we walked in, the volume turned right up, all by itself!"

Aunt Katie looks thoughtful, as she leans on the table, her chin cupped in her hands. "I see where you're going. It's as though something, or someone, was trying to give you clues about Sophie's whereabouts." She shakes her head, trying to absorb everything I'm telling her.

"Yeah. It was a drip feed of information that we only managed to piece together when Sunny happened on the ghost walk information and the poster mentioned that the poltergeist had a fire-starting habit. I wasn't too sure about the Sophie part, but I kinda had a hunch that there was a connection. And, well, you know the rest of it."

"It's amazing, PJ. I mean, we do get good EVPs and results from tests on our subjects in the lab, but I've never come across something that seems so calculated and well put together. I think you might have stumbled on things that are truly unique. We'd have to examine it all a little more closely, to eliminate the possibility that one or more of you were playing pranks and putting on voices, but it sure is fascinating."

"Wait 'til you see and hear the other stuff we have recorded from the investigation, Aunt Katie. You're gonna be convinced, I'm sure. Anyway, how could any of us have created that booming, growly, old man voice?"

Aunt Katie laughs. "Well, go read about the Enfield Haunting. A deep, gravelly voice came from one of the girls who was haunted by the poltergeist in that house. Although it was highly unusual that she could create it, there is a suspicion that somehow she managed to manipulate her vocal cords."

I shake my head and smile. "Ever the scientist, Aunt Katie. I see where you're coming from, particularly as Shuggie was pranking us that night, but it's all too coincidental. I'm certain it wasn't him and anyway, it doesn't explain the rest of it."

"No, that's true, PJ. It could be really exciting. I can't wait to see all of it when it's put together."

*

The reporter arrives at the agreed time and close on his heels are the other Paranormal Pursuers.

He listens and takes notes in a squiggly shorthand and asks us loads of questions. He's fascinated by our investigation and wants to do a full-page feature on us. We agree he can see the footage we captured before it's put on YouTube for public broadcast. It's agreed that he'll come back in couple of days' time to view the debut of our first investigation film.

We're all buzzed and excited that this is going to publicise us as a paranormal investigation group and the prospect that we could get loads of hits on YouTube, Instagram, Facebook and Twitter.

"Aye, this could really launch us, PJ. Ye ken if ye get loads of hits, people want to advertise on yer sites and pay loadsa wonga for it? We'll be famous millionaires soon!" Shuggie can hardly contain his excitement as he dances around the room.

"Listen, guys, I've been thinking," I say. "I'd like to go back to Mrs Anderson's to round things off. You know, just to see if it's all settled down there now. I've asked Aunt Katie and she's cool with it, although she'd like to come in with us this time."

"That's a good idea, PJ," says Freya. "It would be good to get some closure."

A short while later, equipment at the ready, we trail down the staircase, with Aunt Katie following. She doesn't want to cramp our style or affect the investigation. She's just going to be an independent observer. As we reach Mrs Anderson's door, we find Azrael sprawled out on the mat, cleaning his whiskers.

"Azrael! Where the heck have you been?" I haven't seen him since Hallowe'en on the night of the ghost walk. I stopped worrying when I realised this is his *modus operandi*. He meows several times as though answering me, then arches his body and rubs into the leg of my pants. I reach down and stroke him. He looks as though he's smiling. I open the door of the apartment and instantly, I feel it's different. There is no smell, apart from fresh paint, and although the shades are down and the drapes are closed, the darkness isn't as black and dense as I remember it.

We set up the equipment in the den, which this time includes the motion sensitive bear, a night vision camera on a tripod and, of course, we use the digital recorders and K2 meters.

I begin with a call out: "Mrs Anderson? Are you here? We sure would like to speak with you. Can you show yourself?" Nada. Everything is silent. Freya and Shuggie try, but still, it seems that nothing is going to happen. I'm surprised, however, when Sunny decides he'd like to have a go.

"Mrs Anderson, you don't know me very well, but I'd really like to meet you and say hello. I-I wondered if maybe you have a message for me?" His voice cracks a little. I guess he's raised his hopes that maybe he'll hear from his dad.

We wait, listening. Azrael lets out a loud, drawn-out mewling sound, like a baby crying, and I nearly drop my K2 meter. Suddenly, the motion sensor bear lights up and flickers wildly.

"Someone's here!" Freya gasps excitedly. "Sunny – try again!"

He calls out again and, slowly but surely, twinkling lights start to dance around the room. We watch in fascination, as they all gather together and twist and turn, finally forming a shape. Faces appear. Mrs Anderson is first. She smiles out at me and the strange thing is, her eyes look bright and clear and normal. She's no longer scary. Her features dissolve and they form into someone I haven't seen before. It's a woman and she appears in a full body outline. Shuggie cries out as the woman's arm reaches out to him.

"Maw? It's ma maw! Oh, Maw, are ye OK? I miss you. I-I'm so sorry I made you angry the day of the accident. It wis all ma fault!" Shuggie is sobbing in grief and Freya takes his shoulders. The woman shakes her head, smiles, and puts a hand to her lips and blows a kiss to Shuggie.

"She's telling you it's OK, Shuggie. It wasn't your fault. You mustn't think that. She loves you and she wants you to know she's just fine. You're to stop being sad now and get on with your life. She's proud of you."

The woman nods as though in response to Freya's words. She beams at Shuggie, before waving him a goodbye and retreating into the lights, which seem to be billowing into another form. This time, a man with glasses appears within the lights and it is finally Sunny's turn.

"Dad, is that you?" he asks weakly, his voice thick and emotional. The man spreads out both arms as though to reach and embrace Sunny. He too looks happy and contented.

Freya says, "He's telling you he's sorry he couldn't wait until you reached the hospital, Sunny. He tried, but it was his time to go. He's telling you that he loves you very much and that's he's been watching you. He says it's good to be objective, but there is much that we don't and will never fully understand in this life. Oh! He just made a joke. He says he's not coming back as a dung beetle! He's reached his full potential and he's allowed to remain in heaven if he wants to. He's thinking that's what he'd like to do now."

"Oh, Dad! I'm so happy for you." Sunny sobs. "I'll keep searching for as much truth as possible. This will make so many people happy, if we can prove the existence of something, and I'm going to keep working on it, Dad."

Sunny's dad draws his hands up in a prayer pose, nods his head towards Sunny and smiles happily. He reaches out towards Sunny with both arms and recedes into the lights.

I look at Freya and she beams at me. "Look," she says, and points to the lights. There are two faces, Mom's and Alana's. My heart swells with joy as they form into full bodies and they hold hands. Neither say anything. They don't have to. I can tell they are happy and they're telling Freya and me that we all have a connection.

"They're saying goodbye, PJ. *Until we meet again...*" There are tears in Freya's eyes and I stifle a sob as Mom and Alana disappear into the lights. Azrael stands within the swirling column, which is now scattering and dispersing into the walls and ceiling. It vanishes completely and with it, Azrael is gone too. I have a feeling I'm not going to see him too often now, if ever.

I am dazed, happy and sad, all at the same time and as I look around at my friends, they too look shell-shocked, laughing and crying all at once. Instinctively, we draw together into a group hug that has no need for words.

As we separate, I look back at Aunt Katie. She is standing in the doorway, her hand over her mouth and tears are flooding down her cheeks. She saw it all too! I give her a smile and she returns it with a nod. Yup! She saw Mom. I'm happy for her.

Freya says, "They've gone now, PJ. Everyone is at peace. Alana was with me, telling me what everyone was saying."

I feel a tear slip gently down my face and my chest feels heavy. My voice trembles as I say, "Does that mean I'll never see or hear from Mom again?"

"Maybe not in the way it's been recently, PJ. But I think we can be sure that our loved ones are around us and if we really need them, we can reach out for guidance from them. They'll hear us, I'm sure of it." She takes my hand and leads me to the door, Sunny and Shuggie following.

CHAPTER 27

A couple of days later, we're all back at mine to watch the screening of *PJ and the Paranormal Pursuers – The Mackenzie Poltergeist*. Aunt Katie, Donald, Hamish and the reporter are here too.

Some swirling mist bursts onto the screen accompanied by some very spooky music and the title comes up, bold and clear, only to melt like wax from a candle down the screen, eventually disappearing to reveal the opening shot of Greyfriars Kirkyard on a very sunny afternoon.

"Ah got that music from the royalty-free downloads on Amazon. It's a braw theme tune, eh?" Shuggie comments proudly.

"It looks and sounds amazing," says Freya.

We watch Shuggie's typically jaunty introductory piece, with a short tour of the Kirkyard in daylight, and the team biographies. I explain the history of the Covenanters and Bluidy Mackenzie, and move on to the activity experienced in the Kirkyard. Sunny explains how we'll be carrying out our investigations and demonstrates the equipment. Freya explains that she is an empath and is able to speak with spirits.

Shuggie segues off into a short comic interlude in which he shows the film of me hugging the tree in the Kirkyard. He can't resist a joke at my expense.

"PJ has a special ability. He can talk and provide counselling to trees. These trees have witnessed centuries of secrets: happy, sad, traumatic. And they want to talk. Take a 'leaf' out of PJ's book and give them your time. You'll be 'barking up the wrong tree' if you doubt what they have to tell you. If you'd like to donate to PJ's counselling service, call into a local 'branch' of the Elm Bank, or why not make a 'trunk' call to tree, tree, tree, tree, tree tree." The numbers 333333 came up on screen. "Finally, you can text 'YEW O(A)K?' if you prefer."

I can't help but hoot with laughter. It's all a bit Zak Bagans, *Ghost Adventures* zaniness, but it is entertaining.

The film reaches the investigation and I shudder when I see the footage before entering the mausoleum. The mist, the shuddering ground, the growls. It is really creepy to watch. There's a sadness about the Covenanters' Prison but our cameras did pick up the lights and shadows. I feel grateful that those poor folks were trying to warn us out of the Kirkyard. The EVPs are pretty amazing too.

Shuggie explains how my equipment died when I entered the mausoleum and therefore there is no evidence except my narrative about what happened in there. There is a heart-warming moment when Sophie and I emerge from the mausoleum, just before I pass out. Shuggie has a rousing backing track over the part where we stumble out together and there's a montage of scenes as Sophie is reunited with her mom and dad.

Freya wipes her eyes. "It's quite an uplifting tear-jerker." She sniffles into her Kleenex.

"*Finally,*" Shuggie winds up the film, "*ah'd like tae leave ye's with a last wee tribute to oor friendlier resident of the Kirkyard, Scotland's most famous and worst poet, Wullie McGonagall – ah hope he'll pardon me for being so familiar! So, here it is:*

'*Greyfriars Kirk in the dark an' the murk,
Reveal tae us noo the secrets that lurk.
There wus a ghostie that loomed in yon tomb,
But it's no there noo,
It shifted alang wi' McGonagall's coo!*'

"*So, on that note, thanks for watching. Sleep tight and we'll see you for the next episode of* PJ and the Paranormal Pursuers*! Goodnight.*"

The spooky music kicks in and the scene fades to blackout as credits roll on the screen.

"Wow, Shuggie, that whole thing was amazeballs," exclaims Freya. "It was so professional!"

"Awesome, man," I say to Shuggie as I give him a congratulatory slap on the back.

"Brilliant. Well done, Shuggie," Sunny adds. "You did a fantastic job. The viewers are going to love it. It struck just the right balance."

Shuggie beams and glows bright pink. For once, he doesn't know what to say. Taking compliments isn't something he's used to.

Everyone claps and the grown-ups congratulate us on a

great piece of work. The news reporter is delighted with the material and tells us to look out for the feature in a couple of days.

*

We have one final task to complete, but this time, we decide not to film it. I speak first to Donald.

"Say, Donald, we'd like to go back to the Kirkyard one night this week, if possible? We think we might be able to help the Covenanters and, most importantly, make sure that kids like Sophie aren't in danger from the malevolent spirit."

"Aye, I see no problem with that, PJ. I'll make the arrangements for you. I'd keep quiet about it, though – the ghost tour companies will be complaining you've ruined their business!"

"Well, I can't guarantee we'll be successful and I'm sure there will be one or two other restless spirits hanging around the Kirkyard. But I won't tell if you don't." I give Donald a wink.

*

It's another cold but clear night and we're inside the Covenanters' Prison. I call out, "Hi, Covenanters. We've told everyone the story of your pain and loss. We totally get it and understand why you're unhappy. We'd like to try and help you find peace now. We think we have a way. Can you hear me? Two flashes of this K2 meter, if you can, please."

Bam! There are two flashes. They hear us! Freya

continues, "I was here with you the other night. We understand your pain, but holding on to the bad memories isn't good for you, or the visitors to your resting place. We want to help you cross over into the light and leave the horrible man Mackenzie to stay here alone in all eternity. Just think what a punishment that would be for him, having no attention from you and unable to cause you any more misery. Would you like us to help you?"

In the darkness, a host of sparkling orbs of light appear against the sky, thousands of them. They dance like fairy lights against the velvety blackness of the night.

Freya says, "Look, the Covenanters have all come out."

I say to the dancing lights, "Please flash twice if you would like to go to the light." *Bam! Bam!* Two flashes. "OK good. We wish you happiness and peace."

Freya takes over again, her voice soothing, to complete the process of helping the Covenanters to pass over. "Now, look for the bright white light and when you see it, go through it. Your families and friends are waiting for you beyond the light."

We watch in silence and suddenly, the orbs all gather together into one huge orb. A white light appears in the sky, forms into a kind of archway and the huge orb sails into it and disappears.

"They've gone," Freya says, happily. "They're at peace now."

I feel sure she is right.

Next, we go to the mausoleum. I feel slightly nauseous; the last visit all too vivid in my memory. I swallow hard and command the spirit inside, "Sir George Mackenzie, you will be tormented no more by those to whom you brought pain and suffering and you can no longer torment them. Let that be an end to it. We apologise on behalf of all those of us who summoned you with the nursery rhyme. We cannot prevent it happening again, but as a matter of goodwill, we ask that you harm no-one else in return for releasing you from the eternal guilt of what you did to the Covenanters."

We stand expectantly. Everything is still and silent until we hear a deep sigh followed by a raging growl. A black, ominous shadow forms and floats upwards towards the sky, disappearing as it mingles with the stars. I know it was Mackenzie.

"I think it's over," I say. "Let's hope no-one comes back and recites the rhyme anytime soon. He's a bit unpredictable, but maybe he'll mellow now that the Covenanters are away."

"Well, ah think oor work here is done. Anyone fancy the pie shop and an Irn Bru?" It could only be Shuggie.

There is no more we can do. We've tried, and all we can do is hope that some peace might now descend on the Kirkyard, its visitors and the surrounding tenements. We link arms and head off to say our goodnights to Donald, before heading off to the nearby pie shop for some Shuggie scran and, of course, *your other national drink!*

CHAPTER 28

It's Thanksgiving, my first ever without Mom and Buddy. I squeeze my eyelids together, fighting back the tears, remembering the last time we'd celebrated it all together and how Mom spent days before, preparing all my favourite seasonal desserts and sides that she'd put in the freezer ready for the big day.

I recall last year when the Rosenbaums had been there, too. I'm glad I didn't know then, that it was the last Thanksgiving I'd ever spend with Mom. She'd gotten out of bed extra early to get the turkey in the oven. Later in the afternoon, the Rosenbaums had knocked on the door, bringing gifts of chocolate and wine for the table. Mrs Rosenbaum, never happy to arrive without some of her own home baking, brought potato latkes and her own recipe spiced apple cake to add to the already groaning table. To go with the turkey, Mom prepared spiced cranberry sauce, the fluffiest mashed potatoes, roasted sweet potatoes, sprouts and green beans. She made my favourite cauliflower soup and the kitchen was filled with the aroma of freshly baked brown butter cornbread and Parker House Rolls, buttery and sweet, that were awesomely melt-in-the-mouth. The best bit, though, was dessert. Mom's pumpkin pie cheesecake and pecan pie were, well, to die for. Not an expression I will use again anytime soon.

Mrs Rosenbaum fussed over everyone as usual, but especially Mom, who she insisted should take it easy and sit down while she dished up and sorted out the dishes later on. I didn't realise it then, but the Rosenbaums knew that Mom was sick and wanted to make sure she didn't overdo things. Mom was determined, though; it was to be business as usual as far as she was concerned. Thinking back, it was the best Thanksgiving ever. I think Mom wanted to make sure we were making memories, just in case things wouldn't be the same for me next year. She knew, I think, that she wouldn't see the passing of the seasons to reach this magical time of year again.

I lie back on my bed and feel, for the first time in a while, the boa constrictor curl in my stomach. He is no longer angry. He is just a little heavy. I get rid of him by allowing tears to flow down my cheeks, leaving just a hollow feeling in my stomach as I dress and go find Aunt Katie. In Edinburgh, Thanksgiving isn't celebrated.

Katie looks up from her newspaper.

"Say, PJ. What are you up to today?"

"Uh, nothing much, Aunt Katie. No real plans. I think I might take a walk up to Princes Street and spend a little time alone."

Aunt Katie nods. I know she understands.

"Could I maybe ask you to run a few errands for me while you're there?" she asks.

"Sure, I will," I say, pleased to have some normal stuff to distract me for a while. She prepares a list of provisions she wants from the stores and after a quick cup of hot tea, she gives me some money and I pull on my jacket before heading off to Princes Street. It's kinda strange. On her list are things I think we already have at home. Maybe she isn't gonna have time to shop herself this weekend, so I set about picking up everything she's asked for.

It's busy when I reach Princes Street. People are starting to do their Christmas shopping and I find myself caught up in heaving crowds. The Edinburgh Christmas market is in full swing and swathes of visitors clamour into Princes Street Gardens, where colourful huts and stalls are selling all sorts of crafts, sweets, savouries and unusual goodies to tempt in the shoppers. I gaze in awe at the massive Ferris wheel that's arrived in the main street. Perhaps the team and I will take a ride on that soon – a momentary glimmer of excitement taking my mind off the day.

It's mid-afternoon by the time I arrive home. Aunt Katie has obviously been busy making dinner as the apartment is filled with a mix of aromas that make my mouth water. My stomach rumbles, reminding me that I haven't eaten today.

"Thanks, PJ," she greets me at the kitchen door and takes the bags from me. That's kinda strange as I would normally march straight in and plonk everything on the kitchen island and put the shopping away.

"Now, go and wash up and change into something smart," she says.

"Why? Are we going out somewhere?" I ask, bemused.

"Kinda. Now hurry up. Off you go. I'll be waiting in the den for you."

I don't feel much like going out, but Aunt Katie has something in mind, so for her sake, I don't argue and trudge reluctantly off to my room. I sigh, heavily. I really can't be bothered today. I feel tired and too wrapped up in my own thoughts.

Twenty minutes later, after a shower and a change of clothes, I feel a little livelier and dutifully head back to the den, ready to paint a smile on my face and suck up whatever she has in mind.

It's real quiet when I reach the door of the den and push down the handle. As the door opens, I swear my life goes in slow motion at what greets me. Inside, the drop leaf table is extended to its fullest and is laden, absotively, posolutely *groaning* with food. A mahusive turkey takes pride of place at the centre and all the familiar goodies that I last shared with Mom surrounds it. It looks beautiful. So beautiful, in fact, I barely notice that Shuggie, Freya and Sunny are already seated there and another four places are set for dinner.

"Happy Thanksgiving, PJ!" Everyone grins as they raise their glasses of Irn Bru to toast the celebration.

"Wow!" is all I can say at first. "Just wow! This is *awesome*, Aunt Katie. Guys! Happy Thanksgiving!" I return, gazing in wonder at the spread of food and the happy, smiling faces around the table.

The door from the kitchen opens and I glance over, wondering who on earth might be coming through, but I freeze as I hear a major scuffling of something kinda familiar sounding on the tiles beyond. Like a whirlwind, a fluffy brown lump dives from the kitchen, bounds over to me and jumps up, knocking me clean off my feet. As I lie on the floor my face is washed with doggy licks and my chest is pinned down by familiar teddy bear paws. I laugh through the tears of joy rolling down my face.

"Buddy!" I cry helplessly, giggling and sobbing at the same time as my beloved old friend greets me with joy and enthusiasm. "How did you get here?" I ask him, as though he would give me an answer.

From the direction of the kitchen, someone coughs lightly. I recognise that cough! I gently move Buddy off my chest and sit up from the floor to look at the door. Standing there, looking on with tears in their eyes, are the Rosenbaums! Oh, wow! It can't be, I think. I'm seeing things. This is unreal! Everything continues in that slow-motion dreamy way as I get up, Buddy following on my heels, and run towards the two dear, dear people who I love as much as if they're my real grandparents. We all hug and cry and Mrs Rosenbaum, through her tears, says, "Ezra, doesn't PJ look well? He's looking wonderful, Katie. You must be feeding him well. Ezra, say something to the boy,"

"Well, I will, if I can get a word in," he says amiably. "PJ, it's wonderful to see you, boy. We've missed you. Haven't we missed him, Rachael?"

"Missed him? PJ, there's been a hole in my heart since you left. Hasn't there been a hole in my heart, Ezra?"

"There's been a hole in her heart, PJ." Mr Rosenbaum smiles indulgently at Mrs Rosenbaum. "I hear nothing but, 'I wonder how PJ is. Do you think PJ is OK, Ezra?' PJ this, PJ that! I'd never have heard the end of it if we hadn't come over for Thanksgiving."

"You brought Buddy," I say tearfully, bending down to cuddle with my beloved old friend as he resumes washing my face again.

"Yes. Aunt Katie called us up and asked if we would bring him to you. I felt so bad, though, didn't I, Ezra? We had to put poor Buddy in a crate and he had to fly all alone in the hold for seven hours straight. I worried all the way. I thought he would be so afraid down there."

"Oh, thank you. Thank you all," I say through my tears. I gaze round at everyone in the room, my heart swollen with gratitude, love and joy. My new friends mean the world to me and my old beloved friends, here with me now, occupy such a special place in my heart. Here in this room, everyone I could hope to see is gathered around – with one exception. But I feel Mom all around us and my heart lifts. I know – I just know that she's here with us too. How do I know that? Because as I bend down to hug my beloved Buddy, a feather that hadn't been there just two minutes ago is sitting, right there, between his front legs. He kinda winks at me and I know he knows it too. I whisper to him, "Welcome to Edinburgh, Bud. You're gonna have a whole new exciting life here now." I hug him again and he sighs contentedly.

Freya sighs, her head tilted. "Aww, that's so totes emosh." She forms a heart shape with her fingers and pushes it out towards me and Buddy, before drawing it back towards her own heart. Sunny and Shuggie grin. "Aye, that's so sick, man! Ye're almost bringin' a tear tae ma glass eye!"

Everyone laughs around the table. You can always trust Shuggie to bring things back to earth with a thud. I roll my eyes, and smile, shaking my head in mock disdain.

"What? What did ah say? What did ah do?" He shrugs and leans over to grab a piece of cornbread, which he stuffs unceremoniously in his mouth.

Once the shock and the emotions quell, we all sit down excitedly to exchange news and stories, and laughter rings out in our home just as it had in the old days. We toast our loved ones, those present and those no longer with us. I remember what Cass said to me just a while back when we were at the shop.

"*Don't despair, PJ,*" she said. "*You will find your feet again and there are some very happy things to come for you. Next month, I think, PJ. Something good. You'll know it when it happens. Just remember to give thanks to the universe.*"

Well, I *do* give my thanks to the universe because I know now, without any shadow of a doubt, that nothing is forever but nothing truly ends. Of course, I can't prove it. Yet. But no matter. *I* know it. Here, now, in my heart and in my head. We are never alone, even when the inevitable happens. Mom's legacy remains here in Aunt Katie, the close friendship she's formed with the Rosenbaums, my beloved Buddy and the new friends I just know she's brought together. The Paranormal Pursuers will keep trying to find the truth in a form that everyone can share. We'll work tirelessly to bring help and comfort to others, just as we have found it. The adults chat amongst themselves and the four of us Pursuers raise a toast of our own: to the next investigation we'll be doing real soon.

ACKNOWLEDGEMENTS

I would like to thank Jonathan Eyers, author of *The Thieves of Pudding Lane* and commissioning editor for a well-known publishing house, who mentored me through the editing of *PJ and the Paranormal Pursuers*. Thank you, Jonathan, for your eagle-eyed expertise in spotting my errors, repetitions, non-sequiturs, gaps and missing punctuation. I also enjoyed putting the world to rights during our e-mail 'chats. I couldn't have done it without you.